# Stephen's Second Chance:
## Part I

The Chronicles of Fate Book 3
MM Alpha/Omega Mpreg

# Stephen's Second Chance:
## Part I

# Lucas Lamont

# DEDICATIONS:

This book is dedicated to any artist who sometimes find themselves lost in this crazy thing we called life. Don't give up on your dream and stay true to who you are. Your story, in whatever medium you choose, is good enough. The world without art is black and white. Let your color shine through and make this a better place.

I especially want to dedicate and say thanks to the following:

> To "J"—for still being by my side when I feel alone; the friendship you continue to show me is humbling, inspiring, and irreplaceable.

> To "A"—for continuing to show me that love is unconditional and that family is a strong bond which can never be broken as long as love is there.

> To "M&D"—for unconditional love and always supporting me as your son.

> To "M"—for showing me that love is still a risk and it still hurts but it is still very worth it.

To "E"—for not giving up on me and still showing me that you believe in me.

To "JMP"—for still putting up with me in all my crazy madness.

# TABLE OF CONTENTS


Dedications: . . . . . . . . . . . . . . . . . . . . . . . . . . . . . . . . . . . . . . . v

Glossary . . . . . . . . . . . . . . . . . . . . . . . . . . . . . . . . . . . . . . . . . xi

Chapter 01: Working Hard For A Dream . . . . . . . . . . . . . . . . . . 1

Chapter 02: Starting Anew But Remembering The Old. . . . . . . . . . . 29

Chapter 03: Living A Life of Optimism . . . . . . . . . . . . . . . . . . . 52

Chapter 04: Finding Nothing But Dead Ends. . . . . . . . . . . . . . . . 71

Chapter 05: Discovering The One Who Changes Everything . . . . . . . . 97

Chapter 06: Learning To Live With Family . . . . . . . . . . . . . . . . .127

Chapter 07: Discussing The Tough Stuff. . . . . . . . . . . . . . . . . . .153

Chapter 08: Exhibiting Wolf Instincts in Human Form. . . . . . . . . . .197

Chapter 09: Playing The Family Man In All The Wrong Places . . . . . . .218

Chapter 10: Hearing The Call of Temptation . . . . . . . . . . . . . . . .238

Book Club Questions . . . . . . . . . . . . . . . . . . . . . . . . . . . . .267

Author Bio: . . . . . . . . . . . . . . . . . . . . . . . . . . . . . . . . . .269

# CAST OF CHARACTERS

| Characters | Classification | Age |
| --- | --- | --- |
| Robert Daventry (Sur) | Alpha—Type 2 | 51 |
| Nathan Daventry (Veo) | Omega—Type 3 | 50 |
| Alexander Daventry | Omega—Type 3 | 28 |
| Jin Daventry | Alpha—Type 4 | |
| | | |
| Kane Matheson (Sur) | Alpha—Type 3 | 60 |
| Marlon Matheson (Veo) | Omega—Type 3 | 52 |
| Stephen Matheson | Alpha—Type 4 | 29 |
| Warren Matheson | Omega—Type 3 | D. 16 |
| | | |
| Carey Hart | Omega—Type 4 | 27 |
| | | |
| Daniel Harvey | Omega—Type 2 | 25 |
| | | |
| Sean Crenshaw | Alpha—Type 4 | 32 |
| | | |
| Eric Dayes | Alpha—Type 3 | 36 |
| | | |
| Raymond "Rat" Taylor | Beta | 37 |

| Characters | Classification | Age |
|---|---|---|
| Bruce Dawson | Beta | 40 |
| James Dawson | Beta | 38 |
| Dr. Jacob Tyler Erricson | Alpha—Type 5 | 43 |
| Dr. Dustin Cavenbelle | Alpha—Type 4 | 38 |
| Matthew James Whitmore | Alpha—Type 5 | 37 |

# GLOSSARY

**Pre-Wolf Era**—the previous existence of humans evolved from primates and also the only existence of the human female gender

**Wolf Era**—current time, existence of male humans evolved from *Canis lupus* (wolves)

**Rank**—The biological make-up of a wolf-descendant: Alpha—Beta—Omega

**Blood-Type**—a categorial gene system to determine purity of the strongest genes ranked 1 – 5 in Alphas and Omegas

**The 6th Blood-Type**—An evolutionary anomaly in top tier Type 5 Alphas

**Pup**—a wolf-descendent child from birth to age 9

**Adolescent**—a wolf-descendent child from age 10 – 15

**Natural Adult**—a wolf-descendent man from age 16 and older

**Legal Adult**—a male of age 18 and older

**Sur**—formal title given to an Alpha father

**Veo**—formal title given to an Omega father

**Post Education**—beginning of adult and specialized education of 4 Levels in two-year cycles begin at age 16

**Contract**—Legal requirement to form an official relationship bond including commitment, evaluation of assets, reproduction, and authority

**Fated Mate**—a highly sought out bond indicated by primal pheromones to connect with one specific mate or "Fate" for care, love, and reproductive purposes

**Heat**—a 4-month cycle for Omegas at peak fertility where the womb drops for insemination

# CHAPTER 01:

# WORKING HARD
# FOR A DREAM

**"**So, you better turn this place around. Or else!" Eric glared at the Omega, making sure he felt the dominating pheromones fuming off him.

Alexander's shoulders fell as he could barely stand to look at the Alpha coming down on him. In the corner of his eye, he saw his hired help sweeping up the broken glass at the front entry of his bar. Although he was grateful the angry protestor didn't get a chance to break a main storefront window, it still didn't do anything positive for his own reputation as an Omega business owner, nor the bar itself. He glided his fingers through his ice blonde hair, combing out the frustrations. "I don't know what else to do!" he let out. "I've had Bruce and James here since New Year's. They've curbed a lot of the activity that was happening before. But they can't predict if some psycho is going to walk up to the building and throw a rock through my window."

Eric bowed slightly, allowing a canned yellow light to bounce off his shaved head, accentuating his distinguished goatee, dark skin, and black eyes. "You said there was a note attached to the rock?" Alexander nodded. "What did it say?"

Alexander remembered every word hastily scribbled on the crumpled paper. He could have recited each painful passage perfectly to the city inspector but chose to keep it vague, hoping to minimize any damage Eric could impose on him. "The same rhetoric that's in all the hate mail I get and side comments I hear. 'Omegas create pups, not businesses.' 'Omegas support establishments, not own them.' 'Of all things you chose to own a bar? How disgusting! You should be ashamed to call yourself an Omega.' Oh, and my favorite: 'Why don't you sell the bar to an Alpha who knows what they're doing and just become a manager or bartender?'" Heat rose on his cheek bones, and he clenched his fists.

Eric used his thumb and index finger to outline his full lips. "Why *don't* you just sell it?"

"Why? Because I've worked my whole life for this opportunity. Besides, most Alphas who come in here think I'm stupid and try to lowball me an offer as if they'd be doing me a favor by taking it off my hands. It's ridiculous." He shook his head. "Doesn't matter anyway; I'm not selling. And I'm surprised you would even ask that when..." The Omega squinted his eyes, wondering what Eric was really getting at. "Or are you trying to tell me something?"

Eric rolled his heavy shiny pen between his fingers. In his other hand, he held his city inspector's report book. Small empty boxes leered back, tempting him to strike a check in the perfect pattern to easily shut the bar down, eventually forcing Alexander's hand. "I just want what's best for this place. I'm getting nervous is all." The words he spoke trickled down into his stomach, making it tie into knots.

"Yeah, I know what you *really* mean." Alexander turned and hustled his way into the back room, hearing Eric closely behind him.

"Alex!" Eric yelled defensively.

In the colder, less inviting space, Alexander felt backed into a corner with nowhere else to go. With Eric now looking at him with empathy, he chose to ignore his silent partner. Instead, he peered out from the back room into the bar of about a dozen or so patrons enjoying the atmosphere. Lighter music hummed in the background as the heavier upbeat music wouldn't kick in until the weekend. Still, just the same, he slowly started to imagine the long horseshoe counter completely bare of customers, bowls full of untouched bar snacks, bright garnishes locked away in caddies, dusty lights bouncing off the back mirrors and the shiny bottles on display completely unopened. And finally, the music completely silent, turning his colorful dream into nothing more than a pale memory of a failure. "If I was an Alpha, you wouldn't ask this of me."

"If you were an Alpha, you wouldn't be having these problems," Eric pointed out.

"Not true. Bar fights and vandalism happen to any other bar in the city too," Alexander defended.

"Yes, but they don't have the watchful eye of the city breathing down their necks like you do. Plus, they're busier. You got prime real estate here. The city wants as much taxes out of this place as it can get."

Alexander fumed. "They get plenty of taxes! Business is going well. How much better do they need it to be to get off my back?"

"Double."

Alexander's eyes grew wide. Everything screeched to a halt. "*Double*?"

Eric shrugged. "That's what I'm hearing. Not in an official capacity of course, but through the grapevine. They think you owning this place is a wasted opportunity for the bar and scaring other lucrative businesses away who don't want to be around here."

"Oh, please." Alexander waved off. "They didn't think that when they sold me the place."

"You mean sold *us* the place?" Eric corrected.

Alexander twitched his lips and rubbed his week-long stubble along his jawline, the natural dark hair contrasting his dyed hair, light skin, and blue eyes. In his heart, he knew why the bank granted him the loan and why the city approved his liquor license. "I don't really need to hear how you swooped in like a knight in shining armor, okay?"

"As your friend, I would never do that." Nothing else had to be said. They both knew. Eric was the guarantee on the entire venture. Shelling out 30% himself, the Alpha viewed this as an investment to boost his own interests. In exchange for being the watchdog for the city and the safety net, he asked the officials to keep his name off the books to help save himself the ridicule and condemnation for being attached as a secondary to an Omega's ownership. Thus, unless anyone completely dissected the arrangement, the public knew Alexander Daventry as the sole owner of South Street Tavern. But with so many other successes to his name, and Alexander holding 70% of the majority control, Eric was initially satisfied with being his silent partner.

However, since the bar opened a couple years ago, Eric had dealt with a splash of cold water on his face regarding the trials and tribulations of an Omega breaking the glass ceiling and rebelling against the status quo of being treated more like property than a human being, even despite the social advances and triumphs of the modern age. Why was Eric so ignorant? Because he was an Alpha and didn't have to live his life as an Omega like Alexander did. "I'm getting a lot of pressure."

"Why?"

"Because it's a different game now." Eric glanced into the bar, eyeing one bar patron specifically. "Ever since Tauris Medical Center announced their new research addition with its glitz and glamour, the public has been hoping to revitalize the last part of downtown still neglected and overrun with criminals and vagabonds. Now that it's happened, the city is handpicking what it wants, especially so it doesn't tarnish the medical center's reputation."

Alexander was amused by his claim. "News flash: the criminals and vagabonds are still here hiding in the shadows. The only difference is they creep and crawl amongst higher end department stores and luxury apartments now." He paused. "Wait a second. The city isn't grouping *me* into the same category, are they?"

"You are a Type 3, aren't you?" The words slipped out of Eric's mouth.

"Last time I checked, you are too … 'friend.'" The Omega flung the last word with attitude.

"Yeah, and I worked my ass off to get to where I am today." Now Eric went on the defense. "I crawled on my hands and knees just to get here. The number of times I did the shittiest and most thankless jobs, for virtually no pay, and then kissed the hands of Type 4 and Type 5 managers and executives like they were giving me gold is countless. I practically starved in my pursuit to get to the part of the jungle that sees a tiny sliver of light. As of right now, that light is in jeopardy because of this place. And I'll be damned before I let anyone, including you, jeopardize the name and respect I have now!"

The noise of the back room fell to only the quiet hum of an industrial ice maker. Alexander stood there, staring at the drain grate as a minute stream of water trickled in. A crash of newly formed cubes into the chilled basin shook him back to reality. "I'm sorry," he whispered. "I sometimes forget Type 3 Alphas get treated like dirt too."

Blood purity was assigned at birth. Split into "Types," the modern world now recognized a privileged population of wolf-descendants who were biologically dispositioned to be healthier, smarter, stronger in physical and mental ability, and possessing great beauty and potential in society. The final, and most important, indicator was their biological link to the humans who walked the earth before them known as primate-descendants. Believing this connection was the key to the survival of their once scarce existence, wolf-descendants across the world recognized the importance of giving these preferred individuals the best chance at life. To identify them, they were categorized as Type 5, the highest and most prestigious title.

Even though Type 6 Alphas existed in the world, their rarity caused them to be an anomaly to most. A few deemed them a gift from the heavens and a few others deemed them a curse from Hell.

After the chaos of the new world settled, the remains of this practice resulted in a social hierarchy. Now designed more to identify class, wolf-descendants shunned Type 3s, Type 2s, and Type 1s as lesser humans and more like their wild and tameless wolf ancestors, regardless of their true potential. The effects of this prejudice fulfilled its own prophecy, as "Low Types" were given fewer opportunities and lived closer to the world of poverty. With it came the culture of alcohol and drug abuse, high crime rates in theft, vandalism, and assault, and the belief they were all-around dangerous. Type 3s had been spared the worst judgement in recent years as they worked toward developing a standing worthy of the Type 4s and Type 5s. Unfortunately, this has left a Type 3's potential and fate to be determined by their family's history and influence. Some have reaped the benefits from their ancestral line. Some have fought and earned their place at the table. And some have forever been cursed by their blood purity, or worse, their family's reputation.

Eric huffed. "It's bad enough I had to convince every city official to let me watch over this place when they know it's a conflict of interest."

"Yeah? Well, no one asked you to," Alexander snarled.

"You're right. But don't you even think for a second that you'd be open as long as you have without my influence or help." Eric carefully watched Alexander's expression flinch upon hearing his bold statement. "You knew exactly what you were getting into and the risks you faced. I'm sorry that the moment has come."

The Omega's eyes pierced back. "Screw that! The hell it has."

Eric groaned. "Come on, Alex..."

"No! *You* come on! I don't care what bureaucrats want. If I wasn't what they wanted, they shouldn't have sold this place to me or given me my license. But they did. And just like *I* knew the risks of getting into this, so did you! Until my customers dry up or someone can nail me with a legit violation, I'm not selling this place. Not to you. Not to anyone." Fed up with Eric's criticism, he exited back into the bar, but not before Eric stepped in his way to give him one final warning.

"Six months, Alex. The city is giving you six months to see some real results here. If not, they are expecting me to find something wrong with this place. If I don't, they will send someone in here who will."

The warning fell on deaf ears as Alexander pushed past Eric, bumping into his shoulder on his way out. Upon entering the large room, the Omega plastered on a customer service smile, one he had practiced for many years. He then gazed upon a bar patron of the highest interest sitting on the opposite end, his back against the view of the main entrance. "Sorry about that." He pulled out a shiny Glencairn and began filling the heavy glass with another shot of bourbon. During mid-pour, he decided to join the Alpha in the drink and poured himself one afterward.

"No, no. Don't worry about it," the white-collar Alpha dismissed politely. After thanking Alexander for the next round, he sensed the Omega's act. "Everything okay?" His eye caught Eric coming out of the backroom, writing down notes on his clipboard. "Is this about the..." The man pointed to the employee giving one final sweep of glass into a dustbin, choosing to avoid finishing the sentence out of courtesy.

Alexander followed the patron's view, then turned back to Eric for a moment before giving a half-smile in return. "Sort of," the Omega admitted. "City inspectors."

"This late at night?"

The bar owner ignored the question as best as he could. "You know how it is. They're just here to make my life miserable. That's all."

The patron laughed as if he could somewhat relate to the bar owner's woes. "When the Territory's elite come down from Gray City to inspect our labs to make sure we're following protocol, I imagine it feels the same. They're not doing their job unless they find something wrong, right?"

"Exactly!" Alexander nodded as he began doing bar pours for another table's order. "Speaking of, I thought today was the big day for the lab?"

The man nodded. "It is!"

"Then what the hell are you doing here?" Alexander beckoned to his bar help who walked the order over.

"I've been celebrating, giving tours, and surviving off crackers topped with various meats since 9AM this morning. It's been twelve hours; I needed a break." The man arched his shoulders as best as he could in his expensive suit, not his typical wear. Usually, nice slacks and a button down sufficed, especially since he covered it in a white lab coat. But today was the Grand Opening of the Tauris Medical Center's Research Building, headed up by the world-renowned Dr. Paul Birowack.

"Still, Jake Erricson, I think people are going to notice you are gone, no?"

"Nah. Everyone's there to see Dr. Birowack. Besides, I have Dustin herding the crowds there in my stead." Under the leadership of the famous doctor, both Dr. Jacob Erricson and Dr. Dustin Cavenbelle were Paul Birowack's apprentices and second-in-commands.

Alexander gave an overdramatic gasp. "You fed Dustin to the wolves?"

"He's got this." Jake shrugged it off.

"Well then..." Alexander lifted the prestigious bottle of bourbon from the higher shelf once more and filled both their glasses. Lifting his own glass, Jake followed him. "To the new lab and all its successes."

"Thank you! I'll definitely drink to that." Jake knocked back the drink as the Omega had done.

"Another?" Alexander asked, gesturing to his empty glass once more.

"I better take a break. But I will do a glass of water." Jake scratched the stubble beginning to grow on his cheek.

Alexander winked at him. "You got it. So, how long does this reception last?"

"Ha! It's only just begun. The second event started at 7PM tonight. That's when the big guns came out: head doctors from the facility, big names from the territory including Gray City, the board of directors, and the shareholders and investors."

"Damn. That sounds like quite the gathering." Alexander shivered at the thought. "I don't know if I could do that."

"What do you mean? You have this place. You play reception host every night of the week."

Alexander considered his claim. "I suppose. But you have some major people to impress. As a matter of fact, isn't one of your benefactors Matthew Whitmore?"

"Not just one of them, *the* number one benefactor," Jake corrected. "Without him, none of this would be possible."

"Not that it's any of my business, but what has him so interested in the lab, anyway?" Alexander asked with his hands on his hip.

"Matthew Whitmore has always been interested in causes which shape the future. Our research lab is dedicated to investigating every aspect of our species for optimal survival. Once he found out we were focused on research involving Type 5s, which he and his entire family are, and trying to unlock the secrets of the Type 6 Alpha, he was on board to help in any way he could. Once Dr. Birowack told him that having a new medical research center here would put Tauris City as the number one research hospital in the world, the rest is history."

"Wow. I had no idea. I only thought he was interested in politics. He's a great supporter of Omega rights. It's one of the reasons I'm able to own this place. Ten, fifteen years ago, I never could have been here." The thought of only having to go back a decade or so to find a time where Omega business ownership was non-existent depressed Alexander immensely.

"That's not true," Jake rebuked. "There were Omegas who owned businesses back then."

"How about a bar? In downtown Tauris City no less?"

Jake retracted, "I guess you're right about that."

Alexander rubbed his hands through a bar towel out of comfort. "I'm just glad I have patrons like you who are willing to get out of the dark ages and support me in this venture."

"Absolutely!" Jake raised his water glass. "My mate is his own boss, too. He's a skilled builder and an entrepreneur; I wouldn't have it any other way." After chugging the water glass, he continued. "I'll gladly support any Omega who wants to go into business for themselves, even though I'm no Matthew Whitmore."

The bar owner swooned at the thought. "If I was to get support from Matthew Whitmore, it would be a dream come true."

A familiar voice rushed to both men's ears. "I don't know if I can fulfill dreams, but I will certainly try."

There stood the man of the hour, day, month, year, and decade: Matthew Whitmore. In his black suit marked with scarlet detailing, he was a sharp sight and stood out of the general crowd who were equally in awe as they noticed the celebrity in a bar no one imagined he'd step foot into. Feeling the gaze of everyone in the establishment, Matthew took in the moment, not sure how to proceed.

Alexander himself stood there frozen in amazement. "You're... you're..."

"Mr. Whitmore!" Jake jumped up from his seat. He fixed his collar and tie and puffed out his chest like he was entertaining back at the medical center.

"It's alright, Dr. Erricson. I'm just in the neighborhood for a drink. That is ... if I'm welcome here." Matthew scanned the room once more, still noticing everyone staring, and no one formally inviting him in.

Snapping out of it, Alexander took the towel in his hands, reached over the bar, and began wiping off the chair next to Jake's and the counterspace, even though both were already clean. "Of course! Please, have a seat."

The proud Alpha inched his way forward as Jake led him to the corner he had known so well for the past forty minutes. "Nice place you have here..." Matthew began, hoping to get an introduction.

"Alex." He held his hands up, still in disbelief. "Welcome to the South Street Tavern!"

"Thank you." Matthew seated himself and found the chair surprisingly comfortable.

Most of the customers in the bar had gone back to their own business, knowing it was socially unacceptable to approach a Type 5 Alpha such as Matthew, especially when most of them were Low Types. But that didn't stop a few from carrying on, whispering in their small social circles about the celebrity who bestowed his presence on such a place that was beneath him. A few even dared to take out their phones and brazenly take photos of the "caught" moment.

"Mr. Whitmore, what are you doing here?" Jake asked.

"Jake, please. All day and all evening I've been referred to as 'Mr. Whitmore.' Right now, I'd like it if you called me 'Matthew' instead."

The doctor was speechless. "I... I..." he gulped. "Okay, Matthew... I have to say ... I didn't think I'd find you here." Jake glanced at Alexander, hoping he didn't take offense at the comment.

"I needed to get away. I was just going to go down to the Rotary Club lounge when I happened to catch a glimpse of you from the windows." He looked back, taking note of one *less* window but chose not to comment. "Naturally, I didn't think you'd mind me joining you?" Matthew spoke eloquently, very unlike the rest of the patrons here.

"No, of course not!" Jake confirmed. His eyes caught Alexander once again. "Oh! Where are my manners? Matthew, this is the owner of the tavern."

Matthew looked the younger man up and down. His scent permeated his nostrils: mostly nerves. But through it, he clocked Alexander for an Omega without hesitation. He pondered the conclusion and realized now who he was. "You're the groundbreaking Omega who fought the establishment to get his own bar." He smiled. "I'd like to shake your hand."

Blood rushed to Alexander's face as he touched the hand of the celebrity before him. "Groundbreaking? I don't think I've ever been described *that* way. Except for maybe news outlets looking to sensationalize me."

"Nonsense! I've worked the past few years passionately advocating for such things to happen. I cannot tell you how pleased I am to see such a milestone come to fruition."

The bar owner acknowledged with gratitude. He never imagined an Alpha like Matthew Whitmore praising him for such an accomplishment in person, let alone ever felt he was worthy to acknowledge at all. "Mr. Whitmore I honestly should be thanking you for your contributions on Omega rights and changing the opinions of so many in the city on who we are and our worth. You're *my* hero."

Matthew smiled. "I am very honored."

Alexander bit his lip. "Why aren't you running for Pack Alpha of the City?"

Jake focused in with the same curiosity.

The proud Alpha chuckled to himself. "Oh... you and the rest of the city." He squinted as he thought of the right words. "It's just not my calling. Political ambitions change people, and there are so many more rules to follow when you want change to happen. I'm amazed myself on how much people attribute to my dedication without ever holding an elected position." He shrugged his shoulders. "Perhaps I'm worried my effectiveness and success would disappear if I fought it from a political position."

Although disappointed, Alexander nodded, fully understanding his view. "Oh, Wolf-God! Where is my head? Here I am a bar owner, and I haven't even asked you what you'd like to drink."

"Ah, I can't wait!" Matthew finally relaxed for the first time since walking in. "What is the house specialty?"

A couple hours passed and several drinks were consumed between the doctor and elite businessman. Many customers were in and out until only a couple remained, typical for a weekday. Alexander excused himself from the conversations as he aided his staff in closing down. But that didn't deter Jake nor Matthew from carrying on.

"That's why I believe in your research so much, Jake. What an amazing opportunity to not only lead the world in the research for Type 6 Alphas but also to have one living under your own roof, your own flesh and blood!" Matthew saluted the doctor with his glass.

Jake reflected on his eldest son, Roman. The 22-year-old Alpha Type 6 was the center of the lab's research. Ever since he was a child, Roman was subjected to tests and exams to see what he was capable of. Based upon existing research, the young man had proven theories to the potential he could possess. Roman was tall, handsome, smart, and gifted athletically. Despite his small circle of friends, he was admired by many at Ashershire Prep. For those who thought of the elite Alpha otherwise, none dared to face him and deliver such opinion. Thus, he was a celebrity in his own right, possibly even bigger than Matthew Whitmore in some eyes.

The doctor rimmed his glass with his index finger. "Roman doesn't view it like that."

"Really?" Matthew sat there, never imagining a Type 6 Alpha to think of himself as anything less than a god in human form.

"I think he just wants to be treated normal like anyone else. That's the last thing he's ever been considered. Between his undeniable stardom in basketball, his moderately wealthy upbringing, and his ambitions, he's always been in the spotlight, even when he doesn't want to be."

"What are his aspirations?"

Jake sighed. "Right now, he wants to go pro in basketball. But his Veo and I have beaten into his head he needs a backup plan, no matter how likely it is he'd make it in the big leagues. He surprised us both by saying he wants to be a doctor, albeit in Sports Medicine and Physical Therapy, but there are worse professions."

"Huh." Matthew considered his next move, wondering whether to divulge his own private life. "I sense the 'worried parent' in you." Jake shrugged. "I can't say I'm any different."

"Your son? Peyton? No way. He's gotta be doing well for himself," Jake insisted.

"Terrence and I have never doubted Peyton's success career wise. Hell, I think one day he'll surpass me. The kid's too damn smart if you ask me."

"I know what that's like," Jake added.

Matthew squirmed in his chair. "But when it comes to finding a mate, I worry he'll never find success."

Jake slowed to a halt upon hearing the topic. The coincidence was uncanny, even scary. He pressed slowly. "What seems to be the problem?"

The frustration grew on Matthew's face. "He just doesn't seem interested. At all! Terrence and I can't figure it out. Socially, he was a loner all his childhood. But we were both convinced once Peyton started going through heats he'd change his priorities and consider finding his Fated Mate ... or any mate for that matter."

Jake cleared his throat. "Adrian and I worry the same about Roman." A heavy sensation overcame him.

Matthew stared in disbelief. "Roman? The Type 6 Alpha? You and your mate are worried about *him*? I'm surprised potential suitors aren't knocking down his door!"

"Oh, believe me, they are. They call him, text him, incessantly bug him at school. The twins have told me there's even been fights over him. Yet, ironically, I've never heard that Roman was interested in any of them." Jake laughed.

The high-class businessman scratched his head. "You have twins?"

Jake was stunned. After a moment, he realized just how much of his life was about Roman. "Um. Yeah. Rixen and Ryan are twins. Rixen is an Omega and Ryan is a Beta. They were there tonight at the reception."

"Didn't know that," Matthew answered. "So, why is the most sought after and coveted Alpha at Ashershire shunning every opportunity in front of him?"

"He... uh... he's waiting for his Fated Mate." The doctor's eyes circled around, hoping the answer wouldn't get scrutinized.

"I get that. We all do. Obviously, his Fate hasn't shown up at Ashershire. Or if he has, he's done a good job of staying incognito. Has he tried going to formals? Terrence and I went to them all the time before we found each other."

"No," Jake answered.

"How about casual events like at bars, stadiums, other schools?"

"No."

Matthew struggled for other possibilities. "Online dating? Wolf-God forbid."

The doctor's voice dropped to its lowest yet. "No."

"I don't understand then. Is he just waiting for his Fated Mate to walk into your house one day?"

A headache was starting to consume Jake, a mix of stress and booze. "Yeah. Yeah, that's exactly it," he criticized. "He'll go out, especially if it involves his friends or teammates from basketball. But he claims he's never gone to do an active search. And yet, he says his Fated Mate is all he'll ever consider." He sighed, agitated. The doctor was convinced he needed to share the truth. He couldn't keep Matthew in the dark anymore. "It doesn't matter."

"Why do you say that?" Matthew asked perplexed.

Seeing the sparse few that remained in the bar and the employees scattered elsewhere, Jake beckoned to Matthew. "I need you to keep a secret."

Matthew furrowed his brows. "Okay..."

"Roman... he... he can't find his Fated Mate." He felt his mouth go dry.

"You already said that," Matthew pointed out, chalking it up to the booze. "That's common."

"No, that's not what I mean." He paused. "He doesn't have the *ability* to find his Fated Mate."

The words took a minute to sink in. "Oh? Oh. *Oh*. Damn. Poor guy. I don't understand. Why is this such a big secret?"

Jake's heart sank. "Roman doesn't *know* he lacks the ability to find one. Neither me nor my mate have told him." A million thoughts raced through his mind. What would Matthew think? Would he be completely disgusted by his actions as a parent? Would he disassociate himself, or worse, even pull his funding for the lab over it? The suspense of Matthew's silence killed him inside.

"You... *what*? How on earth does a man not know he can't find his Fated Mate? How do *you* know that?"

"It's complicated," Jake attempted, lost in his own frustration. "Through seeing trends in his hormone levels from his blood tests, it's almost like he's missed a part of puberty. I mean, obviously, he's gone through it. But in all the amazing capabilities Roman has ... he doesn't have that one." He gazed at the Alpha next to him, completely stupefied by the claim. "Please, Matthew, you can't say anything. Only Dr. Birowack, my work partner Dustin, and my mate Adrian know this."

Matthew's expression dropped. "Jake... why didn't you tell him? Aren't you going to?"

"Think about it, Matthew. When was the last time you ever heard of an Alpha who doesn't possess the capability to find his Fate?"

He cleared his throat. "I suppose I've *never* heard that before. But there are plenty of Alphas and Omegas out there who have never found their Fated Mate. That's just the reality of statistics. To find that one person in the entire world who was meant to be yours… that's a gift."

"Something you and I both have had the pleasure of doing," Jake added.

"Right." Matthew's eyes shifted. He continued, ignoring the statement. "Who's to say those who never found their Fated Mate aren't biologically disadvantaged like Roman is?"

"You have a point," Jake admitted. "But we as wolf-descendants have been programmed our entire lives knowing there's a risk we'd never find our Fated Mate. I suppose those who haven't just never venture to see if they have that disability." *Disability.* Uttering the word made him sick. "Being a Type 6 celebrity is a double-edged sword at this point. One of the rarest human beings can't perform the one biological and instinctual act we were put on this planet to do. If the world knew this, it would destroy everything Roman has represented to be, whether he wants it or not. As far as telling him… I need to. Soon." He let out a pitiful laugh. "Just be glad Peyton doesn't have to worry about that. Odds are, with your family's good fortune, he'll find himself a great mate one day, Fated or not."

"Don't sell Roman too short, Jake. I saw him tonight at the reception, along with everybody else there. He's going to be a trophy of a mate to whomever he chooses." Jake smiled in return. "I even saw Peyton talk to him for a short while. Between you and me, I hoped perhaps the two would hit it off, or even better, find out they were each other's Fate. Of course, that was before I found out the news about Roman not being able to."

"Wouldn't that have been nice?" Jake equally found the possibility a fantasy. "Believe me, Matthew, there are days where I just hope I'm wrong, that Roman will find his Fate and the issue can finally be laid to rest without me even having to say anything. But then, every time he gets a new blood panel, I see the identified marker staring me straight in the face telling me it's never going to happen. Thus, I'm praying he finds himself a contractual mate. I mean, most Alphas decide by now."

"That's right. With his Status, he's expected to find someone by now. It's bad enough we Type 5s are told to make decisions so early. Honestly, it's the one reason, and only one, why it would be nice to be a Lower Type ... to have the opportunity to leisurely wait for the right mate to come along without the pressures of family or society breathing down our necks." Matthew's comment summed up the unfair expectation.

Part of being of a reputable Type 4 or Type 5 meant success. The public assumption was this "perfection" permeated all aspects of their lives—including finding a mate. There was great honor to the family for their offspring to find a mate, especially a Fated Mate, early in life. But the sacrifices to keep up the appearances meant some were pressured or forced into mating contracts which were undesirable or unwanted. As laws became more liberal and focused on individual rights in recent years, this practice became more of a relic geared toward the aristocrats. However, with Peyton's upbringing and Roman's exceptionality, they were two prime examples of how this custom was still alive and well.

Jake groaned and rubbed his face. "I just need to let this go. Something's bound to come along for Roman. I can feel it. Peyton, too. He'll find his by the end of the year; I know it." He tossed out the optimism, hoping it would stick.

A glimmer struck Matthew's eye. His brain began turning ideas. It was faint at first, but the more he kept on it, the more it radiated into every part of his being and he couldn't concentrate on anything else. "What if Roman and Peyton found each other?"

The doctor squinted in confusion. "Found? They already know each other."

"I know that." Matthew turned his whole body toward Jake and leaned in close, making sure Jake understood every word about to come out his mouth. "What if Roman and Peyton went into contract together?"

Alcohol allowed Jake to be candid in his inquisition. "You... you'd want that? I mean, you'd want Roman and us to be a part of *your* family?"

Matthew smirked. "Unless you guys are secretly hiding the fact you're terrorists or something." He bit his lip. "Or if the whole 'Roman being a Type 6' thing is a sham."

Jake studied Matthew, wondering if that's what all his intentions were about. But it took a backseat to the excitement flooding his veins. To be a part of the Whitmore dynasty was equal to being the final chosen suitor on a reality dating competition show. It not only was highly sought after; it was a dream come true. Quickly, he replied to snuff out any doubts. "Absolutely not! We can prove it medically and legally just like anyone else can."

"Excellent." Matthew's joy was suddenly hushed by the muted expression on Jake's face. "Why am I getting the impression you're not equally enthusiastic about this?"

"Oh, *I* am!" Jake clarified. "I just don't know if Roman is going to be. I already told you what issues we're dealing with now."

"True," Matthew acknowledged. "But you said Roman isn't actively looking and neither is Peyton. The odds of them finding one anytime soon are slim to none."

"So?"

"So... that means we have time to warm them up to the idea. And from what I saw, I think Peyton found Roman quite attractive tonight."

"Hmm." Jake scratched his chin. "I don't know. If we get Peyton and Roman together and the spark fizzles, Roman's going to dismiss this quick, and worse, he'll hurt Peyton's feelings. The idea of going to a courtship only to be rejected would be an embarrassment to your family, anyone's family."

The elite Alpha considered the scenario. Jake wasn't wrong. If Roman boldly said no and couldn't be convinced otherwise, the failed proposition would become public knowledge sooner or later. Being a celebrity like himself guaranteed that. Even more, the devastating effect it'd have on Peyton would ensure he'd hesitate to find a mate to live out the rest of his life, not to mention have someone to trust and enjoy going through a heat with.

Right now, his heat was procedural and being taken care of by a medical professional who used tools and prescription meds to alleviate his son's needs. Without the medical care, Peyton's instinctual urges would consume him, and he'd focus on nothing else other than getting his heat sated. Eating, drinking, and sleeping would become impossible. The final act would be Peyton walking the streets to find an opportunistic Beta or preferably a fertile and potent Alpha to end his agonizing misery. It was nature's cruel joke to have Omegas go through such an ordeal while Betas and Alphas sat on the sidelines waiting to pounce for the sheer pleasure of it all without having to deal with any life-threatening consequences from their own needs.

The thought of it all shook Matthew to his core. He didn't want Peyton to have to go through the dull process of medical alleviation anymore, but he didn't want the latter either. Snapping his fingers, he came up with an idea. "Okay, how about this? How about we don't have them meet up? Instead, we slowly but surely over time warm them up. You know: start with expressing the interest and grow into learning about one another through conversations we'll administer, and when we finally get both of them on the same page, we'll set up the official meet. I even know the perfect restaurant we can celebrate at."

Jake twitched his lips. "I think it has the best odds of success but..."

"But...?"

"How long are you willing to wait? Roman is as stubborn as I am. If we rush this, he's going to back out. His intuition will kick in, and he'll see right through it and know we were playing matchmaker behind his back versus it being a genuine interest from Peyton."

"No worries." Matthew shook his head. "I'll wait for as long as it takes."

As Jake sat there, seeing the plan formulate into conceivable actions, he huffed in disbelief. "You sure are confident."

Matthew pressed his hand onto Jake's shoulder. "We *both* need to be. Confidence begets confidence. If we slowly groom our sons, as if this came down from Wolf-God himself, they'll see this was the right decision."

Like magic, Matthew's touch sank into Jake's soul. Suddenly, he sat taller, face determined, and pheromone glands pumped full of strength and assurance, permeating the room. "You're right. If I helped build an empire for a career, held a mating contract with my Fate for over twenty years, and raised three pups into grown men, I can do this." Jake thrust his hand out to Matthew who took it confidently. "Matthew Whitmore, we have a deal!"

"Fantastic!" Matthew equally beamed from ear to ear. "Alex," he called out, "two shots in celebration, please!"

The call startled the bar owner as he almost forgot the two were still there. "Really?" He took a quick glance at his watch. "We're closing in ten minutes. Last call was nearly an hour ago."

Matthew promptly stood up. The speed caused his equilibrium to falter, a clear sign of just how much the two had consumed already. He fumbled for his wallet inside his suit coat. "Young man, I do believe I haven't paid our bill yet."

"Oh, Mr. Whitmore, I couldn't accept," Alexander insisted. "Your presence here tonight was payment alone."

"Nonsense!" Matthew pulled out a wad of cash from his wallet. He attempted to count out the crisp new bills, but after a couple of seconds, he split the stack down the middle with his thumb and lightly tossed half the largest bills onto the bar. "That should take care of it."

Alexander stood there and gawked at the pile of money before him. He thought it rude to count it then and there but estimated it to be over a thousand. The air drew out of his lungs. "Mr. Whitmore! That's too much!"

"Ugh! 'Mr. Whitmore,' 'Mr. Whitmore,' 'Mr. Whitmore.' Just for once I want to be in a place where everyone calls me 'Matthew.'" He slumped back in his seat.

The Omega picked up the bills and sorted out a generous tip to his closing staff. "Maybe at the family reunion?" Jake burst into a hearty laugh. After realizing what he'd said, Alexander began to blush. "I'm sorry, Mr. Whitmore, that was out of line for me to say. Is there anything I can get you?"

"It's all right. I can handle a joke or two at my expense." He laid back into the barstool and put his hands behind his head. "That is ... as long as it comes with two shots."

With a keen eye, Alexander honed in on his remaining staff. Bruce screeched a heavy table he was moving to a halt while James stopped mid-journey toward the dumpsters in the alleyway to throw out the night's trash. He knew what they were thinking. The scrutiny on his place was bad enough. Risking the chance Eric or another city inspector would serendipitously catch him in the act of doing something illegal to shut him down was a bold move; cops on patrol could nail him easily. But denying Matthew Whitmore in Tauris City was even bolder.

Quickly, Alexander laid out three sets of tips with a few large bills each. In silence, they grabbed their share and understood the message. After, they all resumed their work like it never happened. "Two pours coming up!" Matthew and Jake cheered the announcement on like two men on their eighteenth birthday. "What are we celebrating anyway?"

Matthew choked, looking at Jake for advice. "Well..."

"You can trust Alex, Matthew," Jake reassured. "He's not going to say anything."

"It's against the bartender code to share what customers discuss here—barring anything that's gonna get *me* into trouble," Alexander pointed out.

"Not illegal. Immoral? Maybe." Jake hiked his glass in the air, preparing to inhale it.

Matthew caught his arm before he was able to complete the task. A drop spilled over the edge of Jake's glass. "Hey, don't be doing that without me! We're a team. And that means believing in this. No time for doubts now."

"You're right. You're right," Jake admitted.

Alexander finished pouring Matthew's drink and slid it over. "Boy, this seems like quite the venture." He turned his attention to his staff. "Bruce, is the door locked?"

"James locked it after the last two left twenty minutes ago," he answered.

James jerked. "I thought *you* did it?"

"Wolf-God, will *one* of you do it?" Alexander rolled his eyes. He focused back on his two customers, getting ready to make a toast. He lowered his voice. "What are you two plotting over here?"

"My son and Matthew's son are going to go into a mating contract," Jake whispered back. "But don't tell anyone. No one knows about it." Slowly, he brought his shot glass to Matthew's in mid-air, and a low clanking sound was heard before both men knocked them back.

Alexander rested a hand on his hip, observing the two intoxicated men acting like a ball of nerves. Something was off. "Do *they* know they're going into contract with each other?"

A moment later, the slow creaking sound of the entrance door cut through the room. In a flash, Alexander pulled the open booze bottle off the table and threw it beneath the bar into the sink. The loud crash was more humiliating than getting caught with his pants down. He was convinced Eric must have circled back to the bar, noticed it still open and came to investigate. "Damn it, Bruce! I told you to lock the door!"

"He got to the door before I could!" Bruce replied in defense.

Alexander's heart pounded in his chest as felt the sweat begin to form all over his body. The slow opening of the door was agonizing as he wished the suffering to just be over with. He prayed beyond all hope some innocent citizen just happened to walk in, wanting to use the phone or ask for directions. But not *his* bar. His bar was under the watchful eye of so many who wanted to see him fail. Surely, the man entering was some sort of enforcer. As the moments passed in slow motion, visions of his place disappearing became reality.

"Jake?" the man's voice inquired softly as he gingerly pushed the door open and walked into view.

The doctor turned, recognizing the voice instantly. Upon seeing his face, it was like seeing an old family member for the first time in years. "Dustin!" Jake stumbled up, latching his arms onto him for stability.

"Dustin... man... you have no idea how happy I am that it's you." he hiccupped. Alexander felt himself melt into a puddle. The horrors of his mind were worse than reality.

"Here you are! I thought that was you when I walked by. Where the hell have you been?" Dr. Dustin Cavenbelle, Dr. Birowack's other protégé and Jake's equal, assisted his partner back to the bar. Unlike Jake's blond hair peppered with gray, Dustin's hair was completely dark brown with the stubble to match. The few years Jake had on Dustin worked well in Dustin's favor regarding appearance.

"I've been here. Isn't that what you just said?" Jake chuckled into his stupor.

Dustin sighed in frustration. "Your mate, kids, and a third of the staff walked all over campus and the parking lots trying to find you! You wouldn't answer your phone."

24

"My phone?" Jake squinted. In a smooth movement, he carefully sat up and reached for it in his jacket. He shut his eyes as his screen's brightness blinded his altered senses. After the sting subsided, he saw several missed calls, text messages, and voicemails. "Oh, here's the problem. On silent," he nodded. "No one needs to worry about me. I'm a Type 5 Alpha. I can handle anything!" Jake announced.

"Just be glad people are fussing over you." Matthew hummed. "I bet if I pulled out my phone, no one tried contacting me to see if I was okay." The words hit him stronger than he anticipated. To prevent himself from feeling worse, he chose not to check if he was right.

That was when Dustin finally noticed who Jake was keeping company with. "Mr. Whitmore!" he gasped. "I'm sorry! I must be so exhausted to not have recognized you at first glance."

"We all are, Dustin," Matthew replied. "Just having some good ol' Alpha discussions."

"What about?" Dustin became suspicious. Only hours ago, both Jake and Matthew were side-by-side with Dr. Birowack, accepting praises beyond count while Dustin himself was relegated to traffic control: making sure other notable donors and distinguished hospital staff felt welcomed and knew where to find the internationally acclaimed research doctor and the most generous benefactor the city had seen in years. Having missed so much of the action, he could only assume it was about the future of the lab and research.

Jake examined Matthew, who was staring back intently, waiting for his answer. He cleared his throat. "Just talking about how tonight went and our future visions. I'll fill you in tomorrow."

Alexander took the opportunity to clear off the final remnants of a bar way past its hours to hold customers.

"Good." Dustin relaxed. "I don't know if I could absorb anything you told me at this point." He heard Alexander sift broken glass pieces out of the sink behind the bar and into the trash. "Things going okay, Alex?"

The Omega glanced up. "All is well here. Just a little accident with a bottle. How are you? Congratulations!"

"Exhausted! And thanks. This is a tremendous step forward." Dustin beamed.

"Hey, how come only your mate was there and not your kids, Dustin?" Jake asked slowly, relaxing in his chair. Matthew put his arm on his shoulder, giving the doctor his body to lay on.

"Drew is busy in the evenings with sports and his clubs. He's vice president of his class this year; he's either planning events or attending them."

"Tell me about it!" Jake slurred.

"And Mikaél—this isn't his thing. Spending a few hours at tonight's event would have tortured him, especially if he had to stay as long as my mate did." Dustin stood there awkwardly. "Say, Alex, how about a drink before you close down?"

Alexander hummed. "Sorry, Dustin but I'm already closed. Last call was an hour ago. If I keep you guys in here any longer, the cops are going to drive by thinking we're having a mob meeting."

"Oh. Okay." Dustin felt embarrassed he didn't surmise that himself since the place appeared to be put away already. More so, he couldn't deny he felt let down by his co-worker enjoying the success of the night without him. But being professional, and in front of Matthew Whitmore, meant he had to let it go. "Come on, guys. Let's get a cab to bring you home."

Matthew protested. "My driver can take us. He's still waiting at the medical center."

"No, I sent him away an hour ago. Promised him if I found you, I'd get you home." Dustin prayed to Wolf-God he hadn't crossed a line in doing so.

It didn't faze the man one bit; he closed his eyes and sighed deeply. Opening his eyes again, he surveyed the bar once more, viewing it in a new light. "You know, Alex, you really do have a nice place here—a nice blend of modern and classic—and I feel like *real* people come here to be themselves. I even felt relaxed enough to let my guard down."

Alexander observed cautiously, waiting for a backhanded compliment. "Thank you very much. I like my customers to have a relaxed atmosphere—a haven from the chaos of the streets if you will."

Matthew continued his own train of thought. "I'm actually looking for a venue to host a fundraiser I have planned for Jesse Minh. Perhaps you'd consider us using your place?"

The Omega couldn't believe his ears. "Jesse Minh? Tauris City's Pack Alpha, Jesse Minh?"

"Jesse Minh, Pack Alpha of Tauris City *and* The Eastern Territory to be exact," Matthew corrected proudly.

Alexander quivered in the possibility. It was too good to be true. "Mr. Whitmore, surely you'd want to have someone distinguished like yourself in a much fancier place than the South Street Tavern. I mean, The Howler Steakhouse is just a few blocks down. The audience you'd attract there could shell out thousands if not millions for your fundraiser." He winced, thinking he just gave away the best opportunity he'd been offered ever since opening the bar. But inside, he knew he had a point.

"There's a time for The Howler Steakhouse and there's a time for the South Street Tavern." The Alpha fluffed his suitcoat and adjusted his cuffs. "I've told Jesse Minh that his funds are secure, but his votes aren't. He'll garner a good portion of the High Types, but the Low Types are disenfranchised. This isn't about money as it is more about instilling hope in the population that needs it most. If Jesse wants to win, he needs the support of people like you and the clients you serve. What do you say?"

"I'm honored!" Alexander's face lit up. "I'm going to wake up tomorrow and hope we all remember this conversation."

"I'll remind him!" Jake wobbled.

It eased Alexander back into a grounded phase as he considered his chances with the doctor being in this state. Luckily for him, Dustin jumped in.

"*I'll* remind him."

Dustin saved the day as he helped his co-worker off the barstool for the final time. They said their goodbyes and carefully walked one foot at a time out the door and down the sidewalk to scope out a taxi.

Matthew gave Alexander one last look. "You have yourself a good rest of your night."

"You as well, Mr. Whitmore." The Omega watched the god strut out the door like he owned the place. After it shut, he noticed his staff standing, equally stunned. Smiling like he hadn't in years, Alexander poured himself a shot of dark brown liquor and ran it down the back of his throat. He took a deep breath and shouted. "Holy shit!"

# CHAPTER 02:

# STARTING ANEW BUT REMEMBERING THE OLD

On the border of a dirt pathway, a large gray bus squealed to a stop on the rugged blacktop. The airbrakes exhaled while the sliding door opened. Slowly, the 29-year-old descended the stairs, struggling to recognize the place he called home. To Stephen, nothing was the same. Roots and weeds had overtaken most of the luscious green grass along the unkept driveway and the yard. Trees were overgrown beyond what he ever remembered his Sur allowing. Memories of trimming the red oaks and hickories each spring were now in vain. But even those were second to the once prominent country home with bright white painted siding and blue shutters. From the road, the Alpha could tell the paint was worn and chipped. The shutters had faded from the sun into a mute gray, one of them barely clinging to a window in an upstairs room, his younger brother's old bedroom.

The day was kinder than the sight of his childhood home. Air was unseasonably warm as it rushed through the trees with their tiny buds and young leaves. His brown hair barely covered the curve of his ear, but it was long enough to sway in the breeze. In the distance, a loose shutter clanked against a warped sideboard. High above him, the sun couldn't decide whether it wanted to shine freely or hide behind clouds. A hum from the idle bus penetrated his ear. That, and the deep groan of the bus driver.

"Is this it?" the man asked gruffly.

Stephen didn't respond immediately. He wasn't sure of the correct answer. Or perhaps it was more he didn't like the correct answer. "Ye... yeah," he sputtered.

"Don't forget your bag." After speaking, the bus driver spit the last of chewing tobacco out his window.

To anyone who knew public transportation, that was code for "Get out." Looking down, Stephen had forgotten he even set the bag by his feet. Now that he was back in society, the black duffel bag looked smaller and less impressive. The Alpha didn't have much on him, nor did he have much to his name. How could he? He'd just spent the last ten years in prison.

Like having boulders tied to his feet, Stephen walked slowly off the bus. Rocks, sand, and debris crunched beneath his new tennis shoes, a gift from his parents on the day of his release. The bus driver wasted no time closing the door behind him and hitting the gas. Amid the mixture of exhaust from the runaway transit and the funk emanating from the water-logged ditches lining the road, Stephen began his journey down the long driveway.

As he neared the house, he wondered if anyone was even home. The lack of movement or noises was discouraging. There was no way his family forgot about his arrival, and yet, peering in the window revealed only a dark hallway and kitchen. "Now what?" he said out loud. Ten years ago, he would have thought nothing of it and walked right in. But after being behind bars, every day was a reminder he wasn't welcome anywhere anymore. Now, he was certain his home was included in the sentiment. The Alpha heaved his chest and gave a firm knock on the front door. Nerves simmered inside him as he didn't know which he wanted more: his family to be there or not. He didn't have to think about it too hard though.

Soon enough, an older man with ample gray in his short dark hair and beard sauntered to the door. Latches creaked and unlocked, and the door opened with a thud.

"Stephen." The man held the door open and took a good look at the younger Alpha, his face neutral and unreadable.

"Sur," Stephen replied in an equally bold tone. He didn't like not getting an immediate reaction from Kane, his Alpha father. It wasn't like him. Regardless of how his Sur felt about him, Stephen always knew where he stood growing up. But this lack of expression filled him with an uneasy feeling. Even his scent masked whatever he felt inside. Stephen swore he saw the look of strong disappointment in his father's face. However, he quickly realized time had multiplied and deepened the rivers on his Sur's forehead and around his eyes, permanently etching the look of disdain.

"You knocked on the door?" Kane criticized.

"You locked it?" Stephen walked past him and entered his childhood home for the first time in a decade.

The old man's forehead creased even more as he thought for a moment. "Guess I did. Can't be too careful these days. You never know what riffraff will show up."

Stephen was comforted that the inside of the home was in much better condition than the outside. Clearly his Veo, Omega father, did a good job in keeping up the inside of the house. The view overloaded his senses. Almost nothing changed from the day the authorities arrived to take him away. Inhaling deeply, he was glad to find the smell was also the same. Other than the years of wear and tear, it was as if Stephen never left. Overcome with emotion, his breath quickened and his face flushed. Inside himself, he was screaming, kicking, and crying so loud it could make a man deaf. But he was going to be damned before showing that in front of his Alpha father. Luckily, Kane snapped him out of the moment as he patted his shoulder; it was his version of a hug.

"Welcome home," he said mechanically.

It *was* home. But it didn't feel like home. "Dad, where is Veo?"

"Hm? He and your brother went out shopping."

Hearing his father utter such a sentence hit Stephen's core. If his father had said it eight or nine years ago, he would have exploded instantly and pinned his Sur up against the wall, having him beg for his life for the cruel mention of his lost brother. Years of therapy had changed the Alpha for the better. That was what he wanted to show his parents most. But hearing such a statement, this early, was putting Stephen to the test right away. "What do you mean 'he and my brother'?"

Kane tensed and gritted his teeth. "I didn't say that! I said 'your father'!"

*My brother,* Stephen thought to himself. Automatically, he turned to the hallway which led into the kitchen. There on both walls were still the time capsules of years' past. Several school pictures and family moments were captured in wooden frames and arranged perfectly as if by a professional artist. They were, however, not in the same formation as he remembered it. In fact, several were gone and replaced by others he recalled only seeing in dusty photo albums hardly ever touched except for holidays and birthdays. After carefully scanning, he surmised most of the photos missing were of himself in his late teens. His Veo must have taken those down and replaced them with much younger images of an Alpha who didn't exist anymore. Several photographs of a young pup with bright hazel eyes, short brown hair, and the biggest grin stared back at him. Stephen could hardly believe he was once that boy in the pictures. He didn't know how to describe himself back in those days. Ignorant? Happy? Innocent? There it was. Innocence. That was why the hallway was changed. His family had effectively erased his teenage angst from the hall of memories. How bittersweet it must be for them now to have to face it in person.

Then, he found the reason he walked there in the first place. There, at the top-center of all the memories on the wall, was Warren's school picture when he was sixteen. The captured image displayed a youthful Omega who appeared on the verge of manhood, unaware of the horrors out there in the real world. It was safer in photographs; Stephen knew that much.

Unfortunately, his brother Warren wasn't tucked safe behind the glass and wooden frame all his life. It was a single moment in time, like the rest on the wall. It was the last known photograph his family possessed of him. Shortly thereafter, Warren had passed on.

Stephen swallowed hard as he considered his options. This wasn't the argument to have right now—a conclusion he never came to before being incarcerated. "Why isn't Veo here? I thought he said he'd be waiting for me. He sounded as if he was bound and determined to be so on the phone."

"It's your own damn fault!" Kane growled. "You said you weren't getting here until after 4."

Realizing who the man before him now was, Stephen regretted telling his Sur when he'd be home instead of his Veo. It was the only question Kane asked of him, and the only time he was on the phone in ten years. He sighed. "No, I said I would be here no later than 4."

The old man coughed and tugged at his suspenders, trying to replay the thirty seconds of the call he took part in. He lowered his voice. "I'm pretty sure you said 'after 4.'"

Confirming his suspicion about his Sur, Stephen nodded. "My mistake then." He picked up his duffel bag and headed toward the stairs. "I'm going to take a shower."

"If you're looking for your bedroom, it's not there anymore."

Stephen couldn't comprehend the statement. "What?"

"We turned it into a storage room a few years ago," Kane answered nonchalantly.

"What about all my stuff?"

"Most of it is in boxes. Your Veo went through them and pulled out some stuff for you. They're in the guest room along with a few other things he thought you'd need. You can use the bathroom down here to shower."

It wasn't up for discussion. That much was obvious. Doing as he was told, Stephen walked down to the opposite end of the house. In the corner was the guest bedroom, used whenever family or friends stayed over. Walking in, he felt like he was in a hotel room. In one aspect, it was luxury he was no longer used to: a queen-sized bed, full dresser, wooden rocking chair in the corner, and a window with delicate white curtains floating in the breeze coming in from the backyard. In another, it was completely void of anything that resembled who Stephen was. There were no posters or pictures on the walls except for the faded artwork Stephen assumed had been there since the dawn of time. Visions of having his TV and stereo system back were quickly dashed. The only thing with a power cord in this room was a lamp near the bed. None of his collections of knives, skull heads, and bike magazines were in this room. Thinking back, he knew neither of his parents liked him having those things. He imagined they were the first things to go to the dump—that and his drug paraphernalia.

In the hopes of finding something to cheer him up, he opened the medium-sized box sitting on the bed. To his dismay, most of the box was filled with clothes. Worse yet, he wasn't sure the style he wore was in fashion back when he was 19. Now being 29, he knew for certain it wasn't. Tucked under the clothes was a small pile of reading material he hadn't looked at since he was 12: comics and graphic novels which featured heroes and villains on motorcycles, the start of his obsession. Next to them, a cast iron model of one his favorite bikes, and finally a few trinkets of the sports he loved as a pup. Years before the black painted walls, neon lights, glow in the dark demonic bats, and angry metal music, his childhood bedroom was a sports stadium filled with shrines to his favorite teams and players. Despite not thinking of those passions for years, the sight of the figurines and plaques moved him. He had no idea his Veo had kept any of it, especially after he told him to throw it all out.

"Will the clothes do?" his Sur asked, standing in the doorway.

Stephen jumped and tightened his fists instantly. Sneaking up on an ex-convict wasn't the smartest move. Luckily for his father, better senses prevented him from punching first and asking questions later. "You startled me." His father stood there unchanged. "They're a little dated."

Kane shrugged. "Clothes are clothes."

"They won't fit." Stephen pointed out.

The man studied his son carefully. Something must have changed in the last few years because he didn't remember his Alpha son looking so built. The blue jeans he wore were filled out with thick leg muscles, and his dark gray shirt was stretched to accommodate his broad shoulders and wider arms. Kane remembered the bean pole of a boy who was hauled out of his house in chains wearing black eye makeup, a homemade nose piercing, and spiked hair. That boy was no longer here. If he had met his son on the street for the first time, he never would have guessed the past he had. "I think Veo is bringing you back some more stuff. Did you see the shopping bag of socks, underwear, and the toiletries?"

Stephen nodded. "Can never have too much of that." He laughed.

"Shower is across the hall."

"Dad, this is my home. I know where the shower is."

"Towels are in the cupboard." With that, Kane left his son in peace and headed back towards the kitchen.

Stephen picked up the cast iron model of the motorcycle and held it in his hands. It was heavier than he remembered. To him, it was made of gold. Holding something he called his own meant everything to him now. Proudly, he walked it over to the nightstand and put it below the lamp. He sat on the bed which elicited an unexpected sound of pleasure. The bed was the softest thing he'd sat on for over three thousand days. It didn't squeak, it didn't move, and the comforter was smooth and gentle on his hands, unlike the rough burnt fabric he was used to. He knew he was going to have to take a shower quickly, otherwise he'd find himself falling asleep, and not waking up for a week. Before he did, he took his thumb and rubbed off a little dust on the front and back wheel of the model and watched it like he was guarding it with his life.

Picking through the clothes Veo had brought down from his old room was frustrating. With at least new underwear and socks, he suffered through wearing a pair of jeans he had from his duffel bag and settled on one of his old favorite t-shirts. It was a muscle shirt now. Surprisingly, it didn't smell like cigarette smoke, a habit he kicked in lockup.

Stephen walked into the living room to find his Sur sitting in his favorite chair reading the daily paper. He couldn't believe how the sight mirror-imaged everything from his past. Even with his father's older appearance and grayer hair, the button-down shirt with suspenders attached to dress pants, the wool socks sinking into a pair of house loafers, his right ankle up and supported on his left knee, and unshakable concentration were all the same. To any stranger, they'd think the old man was oblivious to the world around him. But growing up, Stephen had known better; his father always had a keen sense. He knew what went on in his surroundings and had great hearing when it came to catching conversations from another room.

When Stephen and Warren were growing up, all private conversations and actions took place in their rooms, away from his Sur's surveillance. Sometimes the cautious behavior proved futile, and the Alpha found out anyway. Stephen remembered several conversations in which he confronted his Veo, convinced the house was rigged with cameras and audio recording equipment. Of course, his Veo was entertained by such childish notions and always dismissed the allegations. That still didn't stop him and his brother from causing mischief outside the home. But Warren's version of mischief was nothing like Stephen's idea of mischief. Not even close.

For five minutes, Stephen sat across from his father on the couch, waiting for his Sur to start a conversation. But the man never flinched nor acknowledged him. It was as if Stephen wasn't there at all. Stephen thought it rude his father chose to act like he was invisible. But he realized his Sur had plenty of practice with his hobbies without him being there. To cut the silence, he cleared his throat. The man in turn adjusted his posture and flipped to the next page in his paper. No acknowledgement was given. Stephen repeated the action a second time.

Without looking up, Kane finally spoke. "Something you need? Was the shower okay?"

Stephen rolled his eyes. "The shower was fine, Dad."

"Good." Attempting to read the newspaper became difficult as he felt his son staring at him. "Something else?"

"Can we talk?" Stephen was shocked he even had to ask.

The newspaper crumpled and folded together in a disheveled attempt to return it to its original form. "The lawn needs to be kept up weekly. I'm sure you noticed the trees on your walk up the driveway. They need trimming and the branches will need to be hauled to the burn pit in the back. New siding and shingles are in the garage for the areas which need patchwork. Paint for the entire house is in there too. Joe down the street said he'd bring over a truckload of rock to refill the driveway. You can call him when you're ready. His number is on the fridge."

It took a second for Stephen to process what his dad was saying. "Okay?"

"What? You didn't think you were staying here for free, did you?"

"No, of course not." The truth was he suspected part of his return home was going to be reliving chores and work he did when growing up. The heavy-duty tasks his parents and brother joined in. He wasn't convinced he was going to get any help this time around.

"Without paying rent and having another mouth to feed, you're going to have to work it off somehow," Kane added.

Stephen wasn't fond of his father calling him a freeloader. "What do you mean 'without paying rent'?"

The old man grinned. "Plan on getting a job, do ya?"

"I'm going to look," Stephen insisted as he leaned forward and rested his elbows on his knees.

"Yeah, I'm sure," Kane murmured sarcastically. "No one is going to hire an ex-con fresh out of prison."

"Something will happen. I just have to find it." It was hard to look his father in the eyes, especially since he couldn't ignore the truth his father pointed out. He instead picked at his fingernail as he tried to come up with something intelligent, something to impress his Sur with. Unfortunately, his mind was blank now. That led him to the only questions he wanted answers to for years. "How come you never visited me? Why could I barely get you on the phone?"

Kane ran his fingers down his beard. He peered at his son: a full-grown man who had started to sound more and more like the teenager he once knew. The former mental state of being a parent slid back into position instantly. With it came the flow of Alpha pheromones which started to fume out of him, giving his son a reminder of who ruled in this house. "Quiet time starts at 10PM. No friends and no visitors. If I catch you or even *think* you have been using or have drugs on you, the street will be your home. Do I make myself clear?"

The scent of his father's domination filled the room. As if by hitting rewind on his life and then the play button, Stephen looked at the Alpha in the eyes and repeated the same response expected of him ever since he was a pup. "Yes, Sur. I understand."

A moment later, the front door clicked and then opened. Faint sounds of rustling bags and footfalls grew louder until they reached sight of the living room. Stephen looked back and caught a breath of fresh air. He quickly lifted himself off the couch and rushed to give his Veo the biggest hug he had in years. This time without restraints or watchful eyes of those who condemned him. Well... almost.

"You're here!" Marlon shouted in awe. He instantly teared up and dropped the shopping bags. Joyfully, he accepted his son's embrace and returned it full force. He hummed as he closed his misty eyes, trying to replay moments in his head about hugging his son way before any of the past happened. Although memories flooded in, they weren't the ones he wanted. Several instances of seeing his son for the last time before being arrested, arraigned, and convicted flashed in his mind. Each ordeal ended with him hanging onto Stephen for dear life until he was forced away. Today was different, but the pain of those days ran deep. "So good to have you home."

All Stephen wanted after getting off the bus was this. It was the number one reason he wanted Veo home when he arrived. Considering he and his Sur hadn't torn each other apart yet, Stephen still felt it was a great homecoming. He himself found it difficult not to join his Veo in the show of emotion, especially when he could hear his Omega father's voice trembling in his ear. "Where were you?"

Marlon finally let go to get another good look at his son. "I went out and got you some new clothes since I knew what I brought down from upstairs wouldn't fit you." He caught a glimpse of his current attire. "I see you found one of them."

"It's tight in the shoulders and back," Stephen shared.

"You can take those two bags there and try on what I bought you. If anything doesn't fit, let me know."

"Okay." He smiled.

Marlon's face couldn't be happier. "I thought you weren't coming in until after 4?"

"There was a..." Stephen looked back at his Sur who stood there silently, observing, judging. "I said it wrong. I meant to say 'before 4' not 'after.' Sorry about that."

"No, no. It's okay. I'm just sorry I wasn't here when you arrived." He reached down and grabbed a couple grocery bags. "I also thought we'd cook your favorite meal for your homecoming."

"Steak! Nice!" Stephen beamed. He tried not to think about how hard he'd have to work for his Alpha father to consider the meal "paid off".

"Thought we could cook them together," Marlon continued.

"Sounds great. I'll try on the clothes and then meet you in the kitchen."

"Wonderful. Kane, do you want to join us?" The Omega peered over at his mate with an overly stretched smile.

Kane slowly shook his head. "No." With that, he picked up the newspaper and began reading the same stories and events again, shielding his head behind them.

***

"I didn't think you liked to use so many seasonings." Marlon watched his adult son whiz around the kitchen, grabbing cloves of garlic, fresh rosemary, and cracked pepper into a cast iron pan with a large steak searing in butter.

"The options down in Brooks Haven are slim to none." Smelling the aromas of his favorite foods in a way he hadn't in years was like sex. It aroused all his senses and made his mouth water. There was no contest for the food in lockup. "Ketchup, mustard, relish, mayonnaise, salt, and pepper were about it. Working in their kitchen was nice until you found out how they prepared the food. Have you ever had a baked frozen pre-cooked steak?" He shuddered at its memory.

Marlon grimaced. "No. But I'm surprised they served steak at all."

"One day a year," Stephen replied as he turned his steak over, the sizzling sound rushing to his ears like sweet music. "They served steak one day a year: the prison's opening day anniversary. The biggest slap in the face is serving steak like it's some sort of honorary celebration. They treat it like a birthday with cake and everything."

"That does sound grim." Marlon finished whipping up the mashed potatoes with cream and chives. "Okay. Try this."

Stephen grabbed a spoon and dipped it into the pot. The smooth earthy consistency glided on his tongue and then down his throat. "Wow. Just like I remember it."

"I have your seal of approval then?"

With an "A-Okay" sign on his hand, the Alpha clicked his tongue. "Perfect." With a fork, he pierced the meat in the pan and pulled it off the heat onto the board to let it rest.

"That's a pretty thick cut. Are you sure you want it that rare?" Marlon asked.

"Absolutely!" Stephen replied emphatically. "I've never wanted to see a rare piece of meat more in my life."

"Why don't you tell your father it's time to eat?" The Omega wiped his hands on a kitchen towel and flipped it over his shoulder. He watched his son's tepid reaction to the request. Clearly, the two had a discussion before he got home.

Without missing a beat, Stephen walked into the living room. His Alpha father was reclined in his favorite chair with his eyes closed. At first, he wasn't sure if he should wake him, but after a second, he observed him flex his feet and scratch his arm which told Stephen he wasn't asleep. "Dinner's ready."

"I heard," Kane replied flatly.

*Of course, you did,* Stephen thought. "Were you going to join us?" His Sur remained as he was. No response. "Were you going to join—"

The footrest of the recliner snapped back and Kane launched himself off and straight toward the kitchen. He skimmed past his son, creating a slight breeze in the process.

Stephen stared awkwardly at the floor as his father gave him the cold shoulder. Knowing there was going to be sometime in the future where they'd have to talk about things, he just nodded to himself and joined his parents in their first family meal in ten years.

***

The mood of the evening was completely different with Kane present. It was obvious to Kane as well, but not due to the lack of leisure conversation. *That* was normal. His son's presence, however, created an atmosphere which made him feel uncomfortable in his own home. Because of that, Kane's demeanor and pheromone palate blatantly communicated dinner tonight had an objective: to eat and nothing else. All sat there without discussion as they ate. Occasionally, he cleared his throat which caused his family members to look up at him in anticipation, but nothing came. The meal wasn't silent, however. Like a mosquito buzzing in his ear, Kane suffered through Stephen's poor execution of cutting his steak. Sharp shrieks from his knife gliding along the plate ruptured the tranquility normally found during the meal. Finally, the noises were too much for Kane to bear.

"Are you trying to cut through your steak or through the table?" Kane criticized.

Stephen looked up as if coming out of a trance. Embarrassment flooded him as he realized his etiquette was less than to be desired. "Sorry," he murmured. "I've been so used to flimsy plastic, I didn't think about what I was doing."

"It's all right," Marlon stepped in. "I'm sure there will be a few things you'll need to readjust yourself to. Just give it time."

Stephen slipped into a smile as he appreciated the encouragement from his Veo. But a quick look back at his Sur wiped it away just as fast. He changed topics. "How are the Thompsons?" he pivoted.

Kane felt the pressure to contribute from both members at the table. "Rodney and Mike finally built that barn they'd been talking about for years. After their boys moved out, they had a lot of free time on their hands."

Taking a drink of water, Stephen nodded. "I remember them talking about it. How did it turn out?"

Kane reflected, "It's big. I'm surprised you didn't see it from the road when you got here."

"I didn't notice; didn't even think to look. I'll make sure to catch it tomorrow."

Marlon jumped in, "You have any thoughts on what you want to do tomorrow? I figured we could go for a walk around the pond in the morning and then do some light traveling in the city. You can see how much Tauris has changed. You won't recognize it. This city has been growing at an alarming rate. Who knows? Maybe one day we'll be bigger than Gray City."

"That's a little farfetched," Kane commented.

Stephen sat up tall in his chair, focusing on the remainder of food on his plate so he didn't have to watch his parents' reaction. "I was hoping tomorrow to start looking for a job."

Marlon instantly shot a look at his mate. When Kane looked away, it confirmed his suspicions. He sighed. "You don't need to do that yet."

"Yes," Stephen drew out, "the sooner the better. It's important I get back into being a productive member of society."

"*Back*?" Kane huffed. "That implies you were at one time." As he confidently stated the criticism, he felt the fumes come off his mate.

Stephen scrambled for a rebuttal. "I had a job once."

The elderly Alpha flexed his brow. "If I recall, you got fired after a month for showing up late and taking too many smoking breaks."

"Not true. I quit because they wouldn't give me *more* smoke breaks." Stephen cringed as he realized it didn't help him.

"Filthy habit—expensive too," Kane grumbled as he wiped his mouth with his napkin, stroking it on his beard to catch any debris.

"I quit years ago," Stephen mentioned, hoping it would earn some respect back.

Kane lifted himself up and out of the chair and tossed the napkin onto his plate. "Good. Then I won't have to worry about you smoking in the house, or worse, asking for money to buy that crap." He glanced at his mate. "I'm going to bed."

"Now?" Marlon asked, completely surprised.

"It's almost 9," Kane barked.

"It's not even 8 yet," Marlon replied.

The old Alpha stood there and examined his surroundings as if he'd never seen them before. It was then he noticed even though all the kitchen lights were on, darkness hadn't overtaken outside yet. Squinting his eyes at the grandfather clock in the corner and then to his watch once more, he searched his mind for a reply. "I'll read some before I fall asleep. You going shopping tomorrow?"

"For what?" Marlon asked.

"Clothes for Stephen."

Marlon saw his son give him a grim look out of the corner of his eye. Without flinching, the Omega smiled as he did a hundred times before. "Yes."

Kane nodded. "Okay. Goodnight."

"Goodnight, dad," Stephen said, waiting for his father's acknowledgement. Instead, Kane kept walking until he was out of sight. Realizing this was the best he could have asked for on day one, he waited until he heard the door to the master bedroom open and shut. "That was ... interesting."

"Sorry." Marlon frowned.

"For what?" Stephen asked.

"For not being here when you got here, for your father's lukewarm reception—"

"*That's* how you would describe that?"

"Give him time, Stephen. This is an adjustment for everyone. You know that," Marlon defended.

"Yeah, I do. But I've waited ten years for this and so have you. So why do I feel like dad thinks it wasn't long enough?"

"Not true!" Marlon reassured. "He hated you being locked up just as much as I did. It's just... having you back here brings up a lot of memories for him. For me too. And I'm sure it does for you."

Remembering how he felt when he first looked at the updated family pictures on the wall, Stephen understood where his Veo was coming from. "It does." As his Veo stared off into his own thoughts, Stephen took the moment to study him as he had his Sur. The years had been kinder on him by comparison; however, since his Omega father was eight years junior to his Alpha father, it was difficult to judge fairly. In addition, Marlon had visited Stephen periodically at Brooks Haven which lessened the effects of a ten-year period.

Thankfully, Marlon never lost his smile. In Stephen's opinion, it was his Veo's best feature, lifting and shining every part of his face in expression. His brown hair was longer than his Sur's, but his mustache and beard were trimmed close to the skin. The gray had come through more on his face, but it appeared more like natural highlight in his hair versus a clear sign of aging. Stephen was always jealous of his Veo's green eyes, a trait which was shared with his brother Warren. But Stephen inherited his Sur's brown eyes instead.

"Do you remember the time Warren laid back in his chair and put his feet up on the dining room table after dinner like he owned the place?"

Marlon gave his classic smile as he nodded his head. "Your father walked up and pulled the chair out from under him faster than a lightning strike. With the loud thud, I was surprised Warren didn't break a bone."

"I just remember his face." Stephen mimicked his brother being completely stunned and dumbfounded. "Then, Dad made him stand up for the rest of the meal and I think all the next day as well."

"Your father wanted more than that, but I put a stop to it." Marlon chuckled.

"How about the time he went to the pond by himself when he was six? We had no idea where he was. Then we finally ran down there, and he had taken his shoes and socks off and was walking knee-deep in the water."

"Wow, I hadn't thought about that one in a long time." The Omega sighed. "I was so mad at him for that."

Stephen scoffed. "I got into more trouble than he did for that considering I was supposed to be watching him"

"Yeah. I suppose you did." Marlon's smile relaxed as he reminisced about how his boys were raised. They were well-fed, clothed, and kept safe and warm. But that didn't mean the boys were happy—especially when it came to their Alpha father. Kane's dedication to his career kept him from being an active part of the family like he should have been. When he was home, the stress of the job drained his energy and his patience. Thus, the boys were constantly subjected to his misplaced criticism and anger, an area of his life he thought he could control. But the harder Kane squeezed, the more Warren faded into a quiet reclusive state and Stephen acted out.

"How has dad been doing?" Stephen asked. It's not as if he didn't ask over the years, but now Stephen felt he'd get more out of his Omega father than the previous "He's doing okay" line he constantly heard.

Marlon traced his finger in the natural pattern of the wood grain on the table. "He's doing okay."

*Or not,* Stephen thought. "I noticed he didn't have his pager on his belt. As a matter of fact..." Stephen glanced around the kitchen. "I don't see the scanner either. The patrol car wasn't in the driveway; I assume it's in the garage?" He saw the look on his father's face: ominous yet somber.

"He..." Marlon hesitated. "He retired."

The news was a complete shock. "Dad retired? *My* dad? We are talking about the same person, right?" The father Stephen knew was committed to his career for life. All he heard growing up were stories on lowlifes breaking the law and the consequences they brought upon themselves. What once was a bonding experience between him and his father became nothing more than condescending lectures on what could happen to him if he didn't "straighten out." Despite the years of constantly hearing the rhetoric directly from a cop, it did little to tame his behavior. But no one, not even his father, imagined the scenario which put him behind bars. "What about his goal of being a police chief?"

Marlon spoke softly as to not have his voice travel down to the bedroom. "Come on, Stephen. Your father is 60 years old. Did you really think the force was going to invest in him now?"

"I-I guess I don't know. Last, I remember, dad kept saying 'next year' it will happen. That's what we always heard."

"And that's what he kept hearing over the last ten years from his superiors. It never happened. Quite frankly, I'm surprised he didn't retire five years ago. It's not like people usually stay on the force for that long anyway—or any career. We only have so much time on this earth; I don't know why he'd want to only have a few years to enjoy retirement." Stephen gave him a look as if he was saying Kane was terminal. "Hypothetically, I mean."

"Oh." Stephen let the catastrophe in his mind fade. "Why were they hanging the carrot over his head for so long?"

"I'm sure they didn't want to lose him at the time," Marlon surmised. "He spent so many extra hours down at the precinct for the last ten years: early mornings, late nights."

"Why?"

Marlon tilted his head. "Think about it."

It took a moment, but then Stephen felt confident he found the reason. "A distraction." His Omega father nodded. "He sounds like a saint. It couldn't have been easy to constantly tell him 'No.'"

Marlon shook his head as he reflected on the constant disappointment his mate went through. "He was just so different after it happened." He swallowed hard. "I noticed it. You noticed it. His fellow officers and superiors, of course they saw it."

Stephen remembered what it was like seeing Kane after Warren had passed. His Omega father was an emotional mess but his Alpha father? It was as if someone sucked the life and soul of him. All that was left was an outer shell. Perhaps it was ignorance to think Kane overcame the tragedy and moved on with his life like nothing happened. That was stereotypical thinking, making an Alpha invincible to any life problem or challenge. Now that he was thinking rationally, Stephen realized just how much it still affected him today. The way he acted, the lack of persona, everything. It was all due to lingering effects of losing Warren … and something else.

"When did his memory start fading?" Stephen finally asked.

Marlon turned his head away and stared out the window. The streetlight on their property lit up the cool night in a white haze. Everything was quiet, just like it had been for too many years. "If you want to know what I really think, I started seeing signs of it even when you two were kids. But it was probably a few years ago when it became a regular occurrence."

"Is *that* why he didn't get the promotion? Or was it because he's not a Type 4 or Type 5?" Stephen's voice became stern as he recalled all the ridiculous assumptions that his family was undesirable, or they were lesser people because of it. It didn't matter who they were: friends, strangers, employers, teachers… if anyone's Status was higher than his family, a comment of superiority was sure to be uttered.

Marlon stared back. "Both factors made it easier not to give it to him. That's speculation though. No one knows the real reason. Be glad you don't have to deal with that nonsense."

It was true. Stephen may have been a part of an otherwise uniform Type 3 family, but he was the outlier. Somehow, he got "lucky" and was identified as a Type 4 at birth. Although he received praise for his identity, most of the time he received sympathy or worse yet, criticism for being a part of a family deemed beneath him.

Staying the course on his goal, Stephen crossed his arms, annoyed his Veo decided not to tell him of his father's condition sooner. "When did he officially retire?"

"Sixteen months ago, now. Winter Solstice."

A fire burned on Stephen's face. Remembering his Alpha father was still in the house, he kept his voice low, but strained with disappointment. "*Sixteen?* Are you kidding me? You couldn't have told me any of this sooner?"

Marlon rubbed his temples to help deal with the conflict. Considering he knew the reaction his son was capable of, he was thankful this was as far as it went. "Your father and I mutually decided not to tell you; there was no reason to."

"Why?" Stephen answered back in disbelief. "It's not like I could do anything about it."

"That's precisely the reason why we didn't tell you. We didn't want to tell you anything which would cause you to jeopardize your release date. We were worried your anger could get out of control," Marlon answered, hoping his son understood their position.

Stephen grunted. "I told you; I've worked on my anger issues. I'm not that way anymore."

"And I'm grateful for it. But it's not like we knew anything about how it was going for you in Brooks Haven. It was bad enough your father kept telling me stories of the things which happened when he was on the job. Wolf-God, some of the things he told me... ugh... gave me nightmares!" he shivered. "Neither he nor I wanted any of that to happen with you, especially if it was based on something we said or did."

"You mean like getting rid of my bedroom?" Stephen spat back.

Marlon bit his lip. "That was one."

"Anything else?"

Marlon slowly shook his head. "Not that I can think of. Again, we were just worried is all. Your Sur and I wanted you out of there as soon as possible."

Stephen replied sarcastically, "I'm surprised Sur cared so much."

"Stop," Marlon lamented. "He loves you."

"Would it have killed him to say it more when we were growing up?!"

Acknowledging the lack of affection was difficult for Marlon. It's not as if his son was the only one struggling with that issue. "I think we all wish we could have done things differently." Inside, Marlon's stomach doubled over, fearing he pushed too far.

The comment was harsh; point well taken. "Can I help you with the dishes?" Stephen asked, unwilling to push the issue further.

Marlon was relieved at his son's pivot—a new development for sure. Perhaps he was serious about his change in attitude. "Please." He smiled.

---

That night, lying in bed felt unreal for Stephen. To think that 24 hours ago he was sleeping on a worn cot on a concrete slab with nothing but four empty walls surrounding him was inconceivable. Even though he wasn't in his old bedroom, part of Stephen felt like he never left the house and that his time served was some nightmare he finally woke up from. But there were plenty of things today which reminded him the past ten years were no dream: Warren was gone, his parents had aged and so had he, and his Sur acted as if he was a foreigner. That all was second to the fact his father's mental health was failing, a revelation he was still bitter over. However, therapy over the past several years had conditioned Stephen to focus on the many positives in his life instead of the few negatives—a philosophy and tactic he never could have considered before incarceration.

As he turned on his side to face the model bike on the night-stand, he reviewed those positive affirmations: he was alive, healthy, fit, and still had a lot of life to live. He was out of jail and a free man now. He knew trying to find a job was going to be difficult with a felony on his record, but he was determined to find something to show himself and his family he wasn't a waste. He was grateful to have his Veo's support; he hoped his Sur's support would come in time.

The soft comfort of the bed, and knowing he wasn't surrounded by criminals or armed guards, cast a spell of exhaustion over him. His arm grazed the die cast motorcycle as he reached up for the lamp to switch the light off. That's when he thought of it: Crusher. *Wolf-God*, he thought to himself as he immediately sat up in bed. He couldn't believe he almost forgot about his bike, his pride and joy, his former key to escaping the hell he dealt with at home. An uneasy feeling came over him as he pondered its condition over the last decade, or worse, wondered if it was still even here. Had his Sur or Veo sold it? Desperately, he wanted to get out of bed and sneak into the garage. But one thing he remembered about his Sur was his keen wolf hearing. Maybe now his father's condition had deteriorated; but tonight wasn't the night to push his luck. He sated his curiosity on knowing first thing in the morning, he was going to check and see if it was still there. If it was, perhaps there was a minute chance his Sur kept up on Crusher, and he could use it to ride into town. Stephen closed his eyes and commanded his brain to shut off so tomorrow could get here faster.

# CHAPTER 03:

# LIVING A LIFE OF OPTIMISM

"No way!" Daniel gasped in awe. He shuffled alongside on the sidewalk as Alexander recounted the previous night's events at the bar.

"That's like the tenth time you've said that." Alexander laughed at his friend as they fast-paced to his favorite wholesale store.

"That's because this is absolutely incredible!" Excitement tingled throughout Daniel's body all the way up to his styled red hair. Continuing to stare at Alexander in disbelief resulted in him bumping into oncoming traffic. Patrons grunted and cursed him as he took up extra space he didn't need to. He apologized multiple times before finally getting a grip on himself and his surroundings. After sticking near Alexander like a lost puppy in his oversized turquoise sweatshirt, he continued his incessant need to find out every bit of detail of his friend's celebrity encounter. "What did Mr. Whitmore want at *your* place?"

The question was honest, but Alexander couldn't help but feel insulted at the insinuation. "He wanted to know if this was the right place to get an unregistered gun, an escort, and some blow." Daniel stopped in his tracks as his eyes widened. Alexander rolled his eyes. "He's looking for a venue to host a fundraiser rally for Jesse Minh on his re-election campaign." The two finally reached the liquor outlet and walked in effortlessly as the automatic doors opened. Alexander grabbed an oversized cart and separated it from the queue. Then he grinned as he happily told Daniel the best part of the night. "And he wants it to happen at South Street."

Daniel jumped until he was as tall as Alexander and shouted out a hoot and a holler. "Aw, yeah!"

This caused several patrons and a few employees of the outlet store to stare at them awkwardly. Alexander wanted to bop him on the head until he was a foot below the concrete floor, officially turning the Type 2 Omega into a legalized midget. He opted not to, fearing it would garner even more attention. "Hey! For Wolf-God's sake, we're in a store, Daniel."

"I'm sorry, I'm sorry!" The young man's face turned red as he noticed the unamused crowd looking at them as they strolled down the aisles. "But how can you not be excited?"

"Who said I wasn't? I'm ecstatic! I just didn't chug an iced coffee in two seconds like you." It was true; it was all Alexander could think about ever since it happened. The opportunity consumed him so much, he struggled to remember the list of items he came in for or where anything was even though he was a regular here for stocking the bar. Luckily, seeing one item he needed refocused his memory. "Hey, grab six of those, will you?"

Daniel looked at the six-packs and began picking them up two at a time. "When is this happening?"

"In about ten days."

"Stocking up a little early, aren't you?" Daniel asked as he finished his friend's request.

"Are you kidding? I'm going to have to do this trip at least once more after this. I'm only here because there's a few things I can only get here for the prices they offer. I don't know how Brice manages to sell this stuff this cheap."

Daniel snorted. "Probably stuff that falls off the back of the truck."

"Be nice," Alexander scolded.

"What? I'm just kidding."

Alexander looked around, making sure no one heard the rude comment. He leaned in. "Come on, you know how I've had to build my reputation up here. By all means, I should be kissing Brice's feet for even letting me get supplies here. I can't imagine the flack he gets for doing business with me."

The Type 2 Omega raspberried as he disapproved of his friend speaking so low of himself, especially since it implied Daniel himself should be thankful he was even allowed to enter the building. "You know, not every business is Status-driven."

"I find most aren't here in Tauris City. That's not the problem. It's the public perception. I'm just happy Brice has a good head on his shoulders to know better." Out of the corner of his eye, Alexander spotted the man of the hour. "And speak of the Wolf-Devil, himself."

"Alex! How are you doing?" The older gentleman smiled. His bushy eyebrows and mustache matched the light gray sweater he wore, covered by his blue apron.

"Doing fine. Here getting the usuals." His eyes glanced down at the wet mop in his hand. "Uh-oh. Cleanup, aisle six?"

"Just a broken bottle. I know that's hard to believe in a liquor store."

"Right?" Alexander hummed.

Brice noticed the young man next to him. He appeared a little unkept with his wilder hair, holes in his jeans, and old sneakers. Obviously, this was a Low-Type, lower than even Alexander. "And who is this? Is this Sean?"

Alexander laughed nervously. "No. This is my friend, Daniel."

Daniel outstretched his hand like a pup introducing himself to his teacher. "Pleased to meet you."

Brice gave him a firm grip. He saw Daniel wince; clearly he wasn't used to a firm Alpha handshake. "Likewise." He turned his attention back to Alexander. "Are you looking for anything specific?"

"Hmm. No. Any specials I should know about?"

"I have an overstock of vodka you might want to check out in the last aisle. I took a couple extra dollars off that. Make sure when you're ready to checkout you find me so I can get your membership discount as well."

"Of course!" Alexander nodded.

"Well, this floor isn't going to mop itself. See you in a bit!"

"Weird Alpha..." Daniel mumbled to himself as he trailed behind Alexander who pushed the heavy cart down the sidewalk.

Alexander furrowed his brows as he looked back at his friend who had his arms crossed. "Who? Brice?"

"Yeah."

"What's got you all pouty all of a sudden?" The cart's wheels vibrated loudly as it transitioned to the curb near the vehicle.

"How could he ask if I was Sean? Could he not sense that I was an Omega?" Daniel wondered if there was something legitimately wrong with the man or if he was just looking to insult him.

Alexander sighed. "I think he was just teasing you, Daniel." He pulled his key out of his pocket and signaled the rear to automatically open the hatch.

"I didn't find it funny." Alexander lifted items out of the cart and handed them to Daniel who in turn reached into the vehicle as far as he could to start loading it with their items. "So, he hasn't met Sean yet?"

"Why would I bring Sean here?"

Daniel hiked his eyebrow. "Um. Because he's your boyfriend?"

"That doesn't mean I bring him along on my errands. He works too, you know." One by one, vodka bottles were handed out as Daniel placed them in cardboard boxes already neatly set-up for loose bottles.

"Come to think of it, I don't really see you and Sean together doing much of anything," Daniel pointed out.

"So?" Alexander felt his nerves rise, fearing he knew what questions were coming.

"Is there a reason for that? I mean, if I had a boyfriend, I'd be with him every chance I got... wanting to ride him." The Type 2 Omega winked.

Alexander winced. "There's a lot more to relationship than sex."

"I wouldn't know." Daniel groaned.

"He's busy with his career and I'm busy with mine. That doesn't leave a lot of time, especially since my job requires me to be more available on the weekends. That's why." Alexander began pushing the empty cart to the caddy, hoping it would give some reprieve from the interrogation. But Daniel was hot on his heels.

"Sounds like a convenient excuse if you ask me." Daniel observed his friend tense, knowing he hit a speck of truth with his claim, especially when he could smell the nerves coming off his pheromones. "I mean, you guys have been together, what? A year?"

"Two."

"And yet you guys haven't formalized a mating contract yet?"

Alexander gave the oversized cart one forceful push which slammed it to the far back, crashing it into the others. He exhaled and turned to his friend who found no issue sticking his nose into personal affairs. "You really only need those when you plan on moving in together or have assets you need to protect."

"Assets... like a bar?" Daniel pointed out.

Alexander dismissed the claim. "I'm not worried about Sean trying to take the bar." As they casually walked back, he realized they had left the back of the vehicle open. "Fuck, I forgot to close it." Both men hustled back to inspect the inventory, making sure no one inconspicuously walked by to take anything.

"You also should have a mating contract when you're planning for pups." Daniel slipped into a grin.

Alexander scanned all the bottles. Nothing appeared to be missing. Then he gulped down his anxiety. "I don't have heats anymore, so it hasn't been a pressing issue for me."

Daniel couldn't believe his ears. "Whoa! Since when?"

Alexander couldn't believe he was having this conversation right now in a business parking lot. "Since... I don't know... as long as I can remember?"

"Shouldn't you go to the doctor for that?"

Alexander swayed in consideration. "I almost did a few times. But the more I thought about it, the more I just realized dealing with heats and the biological urge to have pups is just a distraction. Ever since owning a bar became a tangible dream, I'm glad I didn't have pups. There's no way I could do this and raise a family at the same time. Plus, Sean hasn't pushed the issue, and I'm glad he hasn't. I think that says a lot."

Daniel twitched his lips. "To me, it says you don't want to have pups with *him*. What are you going to say if he asks you?"

Alexander relented and sat on the edge of the open trunk, crossing his own arms like Daniel. He looked his friend straight in the eye, remembering why they were friends in the first place. Daniel acted immature sometimes, but when he finished fooling around, he was a great companion who wasn't afraid to tackle tough conversations with sincerity. "Look. Sean is a great guy. The man is stable, he has a job, he's intelligent, and he's even a Type 4."

Daniel kicked a rock near his foot. "Good for him."

Alexander ignored the attitude. "He's tall, handsome—"

"Handsome? He's got those big glasses," Daniel criticized as he pantomimed thick frames with both of his hands over his eyes.

"He doesn't like contacts. I've seen him wear them; he looks like a totally different person without his glasses. But I think the glasses are part of his charm."

"Hmph. If you say so. You're the one who has to sleep with him."

"Yes, I do," Alexander replied firmly. "And the sex, even though it's been awhile, is ... all right."

"Ouch," Daniel stressed. "You still didn't talk about the 'having pups' thing."

Alexander relaxed his shoulders and rubbed his eyes. "Please don't tell him this, okay?" He looked towards his friend who appeared to accept the plea. "I'm not even entirely sure what *I* want to do about pups. But when I force my mind into a scenario where I do want them, I can't imagine myself having them with Sean. I don't know why ... but something stops me every time when I try to consider it."

"Wow... what are you going to do about that?"

"I guess if Sean asks, I'm just going to have to tell him I'm not interested. And if that affects our relationship, I'll have to accept the consequences."

"What if it *ends* your relationship?"

Alexander paused, making sure what he was about to say was true. "Then I guess it ends."

"You're really okay with that?" Daniel double checked.

The conversation was becoming uncomfortable. Whatever conclusion Daniel was reaching for, he wasn't going to get it. "You're creating farfetched scenarios here; lighten up. Sean and I like what we have now, and that's what is important. We don't have to be perfect or infatuated with each other all the time. Besides, it's not like we're Fated Mates or anything."

"How cool would that be if you two were?"

Alexander snorted. "Wolf-God, if Sean was my Fate, I'd hope it would be different than what it feels like right now. Otherwise, that would be depressing."

A tall, rugged man in a casual blue suit walked up to the rear of the vehicle where the two Omegas chatted. "What would be depressing?"

Alexander glanced over and then nearly jumped to the moon with a loud fright which startled Daniel next to him just the same. The man was also startled, but nowhere near the two Omegas. Instantly, Alexander put his hand over his heart which pumped rapidly like a hard fist against his breastbone as his lungs heaved. "Sean! Wolf-God! You scared the shit out of me."

Daniel hunched over with his hands on his knees trying to catch his breath. He swore he pissed himself and casually glided his hand over his crotch just to make sure he didn't. "Warn somebody next time!"

"Didn't mean to do that."

"What are you doing here?!" Alexander inquired.

The rugged yet sharp man pointed to the casual restaurant at the opposite end of the parking lot. "I sometimes come here to pick up lunch. As I walked out, I just happened to see you come out of the liquor warehouse. I decided to walk over and say hi." Sean leaned his head in to see the massive amounts of liquor. "You two headed off to a party? That might be a little much for you two, especially you, short stuff." Sean winked at Daniel.

The Type 2 Omega didn't find the same humor in his joke. After regaining his composure, Daniel observed Sean looking very elite today with his perfectly sculpted and spiked brown hair and meticulously trimmed beard. His silver eyes sparkled yet looked noticeably different than usual. "Hey, Sean. How come you aren't wearing those oversized glasses you normally do? They're my favorite." He grinned. Alexander responded by backhanding him into his chest.

The Type 4 Alpha smiled as he admired Daniel's attempt. It had little effect. "You may be disappointed to know that I have reinvigorated my efforts to wear contacts again. I've been receiving so many compliments without the glasses lately, present company included, that I've decided to see if I can make it stick this time."

"You look great, no matter what to me," Alexander complimented his mate and planted a firm kiss on the statuesque urbanite.

"So do you, babe," Sean hummed. "What were you two discussing? Sounded serious."

Alexander glanced back at Daniel who looked like a deer in the headlights. "The Whitmore event coming up. You know, I'm just nervous about it, is all."

Daniel put his hands on his hips. "You told him already? Before me?"

"I texted him," Alexander explained.

"That's wonderful news! I'm so proud of you." Sean came in for another embrace and quick peck on the lips. Out of the corner of his eye, he saw Daniel displeased with the whole thing. "Don't worry about it. It's going to be amazing."

"You're going to be there, right?" Alexander asked.

"Of course, I will! I'll try to be there early to help if I can."

"Thanks." Alexander smiled.

"Is that what all this is for?" Sean nodded to the provisions.

"Most of it is. I'll be back here a couple of times I'm sure."

"You should have called me," Sean stated. "I could have come and helped you."

Daniel stood up straight. "I helped just fine."

Sean smiled at the Omega trying to validate himself. "So, you did." Then, he turned back to his mate. "How about dinner this evening?"

Alexander lit up. "Sounds great. I'll need to finish my afternoon shift, but it shouldn't be a problem. It's Eric's shift tonight."

"Great. I'll text you later, then." Sean gave a quick look at Daniel who poorly concealed a sour look. "See ya, Daniel."

In return, Daniel contrived a pleasantry as Sean walked back in the direction of his car.

"Don't start!" Alexander growled as he and Daniel hauled the last of the supplies into the back storage room of the bar.

"I'm just—"

"I don't really want to hear it right now," Alexander fumed as he put away the last case of beer. He hoped the manual labor would help alleviate the pent-up frustration, but it only exacerbated it. "I have enough of my own problems. I don't really need you adding to them."

"Didn't you hear the comment he made about me being some short lightweight who can't hold his liquor? I mean, is he reverting to 16 and making fun of people by taking cheap shots?"

Alexander closed the walk-in refrigerator and glared at his friend. "I don't know. Are you 5 and doing the same thing?"

Daniel reflected on the moment he threw out the glasses comment. "At least I wasn't overt about it."

Alexander laughed. "Oh, that's right. He's just a dumb Alpha who can't understand nuance."

"I don't know why you're mad at me so much and trying to defend him considering what you told me today," Daniel deflected.

"I was just venting, Daniel," Alexander defended. "If I can't voice my opinions to you anymore without you throwing them back at my face, I just won't share them with you."

The thought scared Daniel to think his friend would do such a thing. "Really?" he spoke softly.

"No, not really," Alexander fumbled his discontent. "I'm just going through a lot of emotions right now."

Daniel curled his lip. "I know. You're right; I was—" A clunking sound echoed from the bar. Once again, both Omegas were startled by the unexpected noise. "What was that?" Daniel whispered.

"Someone's in the bar," Alexander replied. Not in the mood to play games, he hurried into the main hall, feeling Daniel behind him in his shadow. Upon entering, he instantly recognized the man sitting at the end, reviewing paperwork. "Eric?! What are you doing here? Your shift isn't until 6."

The Alpha looked up with the brightest face he'd shown in years. "There's my favorite business partner!" He walked up to Alexander who was now frozen and gave him an uncomfortable look. Ignoring it completely, he continued his goal with arms outstretched before wrapping him up in a big embrace. Eric chuckled to himself and then finally noticed his business partner still unmoved. If anything, he was even more disturbed than before. "What? Can't I give you a hug?"

"What has you all chipper?" Alexander wasn't sure if he ever saw Eric with such joy, not even when they secured the bar or had the grand opening.

"Can't I just be happy to see you?" Eric asked, playing all innocent.

"No," Stephen replied flatly. "Why are you here so early? You're still coming in tonight, right?"

"Yeah, I'll be here," Eric confirmed. "Just came in for a bit to review the inventory. I'm glad you picked up some stuff; it will save me a trip later."

"I was able to go down to Skyline and get some good deals from Brice," Alexander informed.

Eric shook his head. "Man, I'm still surprised you risk going down there. Some idiot is going to accost you at some point. You think Brice is a nice guy now ... wait until he's forced to decide between you and Higher Types. It won't go well."

"I'll worry about that when it happens. Anyway, there's a ton of IPA and vodka back there now and a few of those Top Shelf items I figured we could use for the fundraiser next week."

"Sweet! Awesome! Fantastic!" Eric rattled off as he headed back to his inventory list, hastily making new adjustments.

Alexander squinted as he surmised his own conclusion. "There it is."

"What?" Eric asked without looking up.

"That's why you're in such a good mood. Matthew Whitmore's event coming up."

"Hey," Daniel interjected, "was I the last person to know?" Both Eric and Alexander ignored him.

"Of course, that's why I'm in such a good mood. Are you kidding? This single event could put South Street Tavern on the map and become the number one hybrid location for High Types and Low Types alike. Can you imagine this business's potential if we had both?"

Alexander felt like he was talking to a wall. "We already have both Types coming in, Eric. Where have you been lately?"

"You know what I mean." Eric waved off. "I'm proud of you, Alex."

The compliment shocked Alexander. "Really?" He walked over and sat next to his business partner. "What happened to being the disappointment who needed to double revenue as a last ultimatum?"

"Shit. If this event goes as well as I think it will, the city officials will not only have to eat their words, but they'll be thanking us for being such a shining beacon downtown, especially being so close to the Medical Center. In fact, I'd suspect that as word travels, we're going to be busier than we ever were before in the next few days. Maybe even tonight. I texted every single person in my phone about the event. I suggest you do the same if you haven't already."

Alexander gulped. "I don't know, Eric. Neither Whitmore nor Minh have even announced it themselves yet."

Eric's face went cold. "What do you mean? This is still happening, right? Fuck, Alex, come on! Don't do this to me!"

The panic set in. Alexander held up his hand in a defensive position. "Just calm down! I'm sure he will announce it in a day... or two."

"Or *two*?!" Eric catastrophized.

The ending of the conversation last night flashed into Alexander's mind, especially the part where he worried if Whitmore would even remember making such a proposal from the inebriated state he was in. He tried not to mentally fall to pieces on the devastating possibility this was all pointless.

"How about an hour ago?" Daniel announced, scanning through his phone. Both Alexander and Eric snapped back toward the near invisible Omega and rushed up to him to confirm the monumental revelation.

"Well, I'll be damned," Alexander mumbled as he saw several posts pop up on social media apps from both iconic figureheads.

Eric could hardly contain himself. He vocally gave himself a beat to jive to in celebration. "Who wants a drink?"

"I do!" Daniel bounced.

"I'll sit this one out," Alexander deflated.

Eric stopped his groovy dance and cocked his head at his business partner. "What's wrong? This should be a victory lap for you."

"I'll save it for when the night is here and showing success. I'm not sure how we're going to handle an event like that. We barely survived opening night with the crowds that were packed into here."

Eric rubbed his chin in deep thought. "Hmm. That's a good point. If business is going to go the way I think it is … we need more help here on a regular basis. We're gonna need to hire a new regular bartender or bar back. For the fundraiser, we'll need a couple extra hands as well." He pointed at Daniel. "You available to help that night?"

"I wouldn't miss it for the world!"

"Good." Eric set up three shot glasses and filled them from one of their fruit-infused canteens behind the bar. If he had to, he was going to force the drink down Alexander's throat to get him to celebrate the moment. But like usual, when his business partner was in a crummy mood, Alexander just rolled his eyes in surrender and tossed the drink back like a man. "I'll start making inquiries for applicants, but you're going to have to do the auditions."

"Really?" Alexander lamented. "You don't think I have enough to do around here?"

"I have another full-time job, Alex. When do you expect me to do it? Plus, whoever we choose is going to need to get trained in and comfortable with this place by the time the event rolls around.

That's not a lot of time. The hardest part is going to be getting someone in here."

Alexander propped his arm on the bar and then rested his head on his fist. He thought about Eric's logistics as he pressed his finger to his lip. As the new business on the block, South Street didn't have the reputation nor the finances to pay top dollar. In addition, there was always a difference between supporting Omega rights to own a bar at the voting booth versus being employed in one. Without being a Type 4 or Type 5 Omega, opponents were much more at ease to criticize the efforts ... or worse. "I'll see what I can do."

"That's the spirit!" Eric refilled everyone's glass. "To putting South Street on the map!"

"South Street!" they all shouted before sealing it with their elixir—hoping it would send fate to them in their favor.

***

"And when should we hear by?" Sean listened carefully to his client speak quietly on the phone while carrying a difficult accent. "Uh-huh... uh-huh..."

Alexander sat at the dinner table, patiently waiting as he always had. The waiter slowly crept up and gestured to his glass, so as not to disturb the call. The Omega nodded and silently thanked him for his efforts. Sean pointed to his own empty glass and affirmed another for himself.

"Mr. Yellis, I can't thank you enough for the update. I'll be looking for the funds first thing in the morning. On behalf of T-One and myself, we appreciate your business as always. Uh-huh... uh-huh. Of course! Talk to you tomorrow." Quickly, he hit the "End" button and exhaled. "I'm sorry, babe."

"No, I get it." Alexander's tone reflected this was not an exception, but rather a routine. "Business is business."

"*You* are my business." Sean replied. He found his mate's exhausted hand, laying there on the soft cloth of the round table. He picked it up and brought it carefully to his lips and gave a gentle peck before rubbing it lightly with his thumb.

The gesture eased Alexander back to contentment. He picked up his silk napkin and laid it across his lap, anticipating their entrées to arrive any minute. "Sounds like it went well."

"Getting this client is the best thing that's happened to me in two years!" Sean gloated with excitement.

"Wow," Alexander marveled, "dare I ask what happened two years ago?"

"You know." Sean winked.

The Omega smiled as he indeed knew the serendipitous event to which his mate referred. Right after Alexander and Eric secured the offer on South Street Tavern, they needed a bank to approve the loan. Remembering Sean for the first time as he greeted them both into Territory One, sent shivers throughout his body. The manly Alpha charmed him, and the rest was history. "You're too sweet."

"*You* yourself have a milestone coming up. Any updates on the fundraiser for Jesse Minh? Has Matthew Whitmore reached out to you again?"

Anxiousness once again consumed the Omega as he thought about the upcoming event. The dinner was supposed to be a nice escape from it all, but up until now, the romantic atmosphere of the upscale restaurant was nothing more than patiently waiting for his mate to finish what was the second call which came through since they arrived. It wasn't as if Alexander didn't plan on discussing the once-in-a-lifetime opportunity; it was one of the reasons why they were there that night—to celebrate. But he didn't anticipate this being the first conversation they'd have for the evening. "The only update I have is what I sent you through text: the announcement now both Jesse and Matthew put out. Haven't heard anything directly. I'm just moving forward like everything is still a go. I hope that's a safe bet." Alexander swirled his wine glass to compensate for the nerves before taking his next drink.

"Absolutely. Matthew did what he needed to do in my opinion. Don't take any offense that he didn't say anything to you personally. He's a celebrity after all."

Alexander squinted. "I wasn't taking any offense."

"Are you prepared for it? Do you need me to do anything?" Sean once again picked up his phone and rushed through his calendar, making sure he had the event saved.

The Omega winced. "Not unless you want to be a bartender or bar back." Sean's gaze stayed locked onto his phone, giving off the impression he didn't even hear the comment. Finally, he responded.

"I can't imagine any of those tasks require too much skill..." The words were slow, as if they were inconvenient to share. Putting his phone down, he gave Alexander his full attention. "But unfortunately, I'll be at the bank running a Quarterly for the region. I'm going to try and be there as early as I can, but I don't want to give you an answer and then not be able to make it. Sorry." He gave slight frown to round out his apology.

"I understand." Alexander answered deflated.

"Does that mean you're looking for help?"

The Omega nodded. "Daniel will be there, but we need another guy who can basically run continuous laps around the place. Ideally, he'd be a person with experience who could relieve me, Eric, Bruce, or James at the bar when needed too."

Sean laughed. "Daniel... that Omega sure has spunk."

"Hey, if spunk is all I can get, I'll take it at this point."

"To 'run continuous laps around the place' at possibly one of the biggest events you'll ever host at South Street? The poor guy is going to end up on the bottom of someone's shoe before the night's over." Sean knocked back his glass. He searched for their waiter, hoping he was nearby.

Alexander didn't appreciate the comment. It didn't help he had to defend Sean earlier when Daniel made the claim his mate wasn't giving him the respect he deserved. "Can we ease up on the 'short and feeble Omega' jokes tonight?" he pleaded. "He's my friend and is helping me when I really need it."

Sean sat up and realized the situation was more dire than he originally thought. "Oh. Sorry." He tried finding his way back to good graces. "I'm just playing; he knows that. You know that." Alexander glanced away and gave a half-smile as an acknowledgement. "I get it; you're worried about the event, right?" The Omega nodded. "It will be great. Eric will be there leading the team and you'll have Bruce and James by your side every step of the way." He caught himself. "And Daniel too, of course." His mate stayed silent, proving his words weren't effective. Sean tightened his jaw and then let out an exhale of nerves. "I want to talk to you about something."

Alexander felt Sean's pheromone pallet become thick. He knew that change and dreaded the familiar conversation coming. Relief came when a team of waiters arrived with their entrées. The distinguished men took their time, showing off the meticulously plated works of art like they were having to sell the menu all over again. The eldest, and most experienced, cut the small tenderloin into fine slices. A charred smokey black bled into a pink, red center, juices falling to the cutting board below it. Then, like falling dominoes, the filets of beef were hoisted onto the flat side of the large blade and placed on a bed of bright crisp salad greens topped with parmesan flakes.

Another server transferred stewed potatoes and carrots from a cast iron Dutch oven onto a plate. Then, proudly placed a portion of tenderized beef on top. Over it all, a thick dark gravy rained down from a large ladle high above it, soaking into every nook and cranny it could find before pooling at the bottom of the white ceramic. Then, he placed it in front of Sean who inspected every side and angle of the dish. "Is everything to your liking, sir?" The waiter asked while noting the visual inquisition.

Sean grabbed his knife and fork and pressed into a carrot, then a potato, and finally, his meat. He hummed. "Looks alright." He criticized. "Did the chef get my preferences on the seasonings?"

"Absolutely." The waiter confirmed.

With a tepid disposition, Sean glided his large fork across the layer of gravy and placed it on his tongue. He ignored the look from Alexander as he judged the flavor of the profile. Then, he nodded. "That will do." He looked at this mate, whose pheromone pallet was changing with every moment. "Can we talk?" He tried again.

Alexander broke his concentration from constantly turning over the lettuce and toppings. Anxiousness took over him again. "Oh, it's nothing that needs to be talked about here. Maybe after dinner?"

"No, no. I need to say it. I want to be open with you. I think this is the perfect time to bring this up." The Alpha insisted.

Fear drove Alexander to quickly shove a bite into this mouth. While chewing, he gathered why Sean wanted it here so badly. The atmosphere forced decorum and social expectation to keep a conversation going, especially since their table sat in the middle of the upscale restaurant. Without answering, he focused in and waited.

"Why won't you conceive a mating contract with me?"

The Omega's intuition was spot on. Unfortunately, it didn't initiate any positive changes in his own pheromone pallet. Sean's facial reaction to it said it all. "It's just not something I'm ready for."

"Two years? Some initiate it in six months—most within a year." He saw Alexander's expression widen. "Well, they at least talk about it at least."

Despite Alexander's reservations, he knew Sean had a point. Tonight, what bothered him the most was Daniel's eerie intuition that a discussion was due. Maybe he just jinxed him. "That's fair."

"So, what's holding you back now?"

"I love everything we have together now. Is it needed?" He hoped the comment wasn't insulting.

"Look. I understand your desire to be independent. But is being contracted with an Alpha who wants to take care of you and be your forever mate so bad? I'm not looking to control you." Alexander began to make a rebuttal, but he held up his hand which stopped the attempt. "Let's not pretend, Alex. You wear the rhetoric on your sleeve, your forehead, everywhere. And I've heard you utter the sentiment in the bar before.

*What? The handful of times you've been there?* Alexander thought to himself. He sighed in defeat. "Okay, I admit it. I grip the rhetoric a bit too tight. I can see how you think it's a crutch. It's just hard to not have it there when there's always someone who thinks I desperately need to hear their opinion on how I'm incapable and need an Alpha watching and guiding me. First of all, it's hilarious how each time it's said, every person thinks I'm hearing it for the first time. It's like they think they're telling me wisdom I've never heard before and the revelation will help me see the error of my ways. It doesn't help some of the closet people I have in my life do it too: Eric, Jin, my Sur."

"I get it. I really do. I just hope you aren't including me with that category." Putting himself out there made his stomach knot.

Alexander gave a pregnant pause. His voice finally softened. "Of course not."

"Good." Sean stated in a moment of relief. "Can you... can you just promise me you'll think about it and not leave me hanging this time? I want a future with you, Alex."

The Omega nodded. "I know you do, Sean. I do too. I promise."

Sean brightened, but it was only for a moment. Suddenly, once again, his phone went off. He grabbed it quickly, making it once again his number one priority. "Sean Crenshaw with Territory One. "Mr. Shanahan—how are you?"

Alexander tightened his lips and resumed kneading the now wilted salad.

# CHAPTER 04:

## FINDING NOTHING BUT DEAD ENDS

Waking up in a home versus a prison cell was where the comfort ended for Stephen. For starters, he had been trained to wake up at dawn every morning. The routine held its grip tight, and he tossed and turned until finally giving up and letting daylight win. Today, he didn't see it as a problem since the first thought he had was investigating to see if his parents kept his bike.

He snuck out the front and lifted the heavy garage door in a frightening sound which convinced him he woke up the entire rural area. The garage door springs obviously needed tending. Inside, the space was hardly recognizable. What was once a meticulously cleaned and organized space for two cars, his bike, and a well-equipped work bench was now more indicative of a haunted museum of rusted relics and dusty boxes. Stephen surmised this was where some of his things were boxed up and some of Warren's perhaps. From the looks of everything else, his Sur contemplated being a mechanic for a hobby. But for the life of him, he couldn't figure out what he was even trying to fix.

The collection of junk and boxes easily pushed the cars out into the driveway permanently. The lack of defined pathways made the search for his bike a greater challenge than he thought—until he saw a familiar blue plastic tarp over the exact-sized item he was looking for. Maneuvering through the jungle carefully, he slowly moved and resituated boxes into made-up spaces like an advanced brain puzzle to get full access to what he knew had to be there.

Unfortunately, lifting the tarp didn't yield the results he wanted. Was it his bike from a decade ago? If it was, it went through years of hell to get to the poor condition it was in now. Despite being covered with a tarp, the layers of dirt and dust consumed every nook and cranny it could find. Most of the wiring to the throttle had deteriorated, and the front headlight... what front headlight? Stephen felt a pressure built up inside from the shear disappointment. If there were any doubts this was once his bike, they were taken care of when he used his thumb to brush off the front emblem: a maniacal skull with flames coming off it. *Crusher*. Unsure of where to begin, his next venture in the garage was to find a wrench set.

Hours melted away in seconds. The more Stephen tinkered with his bike, the more he realized nothing about this project was going to be a quick fix if he wanted to get his former pride and joy up and running. This was going to be a labor of love if he ever had one; the focus on such a project was more comforting than anything. He felt he had a purpose for the first time in a long time.

The front door to the house creaked open and shut. Footsteps on the gravel driveway grew louder and louder. Without looking up, he knew right away his Sur was standing behind him as he continued the steady clicks with a socket wrench.

"You coming in to eat?" Kane asked.

"What time is it?"

"8:30. Later than we normally eat. But your Veo insisted we hold off until you got back in the house. Little did we know you were going to choose to live out here."

"Very funny," Stephen replied. He continued working in silence for a minute when he realized his Alpha father was still standing there watching him. "Did you just get up?"

"Hell no." Kane was almost insulted at the notion. "I get up at 7AM everyday rain or shine. Though, today, I was up at 6."

"Why was that?" Stephen sifted through the materials he'd collected below the bike, unsatisfied with the fruits of his labor.

"Kind of hard not to get up when my natural clock is forced awake by the deafening screech of the garage door opening before the sun is even up. You woke up your Veo too."

"Oh. I'm sorry about that. I was hoping that wouldn't happen."

"Hm. Yes. I would greatly appreciate it if you chose to relegate the noise until after your father and I are up, especially if it's to work on ... this?" He gestured with a questionable look all over his face.

"It's my bike, dad," Stephen replied defensively. "Or at least it was at one time."

"Don't I know it," Kane huffed. "That thing was an eye sore when you first got it. The number of times I wanted to get rid of that damn thing, I couldn't tell you. But your Veo insisted it stay here, despite the condition it's in."

"What the hell happened to it?" Stephen stood up.

Kane furrowed his brows. "You don't remember?"

"Remember what?"

The old man didn't expect to be put to the test so early, but here he was, having to unearth memories he was fine without ever seeing the light of day again. "The day of..." Kane paused, trying to find a different way of describing the fateful event. "...the hospital." That was going to have to suffice, and it did according to Stephen's reaction. "You drove that damn bike out of the ER faster than a speeding bullet. Hayes clocked you going at least 20 over the speed limit. He would have, should have, pulled you over and cited you for it."

"Oh yeah? Why didn't he?"

More tough memories. "The event came over the scanner. There wasn't a cop in the entire area who didn't know what had happened by then. He phoned me and asked me what he should do. I didn't say anything; I just hung up." Stephen shifted his weight, dodging even more responsibility, a reminder of the son he also wanted to forget. "You said you made it all the way home when you spun out on the driveway and hit the lamp post of all things." Kane shook his head. "Nothing else in the yard for you to hit, but you nailed the post good."

As the fog started to clear from Stephen's memory, he looked over his Sur's shoulder to catch a look at the sole lamp post on the property. Near the bottom appeared to be some sort of damage; however, today it could have easily been mistaken for any mishap or even weathering. "Okay... that part maybe sounds familiar." He glanced at his bike once more, still in disbelief. "But that doesn't explain the rest of its condition."

"You've really blocked those memories out, haven't you?" Kane surmised. Years of being on the police force had him familiar with assailants and victims who appeared to erase certain events from their memories. Unfortunately, the career also came with the hazard of constantly being skeptical of what truth there was to such a phenomenon. Although Kane recalled his troublesome Alpha son deflecting culpability in his younger years, forgetting events completely wasn't his M.O. Seeing him go textbook on PTSD fascinated him. "The night before your arraignment?" Stephen stood there unmoved. "I don't know if you were having some mental breakdown, considered skipping town, made a poor drunken decision, or just needed to blow off steam. But you took the bike and sped off ... into the backyard of all places. Wolf-God knows what the hell you were trying to accomplish doing that." Kane chuckled, still amused and unsure as to what went down. "Anyway, once you got out of the visibility from the property, you obviously had no idea where you were going. The headlight of your bike was still busted out. An hour later, you came limping up the driveway soaking wet and muddy, telling us you crashed the bike in the bog."

An uneasy feeling overcame Stephen in the moment. He swallowed hard as his eyes shifted and struggled to find any recollection of it happening. Nothing came. "I... I don't remember that."

Kane snorted. "Believe me, I do. Crashing it during rainy season meant we had to wait days for the water levels to go down, even then it was damn near impossible trying to find it. Just be grateful you landed it on the sandpit—otherwise—there's no way you'd be able to do any of this. Your Veo remembers it if you want to ask him."

"Not really," he deflated. The irony of his Alpha father's memory going bad apparently didn't apply to recounting his many missteps and mistakes. Stephen wiped a stream of sweat off his forehead, realizing he probably left an oil stain mark on himself after he looked at the filthy condition of his hands. "I had hoped to find Crusher in some pristine condition and just start her up and go on my way into town to find a job." He heard his father raspberry in response. "What's so funny about that?"

"A pipe dream now, is it not?" He saw his son's shoulders fall. "Your bike would be better off salvaged. The amount of money you'd need to put into it just to get it running wouldn't be worth it. At least, not for a person who has no money and no job."

Stephen started to grow impatient with his father's constant reminders of reality. "I'm going to get a job! I told you that!"

"Wake up, Stephen," Kane criticized. "You're going to have to get on your knees and beg for a job in this city. No one is going to care you're a Type 4 now. You may have struggled between two worlds growing up, but your fate is sealed now. Welcome to the land of Low Types."

"You know... considering the expectations you so clearly outlined for me the moment I walked into that house, I'm surprised you're trying your hardest to put me in the frame of mind where it's pointless to even try."

"I'm trying to prepare you for the real world that is out there, one that you obviously forgot for the last ten years, which by the way, has only gotten worse, not better, regardless what anyone might want to tell you. They'll preach to you all day about how things are getting better for Low Types and Omegas and the middle class, but it's nothing but rhetoric to string people along so that they keep giving the establishment their all until they have nothing left to give."

"That may be how it went for you but it's not me," Stephen spat back.

Kane stood there with mixed emotions. He hated being psychoanalyzed by his ex-con of a son. "I just don't want you to get your hopes up for nothing. I want you to be successful, son. But you're going to have to start off small... really small. This is not going to be easy."

"So, I should be hopeless?" Stephen asked incredulously.

"Not 'hopeless.' Just real." Kane watched his son kick a socket wrench toward the driveway. It rumbled down, skidding against rocks and dirt. "I thought they offered return-to-work programs. Didn't you do that?"

Stephen laughed. "Guess I was just that delusional, dad." His eyes stung as he envisioned what little plans he had disappeared instantly with his father's ominous warning. "Looks like I have to do this the hard way."

Kane realized he wasn't doing his son any favors. Life thus far for his family had been full of unexpected events. Considering most of them were misfortunes, maybe they were due for a good one. After all, it wasn't up to Kane to decide on his son's hire-ability, so who was he to say? Not that he was going to voice that revelation aloud. "You'll get there, Stephen" was all he managed.

Stephen cleared his head. "I know. I'll eat a good breakfast, take a shower, get dressed, and maybe you won't mind me taking your truck into town to start the job search?"

"Do you have your driver's license?"

"Fuck!" Stephen shouted. Kane scrunched his face as he heard another wrench scream out as it hurtled down the driveway.

<hr>

"Thank Wolf-God our territory does same day licensing." Stephen moaned in frustration.

Marlon concurred. "I never knew reinstating an expired license was so involved. Can't remember the last time I had to jump through so many hoops." Situating themselves back in the car, he wondered if he should have let his son in the driver's seat instead. He wasn't going to admit the thought of his son getting behind the wheel after ten years woke his nerves. "Where to?"

"I was thinking you could drop me off down at Tauris Square," Stephen replied.

"*Drop you off*?" A confused look settled on Marlon's face.

"Yeah. I can spend a couple hours down there and cover a lot of businesses in a small area that way. Then, I'll just work my way back downtown if I don't have any luck there. That way, at least, I'll be in a good position to get the bus back home."

Marlon wasn't enthusiastic about the rogue strategy. "I kind of thought I'd take you down to the employment offices on Main Street, and we could get some guidance on any companies or local businesses willing to hire..." He paused with his face flushing red.

"...felons?" Even after ten years, Stephen observed his Omega father struggle with the concept. His Veo bit his lip in embarrassment. "No, this is something I need to do myself."

"This doesn't have anything to do with the conversation you had with your father this morning, does it?"

The pause was more telling than anything. "I need to do this for myself. And Sur is right, this is going to be more difficult than what I initially thought. But it's my burden to bear... not yours."

Marlon bowed his head. He knew his son was right, but it didn't make him, nor the situation feel any better. Regardless, he wasn't going to leave his son empty handed. Reaching into the inside breast pocket of his sweater, he pulled out a folded envelope and handed it to his son.

"What's this?"

His father smirked. "You didn't honestly think I drove you in without considering the fact you'd say that did you?"

"I don't know... maybe?" Even before opening the envelope, Stephen knew it was cash. He just didn't expect it to be as much as it was. "Whoa! What's all this for?"

"To help you get back on your feet. Use it to buy yourself lunch or a snack and get your bus ticket since you're set on doing that."

"Does dad know you gave me this?" Stephen read the look on his Veo's face. He knew the answer without him even saying it. "This isn't necessary. I still have my bus pass that I bought with my 'gate' money."

"Wherever you find a job today, you're going to have to get some type of uniform. Usually, you pay for that upfront. Keep a little cash on you and use your new ID to open a bank account and put the rest in there."

"What bank?"

"There." Marlon pointed. "Territory One. I think the minimum deposit is still a hundred."

Stephen grunted. "Wish I had a wallet."

"Way ahead of you." The Omega pulled out a crisp, brand-new wallet and handed it to him. "Your Type Card is in there too. You'll need that for the bank."

A new perspective on life made Stephen appreciate gifts more than he ever had before. The gesture was not only a reminder of his family wanting him to be successful, but that they weren't giving up on him. He lifted the wallet to his nose and breathed in that classic leather smell which only comes from the first use. Opening it carefully, he unfolded the dollar bills and tucked them inside. In addition, he placed his fresh driver's license in the designated compartment and saw his Type Card, the first time in years. Like all things his Veo kept, it was in pristine condition. Printed in bold on the government card was "**Stephen Xavier Matheson—Type 4 Alpha**" along with his Wolf ID number.

"I'm sorry about your bike," Marlon said, empathizing with his son.

"Is that what all this is for?"

"Maybe a little." He reached over and rubbed his son's shoulder.

"Gives me something to do—when I'm not working that is."

"That's the spirit." Marlon smiled. "Now, go out there, prove everybody wrong, and make something magical happen."

"Gee, no pressure. I'll be right back." Stephen laughed as he got out of the car. Before shutting the door, he looked his Veo in the eyes one more time. "Thank you."

Marlon gestured his head slightly and waited in the car patiently for his son to start his new journey.

***

Stepping into Territory One was a different world entirely. The local branch closer to home felt more suited for down-to-earth hard-working blue collar Low Types. But *this* branch? It was the epicenter for success that only Type 4s and Type 5s could create—business owners, entrepreneurs, and mega corps. The constant suits walking around, contrasting on the white marble floors and walls, only confirmed what he surmised. Even more so, a couple of awkward glances from elite employees disappointed he didn't appear to be an oil tycoon or rich businessman told him he didn't belong. Dark blue jeans and a collared white t-shirt with exotic designs wasn't going to cut it in here. He ran his fingers through his hair and checked his shoes to make sure he wasn't leaving a trail of dust from his country home. Even though he was a strong Alpha wolf, at that moment, Stephen felt like a stray dog.

Finally, a representative had the decency to approach him. His hair, or what he had left of it, was slicked back, his white shirt was free of any blemish or wrinkle, and his tie was set off by a shiny gold clip—real no doubt. "Welcome to T-One. How may we be of service to you today?"

It took a minute for Stephen to even remember why he was here. He shook his head to regain his senses. "Yes, um. I'm here to open a new checking account."

The bank rep plastered a smile on his face. "Of course. Do you have the two forms of identification required?"

"I think so," Stephen replied. He pulled out his wallet and showed the man, clearly an Alpha, his credentials.

After scanning his driver's license, the bank rep took much longer to investigate his Type Card. The ice-cold smile faltered as he scanned Stephen from head-to-toe. Not wanting to make the moment too obvious, like a switch, he snapped back into his former welcoming state. He hummed to himself as if being entertained by a subtle comment or innuendo. "Right away. Follow me, please." The banker pivoted and walked beyond the open lobby to the teller windows in the back. "David," the man addressed, "this young man would like to open a new account with us." For one final time, the banker enacted his best customer service skills. "Welcome to Territory One. We're happy to have you part of the family."

"Thanks." Stephen acknowledged back. Stephen's Alpha instincts surfaced as he sensed something was off. But he took it in stride as to hopefully not cause a scene—whatever the reason. He walked up to the counter and greeted a young, vibrant man waiting with a smile. Unlike the previous encounter, Stephen felt the teller appeared more genuine. "I'd like to open a checking account please and also get a debit card."

"May I see your ID documents?" the teller asked politely.

Stephen pushed the documents beneath the window and waited as the teller inspected and began inputting his information into the system. Trying to remain inconspicuous, the Alpha casually glanced over his shoulder to calm his inner wolf's worries. The curiosity did anything but. On the opposite end of the bank, he noticed the banker who greeted him looking right at him, only now he wasn't alone. Another employee, presumably a higher ranked manager stood very close and engaged in a suspicious conversation. Any doubt that Stephen had about whether the exchange was about him ended when the new banker pointed straight at him.

Then, the banker went to a nearby desk and began dialing the phone. At the same time, the greeter he initially encountered walked over to the entrance where a security officer stood firm with his arms crossed in front of his body. A quick conversation resulted in the officer glancing over, giving Stephen a piercing stare. Before he could even ponder what was happening, he heard the teller's phone go off. Now Stephen knew something was happening. For a moment, David continued rigorously typing on his computer while listening to the call. But then his rapid fingers stopped dead in their tracks. His eyes shot a look at Stephen and then behind him.

The Alpha punished himself by once again confirming his fear as he looked behind his shoulder. Now the elite manager had no issue looking right back at Stephen as if he targeted him as a potential threat. Finally, he set the phone back down.

It wasn't a coincidence David held his breath as he slowly hung up the phone as well. "I'm sorry Mr. Matheson. I'm unable to open this account today."

Holding himself to the best reaction possible, Stephen played coy. "Is something wrong?"

David swallowed hard. "We're having some difficulties with confirming your identity."

"My *identity*?" Stephen was caught off-guard. "But I have my two forms of identification right here."

"I'm sorry, Mr. Matheson. Perhaps if you try another bank, you'll find some success there," David suggested. His customer service aura dimmed as his face became uncomfortable.

"Can you tell me what about my documents appears to be an issue?"

David's eyes fell. "Your driver's license was issued today. Sometimes banks look at it as a potential for fraud." David's answer didn't sit well with Stephen. It was... off. He leaned in and whispered. "And um, perhaps your Type Card."

"My Type Card?" David nodded. "Why would—"

A gruff voice behind Stephen interrupted the conversation. "I think it's time for you to go." The security officer's stern look told him he wasn't going to entertain his presence much longer. Fearing what a confrontation with an officer could lead to, Stephen sealed his lips and snatched his IDs back. A red hue flushed his face as he refused to look at the other two who conjured up his swift dismissal. Besides, he knew they were looking; he could feel their eyes on him. A forceful push of the glass doors sent them flying open as Stephen grunted in frustration.

"High Type assholes," he muttered. David's clue was all he needed to solve the mystery; it had nothing to do with his driver's license at all. The scum who greeted him had the self-proclaimed notion Stephen was a Low Type and somehow conjured up a fake Type Card to present himself as a High Type. But as the theory began to cement in his mind, he stopped on the sidewalk, his feet scraping against the pavement. "Damn it!" The truth finally settled in: his father was a well-known officer throughout the city of Tauris. If the bank had any notion of who his father was by his last name, the banker knew who *he* was.

Stephen tightened his fists and huffed back to the car. The grimace on his face stuck out as he opened the door and slammed it shut.

"What happened?!" Marlon asked.

"Did Sur go around telling people I was released?!" Stephen interrogated, the fumes off his face radiating.

"I—I don't..."

"Tell me!"

"Stephen, I don't know!" Marlon pleaded. He searched for an answer his son could be satisfied with. "Your father takes the car occasionally, and visits with his former partners at the precinct... he'll go to the bar sometimes during the week... I don't know what he has said. Why? What happened in the bank?"

The Alpha exhaled. His voice was a mere fraction that it was previously. "Let's just go." He reached for the seatbelt and clicked it in silence.

Marlon studied his son, his scent somewhere between an angry wolf and a hurt pup. Then he happened to look toward the bank. There, still at the entry, stood a security officer eyeing the car like a hawk. Sensing what must have happened, he clicked his own seatbelt and casually drove toward Tauris Square.

***

Stephen waved his Veo off after being dropped near the entrance of the prolific center. He inhaled deeply, hoping the fresh air coming down from the mountains in the distance would flush out the previous encounter. Every time the scene flashed in his mind, he felt his blood simmer again. The only way to keep the anger controlled was to focus on his next task: getting a job.

Unfortunately, with the bank incident still fresh, the prospects of his next challenge filled him with anxiety. But Stephen knew walking into an interview, especially a cold one, required him to exude strength and confidence. So, before entering any business like an excited pup finding a toy store, he surveyed his options.

To Stephen's surprise, Tauris Square hadn't changed all that much in ten years. Many of the storefronts solidified memories of the past as he walked down the cobblestone streets. The stores here weren't big box brands. No. Tauris Square was known for little shops ran by small business owners, entrepreneurs, and artists hoping to use the desirable location as a launching pad into a lucrative career. Thus, many were focused on a singular product or past time. He remembered a few of his favorites and grinned when he saw the businesses still alive and well: The Honey Pot, The Smoke Shoppe, Smokey Mountain Meats, and his all-time favorite, The Garage Door.

Stephen's eyes lit up. *How perfect would this be?* He stood near the entrance and peered into the large front windows, beautifully displaying the hottest bike brands and most successful tool companies. Shiny metal and chrome sparkled off the sunlight from the street while refracting various colored lights from the neon signs inside. The Alpha closed his eyes and centered his thoughts, clearing any tension or worries from his pheromone pallet. With head and chest held high, he walked in.

Instantly, the smell hit him. It was as if he was here just yesterday—that clean oil smell wrapped in a fragrant layer of freshly polished leather. Even the layout of the store was the same, albeit many of the items were different. Thankfully, his Veo occasionally sent him his favorite magazines in lockup, so many of the upcoming brands and styles were not news to him. He couldn't imagine the embarrassment of walking into a bike shop, spewing facts and rhetoric from a decade ago like it was yesterday.

The hardest part now was praying the owner still remembered him, the good part of him. If only he could remember the owner's name. *Come on, Stephen... come on!* He pondered while he lightly hit his fist against his thigh.

Footsteps of heavy boots walked out from the back and into the main front. A large built man stood there in a black long-sleeved shirt and blue jeans. His curly hair was wrapped with a red bandana which also held up a pair of polarized sunglasses. At first, Stephen wasn't convinced the man worked here, perhaps another customer. The man's welcoming scent was juxtaposed to his intimidating body, though he could have done without bathing in whatever cologne he was wearing.

Squinting his eyes, Stephen noticed the shirt had a name embroidered in cursive. The red thread against the black fabric made it difficult, but he could make out the "G" letter. *G...* Stephen thought. *Yeah, that's what his name started with.*

"George." The man reached out his hand to greet Stephen, noticing his eyes scanning his shirt.

"George!" Stephen exclaimed. "That's who I remember." But just then he noticed something was off. The scent. The "George" Stephen knew was an Alpha. *This* man was a Beta through and through. In addition, Stephen was convinced George should have been older, much older in fact. "I'm sorry. I think I remember you being different."

The Beta looked Stephen over. "Well, considering I don't recognize you myself, you must be referring to my Sur."

Stephen sighed, frustrated at his own stupidity. "That makes more sense. Of course, you are. Man, you look just like him."

George laughed. "I hear it all the time. But I don't hear it in the shop much these days, considering my dad retired a few years ago. I've been here ever since. How long has it been since you were here last?"

"It's been awhile..." Stephen's gaze shifted. He walked on the showroom floor, noticing the two full-sized bikes sitting proudly center stage. "I used to come in here all the time. My Sur would get so mad at me for how much money I'd spend." He laughed. "I don't remember your Sur telling me he had a son."

George scoffed. "Not surprised. My Sur and I didn't get along that well."

"I know the feeling," Stephen empathized.

"Not really," George objected. "Whatever criticism you faced from your Sur, it wasn't because you were a Beta, I can tell you that." He examined Stephen's muscled build and took the essence which read the Alpha was a High Type.

Stephen nodded. "Oh."

The large Beta relaxed. "Ah, that isn't your problem. When my dad decided it was time to let it go, I didn't have the heart to let him sell the place to some unknown who would turn this place into another toy shoppe or shitty secondhand store. So, I moved back down here and took it over."

"I'm personally thankful for that." Stephen lifted a chrome emblem with a flaming skull. *Crusher.* "They redesigned this too?"

"Sure did!" George smiled. "I remember when this company came onto the scene. They wanted the reputation of being the 'rogue' as if the biker community doesn't get enough flack as it is. Anyone who drove around on those bikes wanted you to know they were trouble and not afraid of it."

Stephen wasn't sure if had made a mistake in showing his enthusiasm. It wasn't until George said it that he remembered the company's intentional branding—and that he himself was fully immersed into it. After adoring the ornament, he set it down carefully back into its display box. However, he wasn't going to forget it was here.

"Let me know if you need anything!" George offered. "Something tells me you're an aficionado, so I'm sure you'll be fine." A faint ringing in the back permeated through the showroom. Yet, George stood there unphased.

"Do you need to get that?" Stephen asked awkwardly.

"I don't answer the phone when customers are in here. It's not ideal, but it's so hard to find good help these days."

Stephen's ears perked up. "You're looking for help?"

"Ha! Always," George answered. "The problem is I get a whole bunch of these wannabes who think I have time to teach them about bikes while they are getting paid no less. Or I have professionals who come in and think I'm going to pay them six figures. I don't know what they're smokin.'"

The Alpha inside Stephen wavered as he put himself out there. "Well, I know a lot about bikes. I got mine when I was 16. I'm the only one who has ever worked on it, though I must admit I'm self-taught. Right now, I'm working on replacing the rotor and sprocket." *Not a complete lie,* Stephen decided. *They are going to need repair.*

"Whoa. You must have banged it up pretty bad."

Stephen laughed nervously. "Yeah, you could say that."

George's eye went over to the display case, remembering the previous discussion. "You have a Gunnolf, don't you?"

The Alpha swallowed hard. "Yes. Yes, I do." Deep inside, Stephen wished he had never walked over to the chrome ornament in the first place. He shut his eyes, hating himself for it. He slowly turned, ready to head toward the exit.

Licking his bottom lip, George nodded slowly. "You up for an interview?"

Stephen opened his eyes in disbelief. "When?"

"How about now?"

"Sure!" Stephen's head swirled as his heart pumped in overdrive.

George smiled as he went behind the counter and pulled a flimsy notebook out of a drawer. He scribbled a pen on the pad until the ink pressed through. "All right. How about you do the hard part for me: name, address, and if you have your license and Type Card on you, that'd be great."

The Alpha quickly jotted down the required information and pulled out his ID cards once again. Once he plopped them on the counter, he hid his hand behind his back, hiding the nerves still looming from the trauma at the bank. He prayed to Wolf-God the IDs weren't going to spark the same issue.

Slowly, George squinted and viewed the ID. He surveyed the picture and then glanced back at Stephen to confirm the picture. Holding it up to the bright light on the ceiling, all the right holograms shone through. Then he grinned. "Ohhh, new card today?"

Stephen's shoulders sank. "Yeah."

"Didn't want to smile, huh?" George stood there amused, writing down a couple notes on his pad.

The question shocked the Alpha. *Wait... we're still doing the interview?* He cleared his throat, answering nonchalantly. "Does anyone these days?"

"Probably not. Guys seem to think their license mugshot doubles as an advertisement for a sports position or a photo on a macho dating app." Stephen appreciated the joke. "Type 4? Nice! Haven't interviewed one of those before. I need to confess, I would like help with billing, paperwork, and taxes, but I'm more looking for help that gets your hands dirty. Are you okay with that?"

"Absolutely!" It wasn't new for the Alpha to hear sentiments of 'Oh, isn't this work beneath you?' 'Wouldn't you like to be a C.E.O. or a doctor instead?' But it had been a long time since anyone complimented his Status for being better than the dreams he pursued. Ten years ago, he hated every time someone made the comment. Now, he was grateful for it.

"Okay, Stephen..." George drew out as he finished writing down more information, "...here you go." He handed Stephen a piece of paper.

"What's this?" Stephen asked, looking at the picture of the bike drawing.

"It's a diagram. Fill out as many different parts of the bike you recognize. If you don't know one or aren't sure, skip it. I only want what you know. Then, on the back, answer the few scenario questions," George instructed. "This is how I weed out the posers from the professionals.""Piece of cake," Stephen sang.

"We'll see," George replied. Once again, a faint ringing from the backroom. "Damn it. Go ahead and start on that. I'll be back in a second."

"No worries." Stephen glanced at the paper, excitement overflowing. He hadn't taken a test in years, and now he was taking his second one in a day. Compared to the licensing test, this was going to be simple. Noting there wasn't a whole lot of room to label all the parts he was prepared to write out, he started creating several arrows to the blank margins and then vigorously began marking every little item he could find: clutch, ignition, tachometer, brake, pedal, pipes, levers, mirrors, everything. After a couple of minutes, he realized there was only so much time for showboating. Listing parts of a motorcycle for a bike shop application wasn't any different than an adolescent being asked to label the parts of the body for school. So, he focused his detailed attention to the scenario questions.

The first two questions were listed as stories—customers coming in and complaining their bike had broken down. A mechanic looked over the bikes and noted several errors or clues to reveal what the diagnosis could be. Stephen was relieved to see that both questions were common issues. The first, he narrowed down to worn out carburetor and vacuum leak causing the bike to backfire. The second was a cleaning issue leading to standard replacements of spark plugs, an oil change, and a fuel verification in case the rider used the wrong kind.

The final two questions had to deal with bike laws. Despite just finishing his license test, Stephen wasn't sure if the last ten years had changed the laws regarding motorcycles. With George coming back into the room, he gritted his teeth and wrote down from memory what he did when he was 19.

"How's it going?" George asked, assuming the Alpha was sweating it out.

"Done!" Stephen grinned, handing him back the paper.

"Oh!" George was shocked. None of the candidates finished that early, not even the highly qualified ones. He merely glanced at the bike diagram, amused at the many labels Stephen scribbled all over it. Carefully, he read over Stephen's written answers. By the time he finished, his eyebrows shot up. "Impressive."

"Really?" Stephen asked.

"Yeah, I especially liked your second answer, the one about the cleaning."

"Why? That one seemed like a trick question. It was too easy," Stephen answered.

"Exactly! You wouldn't believe the answers I get on that one. Some guys wanna take the entire bike apart and replace half of it. The customer would get charged thousands for that. If you start at the basics and move your way up, you can potentially diagnose the problem fast and get it repaired even faster. It creates a great relationship with the customer for their future return or referrals, and you can spend more time on bikes that *really* need fixing." Then he scanned the law questions. "Oops, a little error here. They changed this law several years ago. The minimum pass rate is now 80%. The specs haven't been 70% for almost ten years."

"Oh. That must have slipped my mind."

"Not a big deal honestly. I get the new book every year from the DMV. When customers call or I need to reference it, I just open the book and read verbatim most of the time."

"Good to know."

George lifted the page on his notebook to a clean page. "Now that the hard part is over. Let me see if I can get a handle on who you are. I remember you saying 'self-taught,' so do I have it right that you don't have any formal training?"

"Right. I'm sorry."

"Not a big deal. If I move forward with you, we can get you into one of those OTJ trainings and get you certified. Up until that point, I can have you here as my store clerk as we slowly build up your hours."

"That sounds great!" Stephen replied.

"Have you ever been employed as a mechanic before—of any kind?" George asked.

"No."

"Okay." George wrote down the note. "And what is your employment history?"

The world stopped. For Stephen, the moment of the truth was at hand. "I—I don't have any employment history."

The Beta's eyebrows furrowed, wondering if he had misread his birthdate. He saw the license on the counter still and lifted it up. "What are you? 29?"

"Yes, sir."

"And you don't have *any* employment history?" George stood there in disbelief as he wondered who exactly was standing there before him.

"I worked at a fast-food restaurant briefly, but otherwise no."

"When was that?"

Stephen scratched his chin. "Over ten years ago."

George's eyes grew wide. "Were you in school?"

"No."

The Beta circled his pen on the pad, wondering what to do. "I need some sort of explanation, Stephen. This is highly unusual. I'm thrilled at your test results and think you have some potential here, but I can't just go off that."

"I was incarcerated. I just got out—hence why my license is new."

George's body exhaled. "Oh." The store grew quiet. The hum from the wall clock filled his ears, along with each tick from the hands. "Well, look. I get that people make mistakes. Perhaps we can start something on a trial basis, and after a while, we can see how things are going."

Stephen couldn't believe his ears. "I would love that opportunity."

"Good. I mean, you weren't put away for grand theft auto were you?"

"No." Stephen smiled.

"What was it if I may ask? I mean, I'm going to have to do a background check anyway."

Stephen huffed. "It was a drug charge."

"*Drugs*? Oh, hell." George threw his pen on the counter in defeat. "Anything else?" he added sarcastically.

"Negligent homicide of a natural adult." Stephen bowed his head. The writing was on the wall.

"*Natural* adult? That means he wasn't even 18 yet." George couldn't believe the audacity of the man before him. Walking in here like a regular law-abiding citizen expecting to get a job only to reveal that mess. He had gumption—no doubt about that. He rubbed his face. "How long did they put you away for?"

"Ten years."

A thought ran through the Beta's head. Once again, he picked up the license and examined it. "Matheson?" He paused. "I know *you*. You're Kane Matheson's son." Stephen held his breath. "It wasn't just any kid who died. That was your brother, right?" The Alpha nodded. George scoffed. "I'm sorry. I can't help you."

"What? Really?"

"Look. I've been around plenty of guys who deserve second chances. Not everyone is a lost cause."

"I'm not either!" Stephen protested.

George held up his hand. "Be that as it may, I've got my father's reputation riding on this place. Even though having a Type 4 Alpha working here and potentially being my mechanical assistant would be great, you've got quite the backstory here. People know your name and it's for all the wrong reasons. And I can't have this place tainted by that."

"Please," Stephen begged. "Let me prove myself to you."

"I'm sorry." George frowned. He handed the Alpha's IDs back to him and gave him the look that said there was no negotiating at this point.

Curling his lips, Stephen accepted his IDs back and walked out of the store, feeling the "loser" moniker targeted onto his back.

Walking out of the bike shop felt surreal. Things were gradually getting better while he was in there, yet it all crashed so quickly. George's final criticism stuck to him like glue. It played in his mind repeatedly like a broken record. The stunned look on Stephen's face was frozen in time; any passerby watching him would think him shell-shocked. Inside, all that was there was a numb feeling. He was grateful it didn't result in an outburst, but the lack of any emotion prevented him from moving forward both physically and mentally.

Finally, after several minutes, sounds of distant vehicles desperate to find a parking place, people scurrying past him lost in their own conversations, and the wind blowing a cool air across his heated face brought him back to reality. With it, he realized now he had two options: try again or give up. For himself, failure was not an option. And there was no way he could go home and tell his Sur that not only did he not find anything, but he only attempted once.

The harsh end of his interview with George cut his confidence in half, but he was at least prepared to go into his future attempts with a better reality of what he was dealing with. He couldn't change his approach much. Potential employers typically waited for background checks to come through before letting any candidate come to work on day one. Concealing it, hoping the employer would keep him on based on good performance, created a fool's hope he'd keep the job.

With that in mind, he shook the failed attempt off and held his head high. It could get better from here. Right?

Wrong.

Dead wrong.

The afternoon flew by faster than he imagined it could. It was all for the wrong reasons. Time and time again, Stephen was teased with a great opportunity to work in several different businesses in and around Tauris Square. But each time, when his past was brought up, a hard resounding "No" was all he heard. He didn't want to think about the number of rejections he experienced. At the end of his run, he considered just wearing a t-shirt which laid out the entire interview on the front and the surprise reveal about his record on the back. That way, he didn't have to put so much energy into something which led straight to nowhere.

Stephen gave up for the day; it only being a few hours since his Veo dropped him off. However, there was no way he was ready to show his face back at home yet. Feeling aimless, he found the longest sidewalk possible and started walking toward downtown. Every now and then, he caught a glimpse of a business he'd consider for employment, but the lack of confidence stopped him from entering every time.

The walk became second nature, a task he no longer had to think about, especially when the Tauris Medical Center came into view. It allowed his mind to relax, so he didn't have to think about his disappointment. The coping mechanism wasn't too different when he was behind bars. Putting his mind elsewhere kept him from having to deal with the drama and hierarchy inmates chose to impose on each other. Not all of it was avoidable, however. Distinct memories of being involved in physical altercations and reprimanded for such crept its way in to avoid the present.

Before he knew it, he had reached downtown. He damn near missed the Tauris Medical Center and the new research building he didn't see before. Stephen continued eyeing the campus as he walked down the sidewalk. He decided tomorrow he'd consider going inside and seeing if there was a basic level job he could get into: loading docks, custodial, and even hazardous waste disposal came to mind. Ahead of him, he saw a corner with a city bus stop. To his right was a bar which just so happened to have the door propped open to appear even more inviting than it already was. Instead of entering the establishment right away, he decided it best to check the bus schedule first.

To his dismay, although the in-city route was regular every fifteen minutes, the outer-city route showed up in five minutes, but not again for another two hours. Only after that did his route begin a regular pickup until nightfall. Stephen weighed his options and decided it best to forego the bar this time and head home before the rush hour crowds packed the bus. He sat on the lonely city bench only for a few minutes before he saw the large transit pull up. It hissed to a stop and opened the doors, awaiting him.

But right as Stephen was about to board ... it hit him. A faint scent caught his senses. For how weak the essence was, it felt like a punch to his gut. During his incarceration, an abrupt scent change like this warned him of danger and to be alert for any suspicious activity about to go down. However, instead of telling him to stay away or prepare for danger, this was rousing his inner wolf and begging him to investigate the pleasing aroma further. The bus driver asked him if everything was okay and if he planned on boarding. It was then Stephen decided he was going to take the chance that this scent was going to lead to something important, but he had yet to locate its origins.

Just then, the scent came back once more, a hint stronger. He zeroed in as best as he could and barely noticed a glimpse of a man walking back into the bar having placed an advertising tent sign right outside it near the sidewalk. The only description he could make out at this point was a light-tanned individual with bright blonde hair and a forest green polo shirt. Convinced he was the source Stephen needed to investigate, he motioned the bus on and headed toward the establishment.

The Alpha read the street sign first; there were mentions of a couple drink specials written in neon chalk. Then he looked up and saw the large sign. "South Street Tavern," he read out loud to himself. With a deep breath, he entered.

# CHAPTER 05:

## DISCOVERING THE ONE WHO CHANGES EVERYTHING

The bar appeared darker to Stephen than he anticipated it should have for the mid-afternoon. Turning back, he realized all the large windows facing the street had a strong tint on them. Most of the light coming in was from the front door still being propped open. Hence, the farther back he investigated the bar, the more the ceiling lamps tried to make up for it.

The Alpha didn't count every patron, but he concluded there were about eight of them and a few workers in the front and at the bar. Most of them were setting up for the evening and not servicing customers.

"Welcome!" a man announced, giving Stephen a warm greeting.

"Uh. Hi," Stephen replied, trying to appear as if he didn't have an alternative agenda.

"What can I get ya?" The bartender rested on the bar, waiting in anticipation.

It only took a moment for Stephen to know the man was not who he was looking for. This individual was noticeably taller with a much thicker build. Although his hair length was right, the color and style were all wrong. That was to say nothing of his scent being completely off. He recognized the man's scent as pure Beta. Now, Stephen concluded, he was looking for an Omega. The name embroidered on his shirt read "Bruce." Stephen played along, biding his time. "I'll... uh... I'll do that beer special you have on the sign out there."

"Fine choice!" The man whistled as he flung a white bar towel over his shoulder, contrasting greatly against the dark green polo he was wearing. Obviously, a standard work uniform.

Stephen noticed another man just as brute and built on the opposite side of the large room, lifting what was sure to be heavy-weighted tables over his head. He then placed them in a standard pattern across the tiered floor. Inconspicuously, he walked over to the area, pretending to be taking in the sights, but secretly, he was looking to capture the man's scent. Once again, it wasn't right, another Beta for sure. *James*", he thought, was the name printed on his green shirt.

Stephen was at least comforted that all employees were wearing the same shirt. But as the moments went by, he worried he pegged the scent incorrectly or that perhaps the employee he was looking for left the place and wouldn't return. Stephen looked back at Bruce who was holding his beer, unsure of where to place it. In an effort to make his presence less awkward, the Alpha swallowed his impatience and sat at a corner seat easily facing the entire view of the bar. If the Omega carrying the scent he was after was still here, he was going to come out from the back.

"Haven't seen you here before," Bruce offered, trying to start a conversation.

Stephen scanned and tried to pick up the scent again. No such luck. He reluctantly gave Bruce his attention. "I ... haven't been around for quite some time. Last, I remember, this wasn't called 'South Street.' I don't think this was even a bar."

Bruce searched his memory. "Hmm. As far as I know, it's always been a bar. The last owner lost it to the city. A couple years ago, the new owner bought it."

"Yeah? Who's that?" Stephen couldn't stop himself from surveying the room as he answered.

Bruce picked up the awkward vibe. "You mind if I check your ID?"

Realizing he was beginning to lose his mind, Stephen surrendered his surveillance as well as his ID. "I'm getting asked that a lot today," he muttered.

The bartender held his ID up to the light. "Sorry, man. Boss's orders. Alexander Daventry owns the place now. For the next week, he doesn't want any chances of a violation going down." After being satisfied Stephen was legitimate, he slid it back. "Even though you don't even look close to being underage." Stephen furrowed his brows. Bruce laughed, proud of his own comment. "Just giving you a hard time. With being a Type 4 Alpha, you're naturally gifted to have a youthful appearance, right?"

"Sure," Stephen replied, taking a sip of his beer. He wondered if this "Alexander" was the one he was looking for. But an Omega owning *this* place? Highly unlikely.

Another patron's ear perked up at the comment. He was an older gentleman, a good ten years older if not more. His once chestnut brown hair had faded considerably; gray hair peppered his short style as well as the stubble on his chin. With a large beer in hand, he eased himself over to sit next to the Alpha.

Stephen scented the older man as an Omega but nowhere near the pleasing scent he craved. He wished he could describe the scent he was looking for. This Omega in front of him had a fragrance of pear and some sort of spice... nutmeg? It wasn't *bad*. It just wasn't Stephen's.

That was when the connection came through. *Stephen's. His.* The Omega's scent belonged to *him.* Tiny hairs stood on the back of the

Alpha's neck. A rush of pheromones came to the surface as his mind raced with the possibility. "No way," he heard himself say aloud.

"Yes way!" the older Omega next to him sang.

Stephen woke up and stared back in confusion. "I'm sorry?" There was no way the man could hear his inner thoughts.

"I said, 'I would love to buy you your next drink.'" He reached out and put his hand on Stephen's shoulder nearest to him, massaging his hand gently. A musty cologne smell and leather scent from his jacket wafted into the air.

Stephen was caught completely caught off-guard by the proposition and now felt he was in a bind. To make matters worse, he saw Bruce struggle to keep his composure, a smirk forming on his masculine face. Out of the corner of his eye, he also saw a few other patrons sit there, mildly entertained by the encounter. It was then the Alpha concluded that this patron's antics weren't unique. This was a regular occurrence—a well-rehearsed act.

"Call me Craig, handsome." The Omega smiled, a shine coming off his face.

"Okay..." Stephen played along.

Craig waited as he adjusted himself on the barstool. "And what do I call you? Or should I just call you Type 4 Alpha?"

Now Stephen understood. Bruce's announcement of his accolade piqued Craig's interest. Considering nothing else was said about him, it was a sure bet. The Alpha surmised the older Omega must have been a Low Type looking to "rank up" on the Status chain. Passing that judgement aloud wasn't a smart move however—especially if his theory was wrong. To be fair, the other scenario could be Craig was a High Type himself, looking for comradery amongst a sea of Low Type bar patrons. Despite being locked up for a decade, Stephen was still very aware of social sensitivity and acceptable norms concerning Status, especially important ones like: never assume a Rank's Type. To call a High Type a Low Type by mistake was a sticky situation; the Alpha could only imagine what it'd be like in a bar such as this.

"Stephen," he finally responded.

"Hmm... Stephen." Craig sized him up. Very delicately, he licked his bottom lip. "Like Bruce said, haven't seen you here before."

Stephen turned his head in the other direction and rolled his eyes. He was certain Bruce caught a glimpse of it. Turning back, he sighed. "I've been out of town for quite a few years. Just got back home—thought I'd scope the place out."

"Ah..." Craig sang, "well, welcome home, Stephen." The Alpha lifted his glass and nodded in return. "Is the Alpha Type 4 looking to scope a person out, too, or do you have a mate already?"

*If only...* Stephen thought. The Alpha's heart thumped harder as he refocused on scanning the tavern, searching for the Omega he longed for, hoping Craig's distraction didn't make him lose his chance. "No." Stephen spoke in a haze before fully coming back to the conversation. "No mate." As he took his next drink, he scented Craig's pheromone palate change and get richer. He didn't like where this was going. The Omega's eyes targeted him like he was a piece of meat. The last thing he wanted to do now was make a scene and therefore a bad impression for himself. As the minutes slowly ticked by, his hope dwindled on the prospect of meeting his wolf's other half.

"How about the Omega Type....?" Stephen grew desperate to keep the conversation going.

Craig threw his head back, entertained by such a luring question. "Ha!" He slid his beer to the side and laid his arms on the bar. Then he pushed in, getting very close to Stephen's face. "What Type do you think I am? Guess!" He grinned.

*Aw, shit!* Now he was cornered into the one spot he didn't want to be. From this peripheral, he saw Bruce hiding his subtle laughter before he turned away to service another patron. "Oh, I couldn't do that."

"Sure!" Craig encouraged, lightly brushing the back of his knuckles on the Alpha's arm. "Come on, be honest. Don't try to flatter me."

Stephen tried to replay the last ten minutes in his mind and wondered what he could have done to avoid Craig all together. Sit somewhere else? Give a cold shoulder? Ask about the mysterious Omega he saw walk in here? Lie and say he had a mate? No, not that last one. He closed his eyes and gritted his teeth in nervous frustration. "I, uh, I don't... Type 2?"

The older Omega's face flipped like a switch. The sparkle in his eye was doused immediately, and his pearly white smile closed into a scowl. "A ... *what*?"

Even upon the utterance, Stephen feared he made a mistake. But Craig's response left no doubt. A brief reflection reminded Stephen of one courtesy he forgot about social sensitivity: in most situations, when guessing someone's Type, guess high. His eyes widened. "I mean... Type 3?" The attempt at a recovery fell on deaf ears.

Slowly, the Omega stood up and backed away. Craig's pheromone palate burned with rage and disgust. "What a privileged asshole." His voice grew louder with every word until he had the attention of every member in the joint. The remaining group of three he was once sitting with took notice immediately. Their chatter with Bruce ended abruptly which also caused the large bartender to straighten up and investigate.

"What's wrong, Craig?" one of the men asked, adjusting his aged red ball cap.

Craig continued in his offended tone. "Listen up, Eddie! This entitled Type 4 dick thinks I'm a Type 2!"

All three men stared back at Stephen in disgust. The man in the cap, now identified as Eddie, stood up. "Does he now?"

Bruce constantly turned his head back and forth, assessing the looming situation. "Come on, Eddie. Craig did it to himself. If he didn't want him to guess, he shouldn't have asked him to."

"And he wanted my honest opinion. It's just an opinion. He shouldn't get so offended," Stephen added.

Dark chest hair spilled over Eddie's white muscle shirt as he puffed out. He tightened his fists and cracked his knuckles. "What we're missing here are some manners." The remaining members of the group, including Craig, walked a step behind him as he inched toward Stephen.

Craig smirked as he joined Eddie's side. "Wherever he went 'out of town' must not have had Omegas. Otherwise, he'd know how to talk to one." Then he focused on Stephen who was still sitting there helpless. "You obviously haven't fucked an Omega in a long time. Not if that's how you've been trying to court one."

Eddie hummed. "Maybe *he* was the Omega wherever he was. He looks like he's bent over for a few Alphas."

Stephen's demeanor changed instantly. He shot up out of his chair and eyed Eddie like prey in the wild. This wasn't what he wanted to do. But he wasn't going to let Eddie emasculate him in public. Even more so, pheromones pulsed off him which told Stephen he needed to be ready for anything. One more inhale revealed Eddie was no doubt an Alpha. *Good.*

Bruce hunched over the bar once again, but this time with arm outstretched, pleading to get through to Eddie. "Come on, man, I'm warning you. Don't do this."

"We're not going to do anything." The sound of Eddie's voice was to the contrary. He took his wrist and ran it across his full mustache. Finally, he was mere inches away from Stephen. His voice lowered. "We're just gonna talk, Alpha-to-Alpha."

"What do you want?" Stephen growled. All his years of therapy rested on this. In the back of his head, he could see his doctor, plain as day, telling him to think of his mantra and send his brain elsewhere.

"How about an apology, Type 4?" Craig's voice rang out from behind Eddie.

Eddie smiled as he looked back to acknowledge the sore Omega and then to Stephen. "You heard the man."

Everything about the situation told Stephen to attack his enemy, show the entire bar who he really was. Make every patron fear and bow down to him while they begged for their lives. Ideally, they'd beg at his feet for forgiveness and pray he didn't attack their mating glands out of retribution, thus announcing to the public he marked the offenders as his territory: a common practice among inmates in prison as well as perverted and vicious degenerates on the street. But the reformed Alpha knew better and refused to let his anger control him. He shut his eyes, tightened his arm muscles, and whispered to himself, "Calm and concentrate."

Eddie could feel the threatening pheromones exude off the Alpha. He was enjoying every minute of it. "What did you say, Omega?" He grinned, pleased with his insult.

Instantly, Stephen opened his eyes and relaxed, "I said, 'I'm sorry.'"

The room stood still. A wave of shock and awe went throughout the room for anyone within earshot of the concession. Several members of the bar began whispering to each other in disbelief, including those standing right behind Eddie.

But Eddie himself locked eyes with Stephen, studying every movement of his body, every pulse of his blood, every flinch of his eyes, and every pheromone radiating off him. He was looking for even the slightest hint of a ruse or insincerity. The wolf inside him wanted validation to further degrade the Alpha in front of him and incite the anger he knew the man possessed.

However, nothing came. As Craig huffed in frustration, he took in Stephen's scent which mellowed out quickly. Whatever he was bottling up had left him instantly. Eddie swallowed as he couldn't comprehend the phenomenon. No Alpha voluntarily bowed to another Alpha without challenging him first—it was against every instinct of their wolf origins. And even if one did submit to his opponent, the victor always basked in the loser's smoldering pheromones.

It was an addicting sensation all Alphas thoroughly enjoyed; some compared it to marking an Omega. Both experiences, if not kept in check, caused an Alpha to become dependent on the experience like a drug and let it control and then destroy their humanity.

Eddie didn't consider himself one of those power-addicted Alphas, but just the same, his frustration grew as he was robbed of the glory. He was agitated further when he noticed the entire tavern declare Stephen the victor in an unprecedented move. "Listen, wise guy!" Eddie pushed his rough finger into Stephen's chest. All he got in return was the enigmatic Alpha slowly focusing his attention on the threatening gesture. "I don't know what game you're playing at, but—"

"It's not a game," Stephen interrupted. "If I offended him, then I need to apologize. That's it."

Eddie retracted his finger and stepped back. "Some Alpha you are," he muttered.

Stephen watched Eddie back away and the crowd turn their attention elsewhere. As a human, he accomplished all he wanted regarding self-control and stamina. But as a wolf, he was nowhere near satisfied. "Now how about an apology from you?" he yelled across the room.

The light chatter in the place ceased once again. After looking at Stephen in shock, all eyes went to Eddie.

Eddie himself couldn't believe his ears. The blood in his system boiled to the surface and muscles tensed. He couldn't figure out this unknown Alpha. One second, he was a passive follower, and the next, he tried to become pack leader. But that wasn't going to happen, not on *his* watch.

Like a predator in the wild, he eased back into his prey's territory and stayed quiet so Stephen could take in the powerful scent change of the solid Alpha who stood in front of him once again. He spoke softly as his eyes locked onto his target. "What did you say?"

Stephen wasn't surprised at the aggressive response. All he could visualize was how much this behavior was exactly him as a teenager. Years later, to stay on top of the hierarchy in prison, he had to invoke the same persona. But years of practice had turned Stephen from a compulsive fighter to a calculated observer. In addition to taking in Eddie's strong dominating scent and seeing his muscles buff out his shirt, he noticed sweat form at the top of his brow and his overall stance change. The menacing Alpha was losing confidence before his very eyes.

"I said, how about an apology?" Stephen stood his ground, never twitching or losing concentration.

Eddie smiled at his captive audience. The air grew thick. "Apologize for what?"

"I'm not an Omega, nor do I submit like one," Stephen replied simply. "I have nothing against those who do, but I don't like being labeled as something that I'm not. I'd be gracious if you were equally virtuous and apologized to me." The sinister pheromones permeating out of Eddie told Stephen everything he needed to know.

"Sure," Eddie replied in a sly tone. "I'll apologize." He glanced towards the patrons of the bar while also calculating Bruce and James's position. As fast as a lightning strike, Eddie aimed with a loaded fist right at Stephen's head. The amount of force he put behind it could have knocked out any average man. But Eddie found out quickly that Stephen wasn't average.

A mere inch away from his face, Stephen caught Eddie's packed fist in his hand and held onto it with all his might. The muscles in his body throbbed as he maintained a focused expression without any vexation on his face. His eyes observed Eddie staring back in shock.

Eddie realized now *he* had been led into a trap. Stephen *wanted* him to attack. Now he was held between a rock and a hard place; he either had to submit to the Type 4 Alpha's superiority or make Stephen pay for his foolish misstep. Eddie gritted his teeth and creased his lips as he attempted to free his arm from Stephen's grip, but he was locked in place, and the wolf refused to let go of him.

For Stephen, calculating Eddie's every move wasn't difficult; he gave himself away at every turn. A mere second before Eddie's other muscled arm came up, Stephen took the fist he already had in his hand and squeezed Eddie's knuckles down until they became flush with the bones.

Eddie's free hand changed course immediately upon feeling the pain shoot up his arm. He tried prying the Alpha off, but the more he attempted, the more he felt Stephen bear down. Popping sensations and sounds in his hand caused Eddie's voice to involuntary howl as he felt his knees buckle and slowly collapse to the floor. "Stop!" Eddie pleaded. "What are you trying to do? Break my hand?" The Alpha looked down upon him, never changing his focus or expression. Eddie's cries had no effect on the wolf glaring at him.

"Just an apology. That's all," Stephen demanded.

Eddie clenched his eyes shut, hoping he could somehow erase the pain or that perhaps someone would come to rescue. But no one came; no one even moved. Hopes were shattered further as the Alpha wolf now used his body weight as leverage and pushed even more. Snapping and cracking sensations radiated off his fingers. "Ahhh!!! All right!" Eddie croaked.

"All right, what?" Stephen repeated.

"I'm sorry!" Eddie squeaked. Not getting the immediate relief he desired, he looked up at Stephen, straight into his eyes, and gave him the look of submission. "I'm sorry, Alpha!"

Stephen finally let go of his grip. Eddie fully collapsed on the floor as he cradled his hand to his chest. The hypnotic spell which held him faded, and he stared at an audience who didn't know how to process what happened. Stephen had won his first territory battle outside lockup. Inside, he knew it felt good. But now he feared it had gone too far. Was he going to find himself in the middle of a brawl with the bouncers or Eddie's companions? Right now, he wasn't sure, but he prepared himself once again.

"What the HELL is going on in here?" a voice rang out from the back. Every patron whipped around to see a stern Omega staring down the entire scene in the bar, then to Eddie still writhing on the floor, and finally Stephen. "YOU!" Alexander pointed at the Alpha.

"I'm sorry, I—" Stephen began.

"Don't even start!" Alexander growled. "Bruce! James!"

"Alex, I'm sorry," Bruce trembled, feeling the guilt wash over him. "It all happened so fast. I didn't think it would go there."

Alexander scowled. "What do I pay you for if you're just going to stand around and let this shit happen?" He turned his attention to James, walking toward him with his hands on his hips. "And what's your excuse?"

James's eyes grew big. "Well... I... um..." He struggled to come up with an explanation. "I just wanted to make sure it actually looked like something which needed to be contained."

"And?" Alexander crossed his arms.

The bouncer pointed back to Stephen. "It looks like he contained it."

Alexander eyed Stephen from a distance and then walked up, like he was an Alpha himself. "Listen here! I don't know who you think you are, but I have a zero-tolerance policy for fighting in my establishment. If that's the crap you're trying to pull, you're going to have to do it somewhere else." The Omega sized the man up, feeling the heat come off his body, his pheromone palate shifting constantly. He couldn't get a proper read on him. "Is there something wrong with you?"

Stephen stared back in awe. The Omega in front of him glowed in a way he had never seen before. His stunning face with soft cheek bones, sparkling eyes, and dark lashes. Beyond the angry and heated pheromones coming off him, Stephen could still take in the intoxicating aroma which lured him into the bar in the first place. With each inhale, he was cementing the scent into every part of his being. He was never going to forget this Omega's pheromone palate. Quickly, in his head, he identified the scent: a deep pomegranate—aged and darkened like a fine wine. The Alpha wanted nothing more than to taste the Omega's pheromone gland in his neck and imprint his own scent into him—making the man his forever. *What is his name again?* "Alex," he said out loud.

The Omega held his stance. "Yeah?"

Suddenly, Stephen's heart kicked into overdrive and his lungs heaved. "It's you."

Alexander squinted, face concerned. "Are you okay?" he asked inquisitively. "Because despite Eddie on the floor here, you look more out of it than he does." He turned his attention to the nuisance still howling to himself. "Get up, Eddie! Now!"

Eddie grunted as he sat up on his haunches first, finding his center. Then he moaned as he brought himself to a standing position, eyeing Stephen like the enemy wolf he was. Then he turned to Alexander. "Is that any way to treat a bar patron?"

"Is that any way to treat one of *my* fellow customers?" he threw back.

Eddie played dumb. "What are you talking about?" He backed away toward the bar where the rest of his friends huddled together. "He started it!"

Craig joined in. "Yeah, that creep of an Alpha started it." The remaining members of the group nodded in agreement.

Alexander looked back toward the lone, accused Alpha. Something in his expression said otherwise. He rubbed his nose and then looked at Bruce. "Tell me what happened."

Bruce's gaze shifted between his regular customers and his employer—fearing he was in a no-win situation. "Craig and Stephen were having some sort of conversation that got out of hand. From the looks of it, Eddie was trying to defend Craig's honor." The man bowed his head.

"That's exactly right!" Eddie confirmed.

Alexander took another glance at Stephen, observing the Alpha's bottom lip drop. When he looked back at Bruce, he couldn't get the bouncer to look him in the eye. The Omega narrowed his gaze and dug deeper. "What was the conversation?"

"I couldn't speculate," Bruce replied solemnly.

"A private conversation!" Craig snapped.

"Must not have been *that* private," Alexander challenged. "It seems Eddie knew what to defend your honor on." Craig swallowed hard.

Stephen piped up from across the bar. "He wanted me to guess his Type. He was offended at my answer."

Alexander's eyes shifted, knowing where this was going. "And which Type did he guess that had you so offended, Craig?"

Craig faltered. "It's not important now!" He changed subjects. "That brute of an Alpha broke Eddie's hand. You should be calling the police on the psycho."

Alexander wasn't deterred. "Which type did he guess, Craig?"

"Type 2," Stephen offered up.

Alexander walked back over to Stephen, standing only a few feet away. He looked the Alpha up and down once more. He placed his hands on his hips. "I see." After a pause, he lifted his head once more. "Get out."

The words were ice piercing into Stephen's chest. He couldn't believe the cold response the Omega was giving him. *Why is he talking to me that way? Can't he see who I am? Doesn't he know who we are?* The Alpha's voice began to tremble. "But I... you... we..."

"That's right, Alex!" Eddie beamed. "Kick that Alpha in the balls!" Every member of Eddie's group laughed in approval.

Without taking his eyes off Stephen, Alexander shouted back. "The only Alpha I want to kick in the balls right now is you, Eddie!"

"Huh? What?" Eddie wasn't sure if he heard the Omega right.

Stephen himself looked up, completely lost.

Now Alexander turned around to face Eddie and his posse. "I wasn't telling *him* to get out. I was telling *you* to get out!"

"You've got to be kidding me!" Eddie shook his head, laughing the command off.

"I'm sick of your shit, Eddie. You too, Craig! And if the rest of you want to fall on the sword with them, there's the door!" Alexander gestured to it like a showcase.

Craig stiffened. "Alex, if we walk out that door, we're not coming back here."

Alexander nodded. "From where I see it, that will be a good thing."

"Tsk. Stupid Omega," Eddie mumbled.

Bruce reached across the bar and yanked on Eddie's shirt, almost pulling the Alpha onto it. "What did you just say?"

Eddie regretted his words immediately, especially when he felt James behind him. "Nothing! Nothing. We're outta here." With his good hand, he readjusted his shirt and beckoned his crew to follow him. He gave Alexander a neutral look. "It's been fun." Alexander huffed in regret. Eddie gave him a smirk in return, but it lasted only a second as his last look was at Stephen. One final glaring stare at the Alpha ended his patronage at the South Street Tavern.

<hr>

After the group cleared out, Stephen dared to walk up to the bar, standing next to the Omega who captivated him. He started cautiously. "I didn't expect... thank you."

Alexander placed his elbows on the bar and sank his head into his hands. Then he exhaled. "Don't thank me yet. You just lost me a few of my regulars."

"I'm sorry about that," Stephen replied.

The frustration grew as Alexander stood back up. "Who the hell are you?!"

Once again, the Alpha's wolf hurt inside, not understanding the animosity. This wasn't how their first encounter was supposed to go. "I'm Stephen."

"Yeah, no shit. I got that part. What the fuck? Do you just go around to bars and start causing trouble?"

Stephen held up his hands. "I promise you; I wasn't looking for trouble nor did I mean to start it. I'm sorry."

"Bruce. Hit me!" Alexander slapped his hand on the bar. Like an automated robot, Bruce tossed up a glass and began pouring a double shot. He knocked back half of it, closing his eyes and shuddering as the heat flowed into his veins.

Stephen hated seeing the Omega—no—*his* Omega in this state. If he only understood how much. But Alexander was clearly in a different headspace. Perhaps if he could get him to calm down, he'd then be able to discuss what he really wanted to say. "You must have believed me." Alexander stared back at him. "At least a little?"

The Omega licked his lips, tasting the hints of spirits which lingered. He set the half-empty glass down on the bar. "I could tell there was something about you."

Stephen's heart skipped a beat. "Something like..."

Alexander shrugged. "Just that aura that said I could trust what you were saying."

Shoulders slumped, expressions fell, and hopes dwindled; but Stephen couldn't understand why. But he wasn't going to stop now. He couldn't. Not until Alexander knew. "Bruce—I'll take what he's got." He gestured to Alexander's glass. Bruce nodded and finished the order.

"Plus," the Omega continued, "you told me all I needed to know in order to call out Craig and Eddie on their bullshit."

"What?" Stephen looked back perplexed. "What did I say?"

"You said you guessed that Craig was a Type 2, right?" Stephen nodded. "Yeah. That's when I knew."

The Alpha's face twitched. "I mean, I don't blame him for being upset. If someone called me a Type 2 while trying to impress me, I'd be equally turned off."

Alexander nodded in agreement. "Unless you *were* a Type 2." He took the remainder of his glass and knocked it back. "Bruce." He gestured for another one.

Stephen furrowed his brows. "Wait... Craig?" It came together. "No way!" Never in his wildest dreams did he anticipate the whole thing to be a setup.

Alexander laughed. "I told you. Once you said it, I knew who to call out."

"I don't understand. Why did he do that then? Why would anyone do that?" Stephen didn't have any qualms knocking back the entire drink. This day was one insanity after another.

"Territory wars. Wasn't it obvious?" The Omega stared back awkwardly. "Are you even from here?"

"Yes?" Stephen drew out.

"Are you sure?" Alexander chuckled.

"I grew up in this city."

"What's your Type?"

Stephen was thrown off. "I'm a Type 4. Why?"

"Ah. That's why." Alexander took a swig of his drink, amused by the new information.

Stephen however was not equally entertained. "What does that mean?"

"I'm surprised you're even hanging around this bar. Isn't there a High Type place you frequent?"

Now the Alpha was getting annoyed. It was another blast from the past he didn't appreciate. "I've never understood why business owners want to perpetuate the stupid divide between High Types and Low Types, effectively cutting their business almost in half."

"Perpetuate?!" Alexander scoffed. "Please. A smart Alpha like yourself knows how this works. This world is about knowing your place and doing the best with what you have. Not believing it exists or ignoring it is nothing but a fool's end."

Stephen tensed his jaw. "You mean like how an Omega should know better than to own a bar?" Bruce eyed Alexander from the bar, and James looked over the tables in the corner.

The Omega studied the glass in front of him, rimmed it with his finger, smirked, and then looked Stephen in the eye. "Exactly."

Stephen adjusted himself in the chair and rubbed his chin. "My parents are both Type 3. I'm a Type 4. My entire life I've been riding this line on where I should adhere to: my family's Status or my own. Most of the time, it's decided for me. And I fucking hate it."

Alexander nodded. "I can't relate to that. But I do know what it's like having everyone around you tell you who you are and what you should be. And you're right—I fucking hate it too." He smiled.

The Alpha melted seeing the Omega's first genuine smile go across his face. Once again, he inhaled his intoxicating scent and gathered his nerve. *It's now or never.* "Alex..." The Omega gave him his full attention. "Do you... I mean..." He laughed nervously for a moment and rubbed his forehead, unsure why it was going this way. "Please tell me you know who I am."

Alexander stared back in confusion. "I just met you. And as far as I recall, I don't know anyone named 'Stephen'. Know you ... how?"

"No... no. Not like that." The Alpha swallowed. "I'm talking about the connection that only our wolves know."

Within earshot, Bruce heard the comment and turned around instantly. Likewise, James looked more intrigued now than he did earlier during the altercation.

Alexander noticed the pairs of eyes staring back at him. His face began to turn red. "This is some sort of joke, right?" Stephen's expression never changed as he locked his gaze upon him. The Alpha was looking for an Omega reciprocation, one that could only be given in an equal consensual connection. But Alexander scented the pheromone palate coming off the Alpha. It was clear Stephen was referring to more... much more. A sensation came over him which washed all over his body. It made him lose his breath, but once he got it back, he slowly lifted himself out of the barstool. "I think... I think I need to go." He stood up and began walking to the back. After a few steps, he stopped. "Actually, this is *my* bar. *You* need to go."

Stephen stood up. "What? Why? What did I say?"

Alexander shook his head. "Just don't. I'm sorry. But I need you to leave. Please."

If the Alpha's inner wolf could howl at the moon in agony, it would. Stephen's mind raced in several directions. He couldn't fathom what was happening. "But I feel it. You don't feel it?" he pleaded.

Alexander lifted his head high, completely lost. "Feel what?"

"You're my ... Fate," Stephen breathed.

Bruce couldn't hold himself quiet anymore. "Oh, shit."

An uncomfortable silence followed, then an uncomfortable laughter. Alexander wiped his eyebrow. "Are there hidden cameras somewhere I don't know about? Eric talked about installing them." He peered at the far corners, knowing they weren't there yet.

Stephen gulped. "You really don't feel it, do you?" Saying it hurt the most. He didn't know what to do. Either this Omega had the strongest will and best poker face out of anyone he'd ever met, or he was psychotic.

Alexander's face fell. "I think I may have done this wrong. Maybe I should have kept Craig and Eddie here."

"Please don't say that," Stephen pleaded.

"Stephen, I think you are a very nice guy. But you need to leave. Now." Alexander solidified his stance and let every pheromone pouring out of Stephen roll right off.

For the Alpha, the world crashed to a halt in the worst way. He gave the bouncers one last glance as a plea for help. But both stood there, equally shocked at the entire development. Sensing he was at a total loss … he tucked his tail and turned to leave.

But suddenly, a new voice broke the silence and stopped Stephen in his tracks.

"Is that him?" Eric walked into the bar out of breath, eyeing Stephen.

The Alpha froze, unsure of what he was being targeted for now. "I'm sorry?"

Eric approached him with a purpose. "Are you the guy who told off Craig and brought Eddie down to his knees? Literally?" He eyed the fellow Alpha, watching his every move.

Stephen felt like this day couldn't get any worse. Cautiously, he answered back. "That was me."

Alexander felt another headache coming on. The last thing he wanted was for Eric to get involved. Considering what Stephen tried to pull just seconds ago, he didn't need an Eric lecture on top of it. "It's all over, Eric. Stephen was just leaving."

"Leave?" Eric asked incredulously. "Leave?! Hell no. I want to shake your hand, sir!" With a full hand outstretched in a welcome, Stephen slowly gave his in return. After taking it, he enthusiastically shook his hand while pulling him into a bro hug. "Thank you! Thank you! Thank you!" He let go of his unexpected embrace, still smiling from ear-to-ear. "Do you need to leave? Or can I buy you a drink?"

At this point, Stephen's mind was burnt out. "I don't understand."

"I don't understand either." Alexander exhaled with exhaustion. "What's going on, Eric?"

"I come walking down the street when I shockingly see Craig and his pals, walking in the *opposite* direction of our bar, huffing and puffing like their daddies took their toys away and Eddie nursing his hand like he got into a fight with a block of cement. Naturally, I ask them what's going on, and even more interested as to why they aren't in the bar."

"Why's that?" Stephen asked.

Eric was surprised. "I guess you don't know them then."

"None of us here know *this* guy." Alexander added.

"Those guys practically lived here," Eric continued. "Shit, some days we'd find them in the dead of winter, standing at the door almost an hour before the place opens. Then they'd get angry if we opened the door even a minute late."

Guilt rushed over Stephen. He really did lose Alexander a few of his regulars. "I'm sorry. I didn't mean to cause trouble for your clientele."

Eric sat at the bar, proud like he'd accomplished a week's worth of tasks in a day, or as if a great weight had been lifted off his shoulders. "Sorry? Man, don't be sorry! This is great! Now come over here, and I'll buy you a drink. Bruce, get him another whatever he was drinking, and I'll do my usual."

Stephen looked back at Alexander, wondering if he was going to get a death stare which told him *not* to join this new patron. But the Omega's look was equally confused. He used the opportunity to sit next to Eric and let him lead the conversation.

"Can I ask why this is such a great thing?" Stephen snuck in.

Eric smirked at his business partner first. "Alex may not admit it, but Craig and Eddie represent the clientele we *don't* want to have here. Nothing but antagonistic scum."

"That's harsh." Alexander was more offended by the judgement of *his* character versus Craig and Eddie.

"No, it isn't."

Something caught Stephen's attention. "What do you mean 'we'?"

"Oh! I suppose I should introduce myself. Eric Dayes: manager of the South Street Tavern and city inspection rep." This time, the Alpha gestured with his glass instead of a handshake since the formality already commenced.

Stephen saw his drink magically replenished in front of him once again. As he contemplated his own return greeting, he examined Eric's pheromones. The odd combination of being a manager with such an elitist mouth and a city inspection rep didn't ring true to him. But now wasn't the time to criticize the only man he had standing in his corner. Granted, Eric wasn't the man he truly wanted to talk to, but if it got him vicariously closer to Alexander for even a second longer, he'd take it. But learning from his mistakes earlier, he needed to dodge the proverbial greeting. "Why do you consider those guys scum?"

Eric hummed. "I mean, I know Alex has better judgement than to let *anyone* into the bar..."

"Really? Doesn't sound like it," Alexander soured. He admitted defeat and sat next to Eric, who already pushed his chair out so he could have a clearer view of Stephen, not that he was looking for one.

"Now is not the time to act all butt hurt! I told you this place needed to get in better shape, and that means working on the customer base as well. Having bodies in this place does you no good if you allow people in who are going to intimidate other customers. And you and I both know that's what Craig and Eddie do when they're here."

Alexander pursed his lips and took in the criticism slowly. "You're right. I should have kicked them out months ago. Had I known it was going to result in a physical altercation one day, I would have."

"That's another thing!" Eric wondered. "How did it even get that far?"

By the time Alexander, Eric, and Stephen all looked up, both Bruce and James were perfectly standing next to each other behind the bar, being judged like two pups from their parents about mischief or wrongdoings. Also, like pups, both stuck their thumbs out at each other, putting the blame on the other.

Alexander sighed. "Come on, guys! I hired you two for a reason. This is the shit I can't have happen for the next week. We have that huge event coming up, and I can't have things like this fucking it all up! I'm not even sure if the damage from Craig and Eddie alone won't tank this already."

"Oh, please. Do you think the people showing up to that event would even listen to Craig or Eddie give directions to the nearest gas station?"

Alexander's shoulders fell. "Probably not."

"Then, relax, man!" Eric shook his head, enjoying the fact Alexander was taking this all to heart.

"What's the big event?" Stephen leaned in with curiosity.

Eric turned his body and proudly announced. "Matthew Whitmore, *the* Matthew Whitmore, is sponsoring political candidate Jesse Minh for his next run, and he has chosen to host the fundraiser right here at South Street Tavern."

Stephen appeared lost. "That's a big deal then?"

Dark eyes opened, flabbergasted at the ignorance. "Are you kidding me?" Eric stressed. "This alone has not only the potential to put us on the map but elevate us to epic proportions in the city. If it goes well, we'll get the substantial customer base we've been looking for."

"Key word is *if*," Alexander lamented. "We still don't have enough staff for it. Even if we're all here and Daniel shows up, we need another bar back, and quite frankly, one who could occasionally bartend as well."

Eric turned back toward the Omega. "How have the interviews gone?"

Alexander groaned. "Don't ask."

"What's the problem?"

"Really, Eric? Do I have to explain that on top of needing the courage to work for an Omega bar owner, someone who gets hired as a bar back who can also bartend doesn't want to get paid at a bar back wage?"

"Someone's out there," Eric dismissed.

"No one is out there," Alexander rebuked.

Stephen shifted in his chair. He felt an involuntary entity reach into his throat and force the words out of him. "I'll do it!"

Both Alexander and Eric answered simultaneously. "You?!"

Eric continued, "I don't know if I received a proper introduction."

The Alpha nodded. "I'm Stephen. I'm 29 and a native of the city. I'm looking for a job, can work any hours, and know a thing or two about making drinks. I will admit I'd need to learn the ropes at how to properly do all the behind-the-scenes work, but I'm a fast learner and don't give up easily."

Eric studied the Alpha up and down. "You're hired!"

Alexander couldn't believe his ears. "What? No way!"

Stephen furrowed his brows. "Why not?"

"Yeah, why not?" Eric joined in. "You already said there was no one. Here's someone. What's the problem?" He held up his hands like it was a no-brainer.

"You *do* remember he just crushed another patron's hand, right?" Alexander equally gave the expression back.

"*Former* patron," Eric pointed out.

"And you know what? I don't want him to make anyone else we have into a 'former' patron either." The words had little effect. "Come on. This guy randomly walks into a bar and incites violence within five minutes? Who does that?"

"I didn't incite anything. You even said that!" Stephen defended.

Alexander ignored the comment, still trying to convince Eric otherwise. "You can't just hire some Alpha off the street like that. He's probably a criminal or ex-con or something!"

Eric gave the frustrated Omega a look which read he was out-of-line with the comment. But both noticed, with all the quick defenses the Alpha came back with, he was silent on this one.

Alexander read it all over Stephen's face. "Wolf-God, are you serious?"

"I can explain!" Stephen begged.

"Bruce! James!" Alexander called out.

Stephen backed away as saw the two bouncers approach him on command. He wasn't going to initiate his Alpha pheromones; it would have done the exact opposite of his goal. "Please, please! Just hear me out?!" Both Bruce and James turned to see Alexander and Eric waiting patiently for any decent answer to justify his presence. "I—I had a misstep in my past, I can't deny that. Doing a background check on me would bring it up in an instant so I should just be upfront with you. I have a drug and negligent homicide charge on my record that I paid the price for. Despite my record and behavior here in your bar, I am not a reckless, violent Alpha. I've been ten years clean of drugs and have had regular anger management and therapy since."

"Hmph. Might need an extra session in that anger management class," Alexander spat back.

"I'm not violent, but I have the right to protect myself," Stephen defended. "Eddie threatened me to begin with and then he threw the first punch. All I did was contain him."

James spoke up, "He's got a point there."

"Whose side are you on?" Alexander grumbled.

"I want him," Eric announced.

Stephen was perplexed. "I'm confused. Are *you* the owner, or is he?" His gesture flipped between the two, unable to decipher who really had control or final say.

"It's complicated." Eric cleared his throat. "Anyway, when can you start?"

"Now?" Stephen replied, still lost on how to navigate the conversation.

With an Alpha's strength, Alexander yanked Eric out of his bar stool, sending the chair down to the floor. Eric's protests did little to affect the Omega's fuming yet controlled rant. "Do you want to explain to me what the hell it is you are thinking in that warped mind of yours? Did Eddie dropkick you when you saw him out there on the sidewalk?"

Eric composed himself, foregoing a dominant Alpha posture he was more than entitled to as a response for the Omega's brazen move in public. "You said it yourself. We have no one. We need to get someone in on the cheap and fast. You have one week to completely get this guy comfortable with this place."

Alexander shook his head in disbelief and strained his voice. "How am I supposed to get this guy comfortable when *I'm* not even comfortable with *him*?"

"Put him on probation then; odds are he's used to the idea." He glanced over, hoping Stephen didn't hear the tasteless comment. "Give him a week. If he's not up to snuff, can his ass."

Realizing none of his own concerns were getting through to Eric, Alexander tried a different approach. "For someone who is all about this place's image and reputation, why are you so willing to gamble with this guy?"

"Like I said, he's got drive, he's got availability, he's got stature, and he appears to have a brain. What more could you want?"

Alexander threw his hands up. "This guy has a record that includes *homicide*! Did you skip that part? He's probably just waiting to find out all our personal addresses and plans on murdering us in our sleep!"

"No, he won't," Eric sang back dismissively.

"And what makes you so sure?"

"Guys who do that show up at your place of business with resumes that are too good to be true, hide behind thick glasses, talk in a sheepish voice, and speak about their past in vague irrefutable terms. This guy came in and showed all his imperfections to us in twenty minutes and *still* asked for a job—a job we really needed filled like yesterday. And quite frankly, if I'm going to take anyone at face value, I'll take his before the next candidate comes in as a complete mystery asking for double the money we want to pay him. Wouldn't you?"

Alexander hung his head in defeat. "I still don't understand. I really don't."

Eric began walking back to the bar, knowing the agreement was going to be an impasse. "Call it Alpha's tuition; I like the guy. Plus, he hates Craig and Eddie." Along with his own, he took Stephen's glass to the Alpha at the front entrance. Then, he joyfully led them both in a congratulatory toast. "And the enemy of my enemy is my friend." Eric smiled and clinked their glasses together before both finished the drink. Then, he patted the Alpha on the back. "Welcome to the team, my friend."

"Are we even allowed to hire an ex-con? Is that even legal?" Alexander yelled back across the bar.

"I looked it up a minute ago. It all checks out," James replied.

The Omega grimaced back. "Thanks, James. You're a real help," he replied sarcastically.

"Well, I gotta go!" Eric jumped up.

"Go? You just got here!" Alexander's nerves took over.

"I have a city meeting in thirty minutes. I just came to stop by. Good thing I did, right?" Eric's white teeth sparkled as he grinned like a Cheshire cat.

It took all of Alexander's willpower to not punch Eric in the face. He knew exactly what he was doing. "Great. Thanks a lot."

"No problem." He brought up his hand to Stephen, offering him a fist bump. "See you soon, my man!"

Stephen obliged and smiled at his ... boss? Manager? Co-worker? He still wasn't sure. "Thanks again."

"Sure thing!" Eric shouted back, halfway out the door.

Alexander stomped his way to the entrance until he was right up against Stephen, ready to berate him for scheming his way into the job. But as he stood there, looking into the man's vulnerable eyes, the soft pheromone palate took all the ammo away from him. It was hard to acknowledge, but there was some truth to this mysterious man: he *wasn't* typical. Stephen knew just how to elicit the response he wanted. But now, Alexander was showing the Alpha that he, the *Omega,* was in control. Regardless of being in a position of power, the innate ability to switch to a submissive tone in front of an Omega was rare, unless that Omega was their mate. Which—oh, that's right—*that* was another issue. Alexander had no intention of addressing that now. "Who do you think you are?"

"I realize this isn't ideal, but I am grateful for the opportunity."

The Omega was offended. "Opportunity? *Opportunity?!* No, an opportunity is when I offer you a job and you accept it. What you did was come into my business and slime your way into getting this! If I didn't trust Eric enough, I would have let Bruce and James test out the new pool cues on you!" He grunted his frustration. "Just get out of here! And don't come back!"

Stephen wanted to do anything but. However, the Alpha knew the burden to please the Omega also meant no longer hurting him. With the poor position he was already in, he had no choice. The pheromones rushing off Alexander communicated he didn't really have the job as he originally thought. He relaxed his body and began his exit.

"Until ... tomorrow morning at 10 AM," the Omega relented.

A breath of fresh air rushed into Stephen's lungs. The Omega didn't hate him as much as he thought. Or Eric's command finally sank in. Whichever one it was, he'd take it. "Thank you!" It took every ounce of willpower he had not to rush into a full embrace. The pull was too strong. Thus, he felt the conversation needed to be addressed. "What I said about earlier... the whole 'Fate' thing..."

Alexander braced himself, not sure where it was headed. "I was being serious, Alex. The wolf inside me says we're supposed to—"

"Okay. Time-out!" Alexander morphed his hands in the traditional referee position. "If we're going to start this business relationship, then we need some ground rules. Rule #1—No more discussing this 'Fated Mate' thing."

The statement grounded Stephen. "You really don't feel the pull, do you? You don't feel anything."

Alexander gave the same puzzled look on his face. "I don't know what you are talking about. No, I don't feel anything inside me that says you are my Fate. I don't feel anything at all for you… well, except a headache." He crossed his arms.

Continuing to make it an issue wasn't going to help Stephen whatsoever. That much he knew. He swallowed his pride and pretended the last exchange never happened. "What else? What are the other rules?"

Alexander continued. "Rule #2—I may be an Omega, but I am your boss. You will always remember that. If I even *think* you have lost sight of that respect, you are out here. And the same goes for Eric, Bruce, and James. If any of them even give me a hint of a reason not to trust you, you're gone. Do you understand?"

"Understood," Stephen replied confidently.

Still, the Alpha stood there and took a beating from the Omega. Alexander felt Bruce and James's eyes on him. But he knew they were equally in awe of Stephen's willpower. "Rule #3—you are on probation. No late punches, no early outs unless I tell you to leave, no sick days, no excuses, and absolutely no drugs."

"Of course!" Stephen assured him.

Alexander's gaze danced around the Alpha. Slowly he retracted his harsh attitude as he realized the only threatening tone was coming from himself. "After the week trial, I'm hoping you'll be in top shape for the fundraiser. And if that goes well," he paused, "then maybe I'll consider hiring you on as a regular."

"I will do you proud!" Stephen beamed.

"We'll see," Alexander cautioned, effectively pushing the Alpha's excitement back. "Sit over there, and I'll grab the forms in the back for you to fill out. Since you eloquently told us of your past, I assume there will be no *other* surprises in your background check?" Stephen shook his head. "Good. I'm scheduling your drug test for tomorrow morning."

"Drug test?" Stephen asked.

"You got a problem with that?" Alexander interrogated.

"No. I'm just surprised—"

"I'm a downtown bar owner in Tauris City about to hire a felon. You're that surprised?"

"No, I suppose not."

Alexander sighed. "Luckily, no one who has passed through this place yet appears to know you. So, whatever you were convicted of, it was either long ago or didn't hit mainstream media. I'll take either scenario as a plus."

Stephen blinked, unable to argue the necessity of such an outcome. After all, Alexander was willing to take a chance on him. Had his presence come across more like a black-listed celebrity or the entire place crumbled in fear, none of this would have had the outcome he wanted. And the outcome he wanted most was to be with his Fated Mate. Although Alexander claiming otherwise, Stephen was willing to deal with the hand Wolf-God dealt him. The Omega was his. And he wasn't going to give him up so easily. At the bottom of the first employment form, he signed his name in extra-large lettering with flare, declaring unto himself the second victory in over ten years.

# CHAPTER 06:

## LEARNING TO LIVE WITH FAMILY

Stephen walked up the long driveway very much unlike he had the previous morning. Whereas yesterday his legs had boulders tied to them, today he was floating toward the house. Once he entered, he saw it in a whole new light. Instead of the dreary memories of yesteryear clouding his childhood home, he saw a glimmer and shine on the place he refused to take notice of. The sun glistened through the windows and shone off the clean and immaculate furniture. The walls proudly displayed the décor and photographs which were always there. And the warmth in the room took him in like a welcoming invitation. He took a deep breath in and exhaled in splendor. When he opened his eyes, he saw his Veo walk in from the kitchen, glancing at the day's mail.

"Hey!" His tone cautiously matched the obvious delight plastered all over his son's face. Stephen smiled back. "And ... how did today go?" The hesitation on asking the question was pointless; today's goal was clear from the start, and by his son's aura alone, it appeared to be successful.

Stephen contemplated how to respond in the right words. His mind and body never felt so much reassurance his life finally had direction. But still, there were no words to explain how he felt. "Indescribable."

Marlon tilted his head in the consideration of such an odd response. "Does that mean you got a job?"

*A job?* The word was gibberish at first, received in a completely different language. But then his senses pulled through and reminded him of what the original intent was. "A job!" he recalled finally. "Yes! A job! I got it!"

Pure elation fell upon Marlon's face as he ran up and gave his son a full embrace. "Oh, Wolf-God! Congratulations! I can't believe it!"

"What? Didn't think I was good enough?" Stephen playfully criticized.

"No, that's not what I meant. I was just—" The joke finally set in. "Oh, you tease!" He lightly hit Alexander on the chest. "Well, sit down! Tell me all about it." He pushed his son into the living room and sat in the plush chair as he waited impatiently to hear the news.

The Alpha sat satisfied on the couch, balancing his arms on each knee while he clasped his hands together in thought. He had to clear his mind of what he really wanted to say. Alexander was the only focus in his mind—as it should be. His Fated Mate was finally revealed to him at a time he barely felt anyone would consider him even as a casual partner. But with the excitement also came the nerves from understanding that his mate was out there unmarked. Furthermore, there was the predicament of the Omega's steadfast conviction there was no Fated pull. That, however, was a problem for a different time.

He sighed. "Where do I begin? The location is great—downtown Tauris near the Medical Center."

Marlon nodded cautiously, noticing immediately the name or type of establishment wasn't given right away. "Okay..." he drew out, "and this place is...?"

Stephen gulped. "It's a bar. I'm a bar back in training to become a fulltime bartender." The look on his Veo's face wasn't reassuring.

"A bar? A bar." Marlon's volume was controlled but he still couldn't believe his ears.

"Veo, please," he begged.

Marlon crossed his legs and held his head at the reveal. He didn't know whether to support or criticize the news. "You're serious?"

"Yes?" he answered cautiously.

"Do you think that's smart?" Marlon challenged.

Stephen's forehead creased as he didn't enjoy taking in his Omega father's critical scent and harsh expression. He understood the pushback; he just wasn't ready for it. "I think it's actually one of the smartest places for me to be," the Alpha concluded with his head held high.

"How do you figure?"

"It's not as if I have years of experience anywhere else or a full education. If I can only get minimum wage, at least the tips will supplement it to a decent living while I contemplate where I want to go with my life." The thoughts were coming to Stephen on the fly, but the more he thought about his statements, the more he believed them.

Marlon held in his frustration as best as he could. "I can't say I disagree with that rationale, but you know what I'm talking about."

Stephen played coy. "I do?" He saw his Veo toss the mail off his lap and onto the floor. He knew his father meant business and exactly where he was going.

"Yes, you do!" Marlon shoved his fist up to his mouth and bit down on his knuckle. Suddenly, his whole hand shook, his lips trembled, and as his eyes became weak.

It didn't take long for Stephen to surmise the small breakdown his Veo was having. Seeing it on a much larger scale when Warren passed made it easy to recognize the most subtle hints of emotions. "Hey...," he offered in a soothing voice, "it's going to be okay; *I'm* going to be okay. I promise."

A guttural sound choked up into Marlon's throat, indicating minimal success in his son's attempt. "I've heard that *way* too many times for it to be true, Stephen." His voice was on the verge of no return.

The Alpha hung his head. A desperate attempt to find success in the job search didn't put him in the best mind frame to consider what he had done. Even though alcohol was considered separate from drugs by the law, Stephen recalled in lockup the many links to how alcohol consumption or the atmosphere of excessive alcohol consumption could lead to temptation and its foremost conclusion: drug relapse. Incessantly, his parents, and even court sponsors, tried to convince and even beg him to consider Alcoholics Anonymous in addition to Narcotics Anonymous. But Stephen wasn't arrested with alcohol in his system, nor did he have a law violation on his record indicating he abused alcohol, despite him having a social reputation for doing so.

Thus, Stephen threw his Type 4 Alpha Status around and convinced the judge he didn't have an addiction issue much less an alcohol issue. But even so, his release was still contingent on abstaining from drug use or possession. Gaining employment at a bar downtown was the ultimate showdown of self-control, and he hadn't even completed day one yet.

"Why, Stephen?!" A stray tear fell down Marlon's cheek. Even with the emotional plea in his voice and pheromones, one more steady look into his son's eyes made him realize there was no convincing him. "I just," he cracked, "I don't want to lose you again." His hand involuntarily went over his mouth at the mere thought of it happening.

Stephen instantly stood and walked over. As he sat on the armrest of the chair, he embraced his Omega father in a way he hadn't in years. "I promise, Veo, that won't happen again. This is going to be a good thing."

Marlon lifted his head and snorted—a break in his sorrow. "Good?" he chuckled. "I don't know if *that's* how I would describe it."

Finally, the thought of Alexander came rushing back. A flood of happiness rushed to his face, and he felt butterflies in his stomach. "There's... there's something I need to tell—"

The front door opened, breaking up the conversation. Both Stephen and Marlon stared at Kane, who kicked off his shoes and casually walked in.

Wanting nothing to do with the conversation, Kane planned on only giving a quick nod to acknowledge their presence, but the looks coming back to him indicated something was amiss. "What?" An automatic tensing of his neck muscles brought back memories of the two discussing some issue or misstep Stephen got himself into. Their expressions were classic; it couldn't be anything else. "I said, 'What's going on'?"

Like the countless incidents before this, the pair glanced at each other, knowing Kane's temperament. The tone in his voice was unmistakable. Marlon cleared his throat and started in on what was sure to be a tumultuous conversation.

"Stephen found a job today." The words came out steady and neutral.

Surprised by the news, the Alpha's face relaxed and carried a hint of pride. "That's... that's great!" He walked over, still observing his family's uncomfortable disposition. Kane solidified his stance, still perplexed. "Then why does it appear no one is excited about it?" Without anyone rushing in to counter the observation, his phero-mones began their own transition. "He's not some middleman for a crime syndicate, is he?"

A grunt pushed through Stephen's throat. "That wasn't necessary."

Kane's patience ran out. "Will you just tell me what the hell you got yourself into?"

Now, the memories were clear as day. The entire family once again sat in their traditional roles. Some families had game night, others watched movies. But the Matheson family had this: the constant arguments and battles over Stephen's life choices and his future. Ten years of imprisonment erased in a second as if it never happened with each family member falling back into what they were all too familiar with.

Unfortunately for Stephen, his role involved silence and quick dismissals until he was pushed to the brink. But he wasn't near that stage yet.

Similarly, Marlon knew the only way he could prevent his two Alphas from blowing up was to be the scale of reason and neutrality. "He's going to work at a bar in downtown Tauris."

Kane did a doubletake at his mate and son, assessing whether the punchline was coming. When it didn't, he honed in on his son, only remembering the 19-year-old from the past, and not the 29-year-old today. "What on Wolf-God's earth are you doing?"

"Dad, I—"

"Are you trying to get yourself back into jail?"

Stephen held himself together as best as he could. Unlike the pure criticism of the decade prior, there was a hint of sorrow and fear in his Sur's voice. To prevent himself from falling back into his old coping mechanisms and defenses, he concentrated on that as he felt his Veo gently rub his back for support. "I know this isn't ideal and I know the reasons why." Kane's expression shifted to the windows which showcased the serenity outside while biting his tongue. "But I'm not that compulsive and irresponsible teen you're thinking about!"

"I'm not—"

"I can see it all over your face!" Stephen argued.

The strength and nerve Kane once had left him years ago. He couldn't stand over his scrawny teenager of a son anymore; he didn't exist. With time beating him down as well, he couldn't go on his former verbal rampage. Stephen was an adult and he was an ailing wolf on borrowed time. Be that as it may, he wasn't going to hide his vexation. "What are you going to do if you find yourself among dealers and users? A *downtown* bar in Tauris? Practically breeding grounds."

"Then, I'll separate myself from the situation." The response was automatic. Stephen only took a moment to reflect on whether he could. "For a week, I'm in training. If I feel it's not a good fit, I'll leave." Kane furrowed his brows in disbelief. "I will!" Deep inside, Stephen's entire chest hurt at the thought of walking out on Alexander. That was something he *couldn't* do nor would he ever want to.

"There are hundreds if not thousands of jobs out there you could apply for that don't put you in the compromising position you are getting ready to subject yourself to," Kane rebuked.

Stephen rubbed his face with both hands. The discouragement of his previous attempts before the bar made him wince. "No, Dad. There's not. *You* know it, and *I* know it. Nobody's looking for ex-con right now," he said sarcastically. "Hell, they'd probably hire a corpse over me." The Alpha stood up and walked toward the large windows, mirroring his Sur.

"Except this one. How did that happen?" Kane pointed out. "Do they know your history yet?"

Rolling his eyes, Stephen answered. "Yes. I told everyone. No sense in getting my hopes up about a job prospect just for them to take it away from me based on my record."

Kane glided his fingers against his beard. There was indeed a change in his son's maturity level. Thought and consideration had worked its way in. However, there were still plenty of reasons for skepticism. "You didn't answer my first question."

Having the extra scrutiny wasn't something Stephen was prepared for. But he needed a way to come up with a way to minimize the drama. He hesitated. "I ... got scoped out by one of the owners." Both Kane and Marlon looked at him in confusion. "I went there after being unsuccessful at other businesses."

Once again, Kane looked at his mate to see if he was alone in his confused state. "You moped in a bar to the point where an Alpha asked if you wanted a job?"

The natural wolf instinct inside Stephen released a growl at his father's notion he was hired out of pity. "No, it wasn't like that!" he growled.

Remembering himself, Marlon stood up, ready to be the natural barrier between the two Alphas as he had been before. "This is a good thing. I don't think the details on how he got the job are that important, Kane. Like he said, they know about his record." An audible sigh of relief escaped Stephen's lungs. "Plus, right before you came in, I got the feeling Stephen was going to tell me some more good news?" he encouraged.

Marlon's approach surprised Stephen. As much as he wanted to share the sacred discovery with his Veo, he was hoping to gauge his reaction before approaching his Sur on the topic. Now, the Alpha had no choice but to come clean about the reveal. "I don't know how to say this any other way but," he paused, "the bar owner... he's... he's my Fate."

"Your Fate? Stephen, really?" Marlon's face brightened.

The look on both of his parents' faces was expected. In addition to the natural shock and awe of such revelation, there were reflections on the information already given which only raised questions. Kane started first.

"Wait. That doesn't make sense. You fated an Alpha bar owner? You can't fate an Alpha."

Stephen closed his eyes in frustration. "Dad, I know that."

"Wanna clue us in on what we're missing, then?"

After tightening his fists and releasing them, Stephen continued. "There's two bar owners. Only one of them is an Alpha, and as far as I can tell, he's absent from the place most of the time. The other owner is an Omega and appears to be the one who runs the show."

Marlon squinted his eyes as he tried to make sense of what he heard.

Kane, however, knew exactly where his son was going with this. "Oh, hell. You're really going to drop that on me now?"

"Drop what?" Marlon asked, still completely lost.

Kane huffed, annoyed he was having to associate his family with such nonsense. "He's talking about South Street—*the* South Street."

"South Street..." The Omega rubbed his earlobe as he struggled to remember why it sounded so familiar.

"What do you know about it, Dad?" Stephen inquired defensively. "You've been off the force for a while now."

"Don't get an attitude with me on things you don't know about, son!" Kane retorted. "The drama with that bar and its 'owner' has been under the precinct's radar ever since he petitioned the city to hand the title and liquor license over."

"Petition? You just purchase the property and apply for the license. What does petitioning the city have to do with anything?"

Kane rubbed his forehead as he tried to remember the convoluted story from his work partners, the newspapers, and occasional local news story on TV. "South Street was deemed such a loss from its former reputation, nobody anticipated it to be bought as a bar again. They figured some conglomerate would buy the property just to renovate it and tear it down—maybe even the Medical Center—to turn it into something else entirely. Not that it was ever said on record, but the story goes that whoever was initially handling the sale and paperwork didn't know the buyer was an Omega and that the city tried backtracking on the whole thing, all the way up to denying the liquor license."

"On what grounds?" Stephen asked.

"That's the problem. There was nothing the city could do to prevent the liquor license from being issued, and the property was already purchased. I suppose they were waiting for someone to come swoop in and buy the property off the Omega or hope there was some unturned stone in his past so the liquor license couldn't be issued. The best they could do was delay it all until they couldn't any longer."

"Why?"

"At that point, you're not just dealing with the legality of what is rightfully owed, you're dealing with politics. If the city as an entity chose to show its colors that it didn't want an Omega bar owner in downtown Tauris, then that was going to open a whole can of worms they didn't want."

"From what I remember years ago, most of the city is against an Omega bar owner. Alexander only confirmed the rhetoric today to me. So why would taking that stance be such an issue?"

"Think about it," Kane said. "The majority isn't everyone. And the minority has some strong leadership which can't be ignored. When you have proponents like Matthew Whitmore saying it's time to let Omegas own *any* type of business, including a bar, people listen."

Once again, Stephen heard the name which commanded attention and respect, yet he had no idea who he was. He was going to inquire about the businessman but his Veo cut-in before he could.

"'Alexander'—Is that who—"

"Yes, that's my mate... my Fate." Stephen deflated.

Marlon smiled cautiously. "I don't understand. If this is your Fate, then you should be ecstatic. This could potentially be the happiest moment in your life—both of your lives."

Stephen massaged the taut area between his neck and shoulder. "Have you... have you ever heard of someone doubting that the connection exists?"

"Usually, it's a disgruntled Alpha or Omega parent who doesn't wish to see their son with a particular Type or family." Kane smirked at his own commentary. "Why? Are you already having problems with his parents? If so, that was fast."

"No," Stephen exhaled, "not with the parents... the Omega."

Marlon treaded lightly. "Babe, are you saying that *Alexander* doesn't think you two are Fates?"

Just like in the bar, having to accept the notion hurt the Alpha to his core. "Yeah, Veo. That's exactly what I'm saying."

Kane gazed at Marlon in disbelief and then proceeded cautiously. "Stephen, you know Fates only work if both feel the connection. It's unmistakable. You don't get to just walk up to any Omega you want and declare them yours."

"Is *that* what you think I did?" Stephen asked, offended.

Marlon stepped in. "No! No, we don't think that." He hoped his words were enough to cool the heated accusation.

"Then what did you mean?"

A look of consternation fell upon Kane's face as he attempted to reorganize his thoughts. "This is a very delicate process and fine line you are walking. The one Wolf-God given right all Omegas have is to equally say who is and who isn't their Fate. Legally, there isn't anything you can do if this Alexander says you're not the one."

Stephen couldn't believe his ears. "Wow. Thanks, Dad."

"What?" Kane asked, lost from his son's attitude.

"I tell you that I think, no, that I *know* I've found my Fate, the one who I'm supposed to spend the rest of my life with, and the only thing you can think about is whether or not my claim is even legal?" Kane dimmed his expression. "What about my happiness? What about moving on from my past and beginning my future life—a life which is supposed to be the ideal every wolf-descendent hopes and prays for?"

"A life which can't happen unless he legally says *you* are his Fate!" Kane defended.

Stephen began pacing back and forth on the carpet, wondering if his initial fears were right. Maybe he was going crazy; after all, it appeared he was on an 'island of one' when it came to his train of thought.

Sensing his son's pheromones heading down a dark path, Marlon approached his son, and placed his hands on his shoulders, centering him. "Listen to me; we get it. We understand. Your father's approach comes from an entire career in law enforcement. Nothing about that should shock you. Whether or not you are talking about the law, the message is the same: do you *really* think Alexander is your Fate? Is this *really* something you want to fight for?"

For Stephen, the sincere care and tone in his Veo's voice melted away the angered and frustrated pheromones as he once again reflected on his intuition and the instinct he possessed since birth. After a beat, he slowly nodded. A gentle smile swept across Marlon's face which allowed him to do the same.

"Then fight for him."

Stephen furrowed his eyebrows and searched his Veo for the magic trick in how his Omega father spoke without moving his lips. But the look on Marlon's face confirmed his equal confusion. It wasn't his Veo at all. It was his Sur. Both men gave Kane their undivided attention. "What?"

"If this ... Alexander ... is who you say he is. Then fight for him." Kane's words were strong and sure.

Once again, Stephen found himself looking at his Veo, making sure he wasn't the only one who heard his Sur's words. "You... you really mean that?"

For a moment, Kane had to acknowledge he startled himself in the response. It wasn't however the insistence on Stephen's plan of action which had him the most, it was the finally having something to agree with his Alpha son on. "Look... I've seen you chase some foolish and wild dreams over the years—most of them self-serving and stupid."

"Kane..." Marlon sighed, fearing he was about to destroy a pinnacle family-bonding moment. Stephen equally began to pull away from it.

"Just wait," Kane insisted. "You're right, son. You're not that careless waste of an adolescent anymore. In a matter of days, you secured a respectable job and have found perhaps the purest thing in the world to fight for." He began to think philosophically. "Maybe this is the way it had to be for you; I don't know. Our fate on this earth is one strange journey where the more we try to find the answers, the more questions we have. But if he really his your Fated Mate, then you have the right to find that happiness and claim it as your own. Even after all you've been through," he paused, "even after all *we've* been through," he frowned, "you still deserve that."

For the first time in years, Stephen was truly lost for words, something he rarely experienced with his Sur. "Dad, I... I don't know what to say."

Kane's face brightened. "Say you're going to fight."

Stephen laughed. "I will. Wolf-God, I will." As if feeling a gentle push from behind, Stephen walked over to his Alpha father and embraced him.

Kane slowly accepted it and returned the gesture in a way he had thought long gone. As they parted, he continued. "You understand this isn't going to be easy, right?"

"Oh, I know. But I have no clue where this is going to go. Can't believe I feel this strongly for someone who doesn't feel it back. What do I do?"

The old man played the consternation over and over again with the years of legal experience he had in law enforcement. Having the pressure of his son truly caring about his opinion had him equally stunned. "You're going to have to be persistent but patient. You're going to have to be strong yet gentle. Everything inside you is going to want to claim him; it's the instinct we all have. We fear our Omega's safety when they're not claimed. It's a troublesome trait you think we would have grown out of since our wild wolf days, but here we are. Just remember: it's an irrational thought. Alexander isn't in any danger just because you haven't made him yours yet."

Instantly, Stephen's thoughts went cold. "What about when he *is* in danger?"

Kane paused. "You told us for the last couple of years you've learned how to handle confrontation? The law is clear: you have the right to defend. But once you step outside that line, you're gambling a lot more than just your Fated Mate. Remember that."

———

Jin continued his belly laughs as he listened to his older half-brother retell the ridiculous events which occurred earlier in the day. Tears filled the corners of his narrowed eyes, as he struggled to sit upright in the wicker chair. His laughter echoed off the front porch, accompanied by the sounds of crickets and other insects. Once his body relaxed, he picked up his glass of white wine and finished it off, adding the empty bottle to the empty plates shared on the small table, a sign that another successful dinner had taken place. "There is never a dull moment in that joint, is there?"

Alexander cocked his head. "Wish there was. Would that be so bad?"

"Who knows—maybe it's the craziness which keeps it open?" Jin offered.

Alexander's face dimmed. "Yeah. Maybe."

"Hey, I didn't mean it like that," Jin clarified.

"I know. I know." Alexander batted the fear away. He knew Jin meant well; he was the only member of the family who vocally approved of him owning the bar. There was no way Alexander was going to make an enemy of his sole family constant in his life. He exhaled, looking at the few remains of their meal. "Jin, that was amazing."

"Thanks, bro," he replied.

"No, really, I mean it," Alexander emphasized. "If all your recipes turn out like this, you are going to go far!"

Jin slowly nodded. "And if we had more wine, I'd drink to that." He laughed again.

"You want me to go in and get the other bottle?" Alexander offered.

Jin shook his head. "Nah. I'm good. I just want to sit out here a little longer." He pulled out a pack of cigarettes and lit one like he could do it in his sleep.

"You and me both!" Alexander couldn't deny one of the many reasons he liked spring so much was due to the fact it allowed him and his Alpha half-brother to plan "private" dinners on the covered patio, effectively alienating their parents from the affair. "Hey..." He gestured to the cigarette in Jin's mouth.

Jin creased his forehead but honored the wish. Leaning forward, let his brother take the cigarette from his mouth and watched him take a couple puffs, knowing full well his brother wouldn't finish it. Finally, it was offered back to him. "You smoking now? That's not you," Jin criticized.

"I know," Alexander acknowledged. "It just sounds good every once in a while. Needed something in my mouth is all."

"Isn't that what you have Sean for?" Jin winked.

"Pffft. Yeah. Sure," Alexander laughed back. He relaxed back in the cushions of the wicker chair and hiked his feet up to the railing as a footrest.

"What issues are you two having now?"

"Now? There's nothing new I haven't told you. What made you ask that?"

"Because that's the only reason you ask me for a cigarette: when there's something wrong you can't figure out or resolve on your own."

Alexander grunted, amused at the keen observation. "I don't think anyone can resolve this one."

Jin blew out a cloud of smoke, holding a look of intrigue. He flipped his jet-black hair back and then handed the half-spent cigarette back to him. "Oh? Do tell."

Alexander took one more drag and signaled he was done with it. "The same guy who roughed up Eddie?" Jin nodded as he followed along. "We hired him."

Jin choked on his inhale. "You did what? You hired some brute off the street? As what?"

"Our new bar back and quasi-bartender," Alexander replied simply. "Why?"

"Because we need a barback and quasi-bartender."

Jin finished off the cigarette and flicked it into the lush grass off the patio. "Why him?"

"Because we're desperate."

"How desperate?" Jin inquired.

"Like hiring a stranger off the street, desperate. How much clearer do you want it?" Alexander's voice grew tense.

"You think that's a smart move?"

"Me?" Alexander grunted. "No. Eric, however—"

"Eric is an idiot!" Jin spat back.

Alexander closed his eyes and held his patience in. Jin's opinion of Eric was familiar. In addition to thinking Eric didn't have enough business sense to earn a dollar, he was not a fan of Eric also being a representative of the city. On many occasions, Alexander had to keep Jin from hounding Eric concerning his irrational accusations about Eric trying to pull the tavern out from underneath him and claim it for himself. "Regardless of what you think, he is still my business partner. And I couldn't get someone hired within the reasonable amount of time he gave me, so he wielded his power and hired him."

The Alpha smoldered but conceded his position. "Who's the guy?"

"Stephen Matheson," he replied. "Recognize the name?"

He shook his head back. "No. Should I?"

"No. I don't think so anyway. I've bounced the name off a few people. No one's said anything."

Jin squinted. "You don't trust the guy?"

"A guy who assaults a stranger in a bar? No. Of course not."

"Get his background check then. That will tell you all that you need to know." Jin eyed his brother's pained expression. "What aren't you telling me?"

Alexander lifted his legs from the railing and sat upright, slouching over so he could look anywhere else other than his brother's critical stare. "He's a convicted felon."

"A *what*?!"

"I know! I know!" Alexander yelled back preemptively. "Whatever you could say to me right now, I've already said it ten times to myself, I promise you!" He prayed the answer would curb some of the judgement he rightfully deserved.

Jin stared out into the pitch-black night sky to register the news. The reveal, as well as his brother's acceptance, blinded him. "And Eric knows this?"

"That's the beauty of it. So do Bruce and James. As a last-ditch effort to help 'convince us' to hire him, Stephen laid it all out there for us." Alexander shook his head, barely believing it himself.

Jin massaged the bridge of his nose. "Don't tell Sur this. Hell, don't tell Veo this."

"Really? You don't think I should rush in there with a smile on my face and tell them in a voice like I won the lottery or something?" Alexander replied sarcastically. "I already get enough flak from Sur about using Grandpa's inheritance to buy the bar. Do you really think I'm going to tell them this?"

"It would be the cherry on top, that's for sure."

"It would be the fuse and lighter to the ticking time bomb. *That's* what it'd be." The Omega massaged the back of his own neck, moaning as he felt the stress of the day set in. "How are things with school?"

"Almost done. In four weeks, I'm buying a plane ticket overseas and getting the hell out of this city."

Alexander's face fell. "That's still your plan? Up and leaving with a culinary degree hoping to make it big in a 4 or 5-Star restaurant?"

"To get me away from Sur and Veo and everything they've touched in this city? You bet your ass, that's my plan."

"Then just go to Gray City! Move in with me and my apartment and take the light rail back and forth. It's a 50-minute ride to the heart of the city." The idea was more of a plea versus an offer.

Jin shook his head. "It's too much the same. Doing that keeps me tethered to them."

"That's your own damn fault. You could have moved out a few years ago. Hell, we could have gotten an apartment together. But you decided you wanted to stay here and live with them. Well, look what that did!" He pointed at his brother. "I guarantee you that if you had moved out, even just one year ago, you wouldn't feel this much of a need to go thousands of miles away in a plane to feel better about this."

"That may be true. But I'm still doing it."

"Why?!" Alexander cried out.

"Because I just need to, all right?" Jin's pheromones grew tough as he told his brother with his body, he wasn't going to justify himself anymore. "You needed to buy a bar, and I need to get on a plane and get the fuck out of here."

The Omega tensed, feeling betrayed by his brother. Sure, he had mentioned this insane getaway plan for years. But time was running out, and it only strengthened his resolve. Losing Jin like this was going to be tough. And the more it became a reality, the more it scared him. "What are you going to do for money?" He threw out as a last-ditch effort.

"I didn't spend all my inheritance on a bar like you did. It will keep me going until I find something steady." Jin's words were calculated and confident.

"Fine," Alexander croaked.

"Don't get an attitude with me, bro. I wasn't allowed to 'knock some sense' into you when you thought of your stupid bar idea. So, don't expect to get anywhere with me by telling me my idea is any crazier."

"A-ha! You *do* think your idea is crazy!"

Jin looked back deadpan. "Nice try."

Alexander relaxed. He was going to have to settle on a truce now. But the conversation wasn't over. A future discussion. At the moment, he had a more pressing matter on his mind. "Jin... there's something else I have to talk to you about."

His brother continued his attitude. "And what's that?"

"It's about this Stephen guy." Even thinking about the situation earlier made his chest tighten and his brain swirl in circles. He hunched over and held his head for a moment, focusing his thoughts. When he looked up at Jin again, he finally let go of the anger pheromones he had previously and replaced them with concern. "He said... he told me... he thinks I'm his Fated Mate."

A look of bewilderment fell over the Alpha. "Whoa. Really? Wait. What do you mean 'think'? An Alpha doesn't *think* that; it's something he *knows*."

"And what about the Omega?"

Jin considered the question. "The Omega should too."

"Exactly."

"Are you trying to tell me you don't know?" Jin prompted, furrowing his brows.

"One step further, actually. I *know* he's not." Alexander flopped back in his chair, reflecting on the predicament he was in.

"You're telling me there's a guy who declared you as his Fated Mate and yet you feel nothing?" The Omega nodded back. "Then it's a dead subject."

Alexander turned in astonishment. "No, it's not a dead subject. The Alpha works for me now. Every shift I work with him on, I'm going to see that look in his eye and know what he's thinking."

"You *did* tell him, right? That you don't feel it? That he's wrong?"

"More than once." As much as he didn't want to think about it, Alexander remembered Stephen's reaction every time he affirmed it: his face shattered and his pheromones dulled to a sour pain. He never realized how much impact words had until he replayed the situation again and again. And what about tomorrow morning? Was it going to be nothing more than a sad song on repeat? Not if the Alpha held up his end of the bargain and avoided the conversation as such. Otherwise, there was no way he could keep Stephen there. It would crush him otherwise.

"Then don't worry about it." Jin shrugged simply.

"Really?" The nonchalant responses intrigued Alexander more than anything.

"Didn't you used to tell me drunk guys came up to you and said the same thing at the bar?"

"Yeah. They did."

"The loser probably got himself wasted before talking to you."

Something about hearing his brother call Stephen a "loser" didn't sit well. However, the next immediate thought was wondering *why* the comment bothered him. Shaking his head, Alexander snapped back to the conversation. "No."

"No, what?"

"No, I don't think he was drunk. Everything about him was lucid and sincere. There's no way."

Jin caught his brother's torment in the light shining down from the porch. The water in his eyes sparkled. "What's wrong, Alex?"

"There's just something about this guy, Jin. I can't put my finger on it." He faced his brother, making sure he understood the candor in his words. "You're right; bar drunks have come up to me and irrationally stated I was their Fated Mate. In every one of those scenarios, I dismissed them instantly and never gave it another thought."

"But..."

Alexander exhaled in exasperation. "I can't shake this one." His brother's face was neutral. It was a blessing and a curse not being able to see what he was thinking. "I can't explain it. I wish I could. It would make life easier, that's for sure. And believe me, I don't need it to be harder right now."

"What about Sean?" Jin posed.

Alexander snorted. "In all that happened today, he's been the last thing on my mind." He groaned.

"Seriously, bro? An ex-con randomly shows up at your bar and declares you his Fated Mate, and you're telling me during all that time you never thought of your boyfriend?" The Omega curled his lips and gave off a look of guilt. "Now that speaks volumes."

"Please don't do this... I'm not in the mood," Alexander whined.

"What do you hope happens with Sean, exactly?"

After crossing his arms, Alexander huffed. "Honestly, it wouldn't bother me that much if he went behind my back, got another Omega pregnant and became somebody else's problem at this point." An uncomfortable silence immediately followed. It communicated to him he ventured down a road completely unwelcomed. "Jin... I'm sorry... I—"

The Alpha quickly jumped up from his chair, ignoring his brother's apology. He stacked several pieces of silverware onto his plate and with his wine glass headed back inside the house. Before he reached the door, he heard Alexander do the same.

"Jin, wait! Please!" In the rush of trying to get the same task done faster, he dropped a butter knife onto the wooden board of the porch which perfectly fell through the open slit and hit the ground below with a thud. "Shit!" He considered it a loss and walked inside, chasing his brother to the kitchen. Once there, he continued his efforts. "You know, with every part of my being, I didn't mean anything by that."

Jin cleaned up odds and ends throughout the kitchen, refusing to look up. "Sure, bro."

Alexander ran his fingers through his hair. "Jin, I'm just venting. Everything before today was stressful enough, but it went to a whole new level. Can we please just chalk this up to me using a poor choice of words?"

"You might want to talk to Sean if that's how you really feel about him."

The Omega grunted. "Look. I love the guy; I do. It's just easy to point out the shortfalls of our relationship and make disparaging comments when I'm in this mood and feel safe to the person I'm talking to. That's all." No response. "Tell me you haven't ever come to me spouting off about one of your past relationships and then gone back to them the very next day while whistling, and I'll retract everything I said."

"That's not what this is about."

Alexander bowed his head and softened his tone. "Right." The poor choice of words he used earlier shined a spotlight on what made the two half-brothers so different.

Nathan, Alexander's Veo, was a devoted mate to the boys' Sur Robert ever since they met decades ago. Unfortunately, the same could not be said about Robert. The Alpha's views on all Omegas, including Alexander, could be described as misogynistic when comparing male primate-descendants' harsh and inadequate views toward women when they existed. As Alexander grew up, he slowly observed his Alpha father treat his Omega father more as a wild pet that needed to be trained to obey versus being a mutual companion. Thus, it wasn't hard to see the damaging effects which took place when Nathan didn't live up to the irrational expectations Robert set in his mind. Even worse, starting at a very young age, Alexander also was subjected to these unrealistic ideals which he frequently failed to achieve.

Although there were many memories and scars of this abuse, there was one in particular which was the strongest. Alexander remembered the day he was told he was going to have a younger brother. He neither anticipated it to happen so fast nor understood why it was accompanied by such dread. Days later, Jin arrived home, looking very unlike how he imagined. His skin was a completely different tone, his eyes were shaped, and he arrived with a full head of black hair which no one in his family shared. It took the next couple of years for Alexander to comprehend the idea of what a half-brother was and even longer to understand why it happened.

Years later, in a weak moment, Alexander's Veo revealed to him their Sur had been secretly in a relationship with another Omega for a significant amount of time. The reveal of the late-term pregnancy also came with the news Robert planned on leaving Nathan for this new mate. But Jin's Omega father didn't survive the birth; he had succumbed to the risk all High Types take when considering reproduction—the significantly higher mortality rate affecting both the Omega father and pup. Veo had said the loss of his Sur's new mate was devastating to him. And despite Robert already declaring Nathan a total loss, he begged to come back to the family while bringing his newborn pup with him. Although this revelation cleared up much of Alexander's childhood confusion and speculation, this also shattered the cracked image he had of his family.

It was even more disheartening when Alexander observed first-hand what it was like to be the Omega son in the family after an Alpha son was born. Jin was regularly attended to and praised by his Alpha father whereas *he* became the burden and nuisance. Criticism, among other things, only worsened once he found a voice and could easily communicate his feelings about being treated unequally compared to his younger brother. The ability to move out of the family home and away from the darkness which permeated everything didn't come fast enough.

Jin pushed dishes into the sink—harder than he should have. The sounds pierced his ears and radiated outward. Quick and static looks went to the hallway, and ears perked up, listening for their Sur or Veo's descent into the kitchen. Alexander was no different.

Finally, after a few seconds confirmed no such ordeal was on the horizon, both young men relaxed.

Back at the sink, Jin examined the pile of plates, wondering if any had busted into pieces, but he was lucky this time. Turning his body back to his brother, he calmed the pheromones he was fuming and let them wash down the side of his face in a bead of sweat. His voice was low and without vexation.

"I know things weren't good for you growing up." He swallowed. "And there's a part of me that feels guilty I didn't stand up for you more." Alexander's face saddened at the thought his brother held any responsibility for their Alpha father's actions. "But you weren't the only pup in the family growing up who was hurting."

Alexander nodded. "Very aware I wasn't."

The obvious differences Jin possessed made every ignorant person conclude the exotic-looking Alpha was adopted or perhaps a distant relative. Neither were necessarily an insult to assume; it was just frustrating to have an entire childhood of questions and explanations the entire family could repeat in their sleep. Unfortunately, the idea of adoption itself came with a reputation. Everyone knew to conclude the scenario was due to mortality. Any scandalous reason was typically kept behind closed doors, never to see the light of day. The same courtesy naturally would have been extended to Jin as well, but Robert's unabashed personality and lack of consideration for anyone else in the family forced the scandal into the spotlight. If the Daventry family wasn't upfront about Jin's origins, enough gossipers and whisperers were always there to set the record straight.

Jin's face faltered as he turned back around, able to face stained dinnerware better compared to his past. His rough hand movements in the scalding sink matched the frustration in his voice. "Robert the Alpha Sur ... Nathan the Omega Veo ... Alexander the Omega pup ... and Jin ... the bastard son." Without thinking clearly, he forgot he had placed a steak knife at the bottom of the sink. As fast as he felt the sharp metal cut through his now water-softened fingers, he lifted it and flung it onto the countertop, water and soap suds flying with it. "Fuck!" He started huffing, breathing heavily in and out. He splayed both of his hands on either side of the sink and held his head over the water steaming back onto his face.

Alexander walked over. "Are you okay?" he asked cautiously.

"It's just a scratch," he gritted back. "No big deal."

His Omega brother paused. "That's not what I meant."

Jin's inhales and exhales slowed to a halt. He swallowed. "I know."

Alexander tossed and turned in his bed. Whatever stress he had before dinner tonight amplified after his heated discussion with his brother Jin. He forgot how much talking about their childhood reminded him of how much it still affected him today. In addition, it reminded him that it still affected Jin the same way. The conversation impacted Alexander so much, he offered his brother to come back to his apartment with him for the night and drop him off at the academy before he went into work. But Jin declined, as he always did when his brother asked. The decline only exacerbated all the antagonizing thoughts going through his mind: his brother, his parents, his business partner Eric and their event coming up, his boyfriend Sean, and his friend Daniel's opinion *of* Sean.

Lying in bed, he exhaled. "A mating contract." That was all he could say or think about regarding the matter. He prevented himself from going further. He couldn't, not right now. To justify it, he decided he'd wait until *after* the fundraiser. *That* was a more appropriate time to think about it. And then, as if someone flipped a switch, he thought about Stephen.

At the mere thought of the Alpha, Alexander's mind shut off every other worry running through his mind. He sighed and moaned to himself. "Why am I doing this?" After closing his eyes tight with a grunt, he opened them and stared out his bedroom window. The moon was shining brightly, down across the floor and up to the blankets covering his body. Slowly he let his arm glide down his bare chest to the soft sheet covering his waist. It was there the moon beams caught his hand; he maneuvered it with the light, casting shadows across the room. He swayed his hand back and forth, trying to figure out which angle gave him the longest silhouette; for a moment, it was a joyous distraction. But as his hand drifted to the right, he noticed a perfectly untouched side of the bed and a pillow which had no head laid upon it.

Sean had slept there several nights in the beginning. Then, slowly, but surely, their careers pushed them to where it was easier to stay at their own places—at least—that's what Alexander told himself. The sad part was, thinking of his boyfriend laying there next to him didn't do anything for him. Maybe Daniel was right; maybe he and Sean weren't the mates they were supposed to be. However, there were plenty of reasons to keep Sean around. For starters, he was one of the few Alphas he knew who didn't mind being with a headstrong Omega. *Stephen couldn't handle that.* He thought to himself.

The mere stray acknowledgement of the man jolted Alexander up as he wondered why on earth Stephen crept in as the very next thought. "Wolf-God, Alex!" he sang out. Throwing back the covers, he hoisted himself out of bed and walked to the bathroom. The brilliance of the moonlight coming in didn't make the bright yellow bathroom lights hurt as much—especially since he was so awake already. A silver cup sat next to the sink; the Omega thrust the cup under the faucet and gulped it down like it was several shots of liquor. The comparison of such soothing therapy made him bite his lip. Then he shook the foolish consideration out of his head. He could not wake up with a hangover, or worse, drunk. Criticizing Stephen for even looking at him wrong tomorrow wasn't going to fly if he himself was a mess; the hypocrisy. Coincidentally, he felt a headache and uneasy feeling come over him as if he was inebriated already. That's when it him. "Oh, fuck!"

# CHAPTER 07:

# DISCUSSING THE TOUGH STUFF

"Bruce!" Alexander called from the back.

"Yeah?" he called from the front as he began to pull down the bar chairs.

"Where did that med bag go?"

Bruce aligned a large table on the main floor. "It should be in your office."

"Office," Stephen scoffed as he shook his head, reminding himself it was nothing more than a couple file cabinets and shelf unit in the back hallway. He walked over for the third time and tracked every item with his finger before thrusting the metal drawers open—already knowing the bag wasn't in there. It was still disappointing to him just the same when he confirmed it. "It's not there. Did James need it for something?" he yelled.

"Not that I know of. What about Eddie's hand? Did anyone help him with that?"

Alexander walked out to the front where Bruce finished setting up. "I don't think so," he snorted. "I know *I* didn't."

The front door opened and a voice called in. "Hello?"

The Omega thrust his hips in a defensive stance, as if the Alpha never left. "You're late."

Stephen looked at his phone. "By one minute?"

"Hmph. If I were you, I would have camped outside the bar and slept in a sleeping bag to get here on time before being late—especially on your first day." Alexander stared the Alpha down. In addition to giving him the condescending glare, the Omega had plenty of time to notice Stephen had showered and shaved this morning. His arms were bursting out of the white t-shirt, and his legs pressed hard against the fabric of his jeans. A belt sat snug around his waist, but he chose not to focus on that. Instead, he noticed Stephen's gentle look back. He wasn't like a typical Alpha who would have spat back and told him to mind his place as an Omega. The shock it wasn't said made Alexander reflect on his own tone. Finally, he removed the teeth from his words. "You took the bus here?"

"Yeah," Stephen replied. "Once I get myself situated, I plan on getting my bike back up."

Alexander nodded. "A little tip: instead of taking the one downtown, use the line that goes to Chad Ave and Hubbard Street. It's only three blocks down, but even if you walk the rest, it will save you fifteen minutes. I mean, until you start bringing your bike."

Stephen smiled back, a twinkle gleaming in his eye. "Thanks. Will do."

Alexander felt his face equally give the expression back. For a moment, it was as if nothing else mattered. But then, he remembered, it did. He slipped back into his boss voice. "Okay. You have work to do. This is going to be a lot and it's going to be fast. I have a good week to get you into shape like you've been here a month. So, it's going to be your job to keep up and ask questions because otherwise we're moving on. And if you have a problem taking orders from me," he pointed with his finger, "there's the door."

Stephen examined the Omega, holding his own like any Alpha who owned a business. The expression was cold, authoritative, and straight forward. Upon hearing the words, Stephen felt his heartstrings tug, worrying if the Omega was right, maybe they had no connection at all. But one more deep influx to his lungs, and

Stephen felt his wolf purr inside him. No. He was still his—whether the Omega knew it or not. "I'm ready."

---

The Alpha didn't find any of the tasks arduous or above his ability, but he had no idea of all the different moving parts required to run such a simple concept as serving a customer drink. But like the lifecycle of every creature on this earth, Alexander spared no detail and skipped no corners when it came to giving him a thorough rundown of every process and procedure the South Street Tavern needed to operate its best at all times. At one point, Stephen wondered if he was being groomed to be a manager. However, his keen Alpha wolf knew better; this was all a test. Alexander was intentionally trying to see how far he could push him before he lost his resolve. Once he caught on, he doubled his efforts to show the Omega he wasn't going to break easily—in spite of how he handled himself only yesterday.

A couple hours later, both sat at the bar and were handed a couple soda-waters with lime by James, holding a very entertained expression on his face. "How's he doing, boss?"

Alexander sat in the chair next to Stephen. "He's doing okay." Stephen smirked, then looked at James who read through the comment just as easy. "Now, here's the real challenge." Alexander swiveled his chair. "What all needs to be done before the first customer walks in?"

After a long drink and noticeable swallow, the Alpha took a second to prepare himself. "Check the perimeter, check the bins, lights, floors, bathrooms, tables, chairs, freezers, fridges, stock counts, order status, glasses, prep, daily specials, and boss's demeanor." The final criteria slipped off the tongue easily.

The Omega choked on his drink as he heard James stifle his own laugh. "Do you think this is funny?" He used his cocktail napkin to clean up the few drops on his chin.

Stephen adjusted himself back to attention. "No. Not at all."

"Good. It's a thankless job where you constantly have everyone needing you at a moment's notice and wanting the request done five minutes before they even asked for it. Everything we did needs to be done in about half the time we did it. And on our busy nights, as soon as you finish the list, you just go back through it again and again until the night's done. Most people looking at you doing this job are going to say this is beneath you and that you should be running this place." He saw the Alpha's serious demeanor fade. "But that's not gonna happen. This is *my* place." Scanning the room, he proudly took in the sight of his establishment, his realm, his playground. "Besides, you missed one anyway."

Stephen searched his mind. "I did?"

"Hit it, James."

Grabbing a remote, the Beta punched a button which released a wave of modern music seeping out of large speakers fastened to the corners of the ceilings.

"Music?" Stephen questioned.

"Yes, music!" Alexander replied enthusiastically. "This alone creates the atmosphere you want. Whichever way you want your customers to act is the music you play and how loud you play it."

"And what music did you play yesterday while Eddie was looking for trouble?"

Alexander grunted. "Well, there are *some* exceptions to the rule." His gaze fell to a red bag behind the bar. "There it is!" He jumped up and hurried over and grabbed it. "James, I've been looking everywhere for this! Where was it?"

James looked in the direction it was found. "Right there?"

"Ugh. I swear sometimes." He unzipped it, scurrying through several items. "Did you use it on Eddie yesterday?"

He laughed. "No. But I felt like I needed to go through the motions."

"Good call," Stephen interjected.

"Yes!" Alexander gasped. "Thank, Wolf-God." He held in his clutches a prescription bottle. Throwing the bag onto the bar, he twisted the cap off, measured out two pills, and grabbed his drink to wash it down. A sigh of relief and relaxation melted over him. He peered over and noticed Stephen staring at him, full of concern. A dozen scenarios came to him on how to address the situation but before he could, a call came through his cell phone which gave him the freedom to walk away without explanation. "Oh. This is our delivery order. I hope they're not telling us anything bad. I'll be right back." He rushed out to the back with the call in progress.

When Alexander was completely out of sight, Stephen caught James's attention. "Hey," he whispered, beckoning him to come closer, "what's that about?"

James furrowed his brows, whispering back, "What's what about?"

"Those pills."

The Beta shrugged. "It's just a medication he takes."

Stephen couldn't understand the nonchalant response. "Why does he have a prescription bottle in a standard med bag?"

"Probably an emergency stash. Most likely he forgot to refill it. It happens periodically—he's just under a lot of stress right now."

"Any clue to what it is he takes?" Stephen hoped the question wasn't too personal to ask his boss's loyal employee. The last thing he needed was an additional person in the establishment rallying against him. He tried with every part of his being to convey the feeling of concern versus nosey curiosity—especially considering his past.

James tapped his fingers on the bar. "Uh... the most I know about it is something to do with his heats."

"So, they're just suppressants?"

A perplexed look fell upon the Beta's face. This wasn't the first time a conversation had come up on the subject, yet the answer wasn't any clearer. "No... I don't think so..."

"Whew!" Alexander breathed as he came out and found his seat again. "False alarm. They just wanted to confirm the order was right—since it was so large."

"You really anticipate this event to be a big deal, don't you?" Stephen inquired.

The Omega's face grew serious. "If this goes like I hope it to, this place will be filled at maximum capacity from 6PM to 2AM. If I can manage to get 1 out of 4 of those customers to come back on a regular basis, I could afford to retire and turn this bar into a diamond-studded rail."

"Wow. I had no clue."

"Which is why I need all of this to be perfect from here on out. I know it's not realistic, and I know it's not fair, but that's just the way it has to be." The Omega changed his tone. "I'm sorry I blew up on you so much yesterday. That also wasn't fair." Slowly, his eyes followed up the Alpha's chest, to his face, and into his eyes.

"Hey, it's okay," Stephen reassured. "Believe me, I don't think there's one person here who would blame how you acted." He paused. "I know what I told you yesterday didn't help matters." His stomach hitched, hoping he didn't compromise his already fragile position but also not ignoring the incessant desire to know where he stood.

Alexander's gaze fell as he pictured in his mind all over again the Alpha's unwavering confidence in his claim they were a Fated pair. Even worse, Stephen's reaction when he claimed there was no connection. But focusing on that wasn't an option today. "Take a lunch and meet me here at 2. The early comers typically come in at 3 and it only gets busier from there. Happy Friday." Even before Stephen could respond, he lifted himself up off the barstool and headed toward the back, avoiding any possibility the Alpha would break one of the rules he established yesterday and have to face the conundrum again.

---

Very quickly, Stephen realized his job at the bar was no joke. It made the Alpha recall the days of practically living at a few local joints in the city for the two years he was legally able before his incarceration. Ignorance had him under the impression bars were magically built to be well-oiled machines which had imaginary elves do the grunt work sight unseen. The only part he remembered witnessing was a bartender or two exercising that delicate balance of quality customer service and edging on the brink of a mental breakdown from the constant demands and challenges of the clientele. Even then, the Alpha only cared to notice such things when he wanted his own requests taken care of.

Now, he was on the other side, being an official member of a club who lived by a code of "Never let them see you bleed" as well as "Yes, and…" His empathy went out to Alexander specifically, who dealt with stereotypical degrading rank comments as if he was there specifically as a spectacle to Alphas and Betas who found it nothing more than entertainment the Omega was not only giving orders and ultimatums to pretentious and shady patrons, but also owned the place. Most of the time, Stephen was just plain confused, wondering why so many customers reveled in the joy of it like it was breaking news considering Alexander had owned the bar for so long.

It wasn't all criticism, however. Several comments from the bar staff and patrons confirmed Stephen's theory. Matthew Whitmore, whoever the man was, single-handedly ushered in a new clientele for the bar with the anticipated fundraiser coming up. That made Stephen happy for Alexander, the trailblazing Omega. *His* trailblazing Omega. Stephen swallowed hard at the thought—not that his new boss let him think for any considerable amount of time. If the customers weren't keeping the Alpha busy, the Omega was.

"Stephen!" Alexander yelled through the noisy crowds and pulsing music as he attempted to finish an entire tray of shots.

"Where's that cinnamon whiskey I asked for?" If the noise level was lower, Stephen could have heard the discontent in his voice. The frustration exuding off his pheromone scent made it clear enough.

The Alpha walked toward him to make sure his response was heard. "The shelf was empty as well as the bulk box you had on the floor."

The Omega wiped his forehead. "Shit, this stuff is going like fire!" He growled at his predicament, mentally kicking himself for underestimating just how much one man's social media post for an event a week from now had changed the entire status quo. "Go to the walk-in. See if there's another box in there. It would be on the left side with the rest of the pours." Stephen nodded as he made a straight shot to the back.

Alexander switched to a different order. A few customers had no problems parking themselves right in front of the Omega bar owner, entranced at the whole set-up: two Alphas and a Beta. As Alexander finished off the first Alpha's drink, he heard the sly ridicule he was waiting for.

"Man, you got that Alpha by the balls, don't you?" Siro grinned as he gave off the "Pack Leader" scent.

The second Alpha, not to be outdone, joined in. "Maybe the Alpha doesn't have balls anymore." All three men laughed in satisfaction.

Alexander countered, "That Alpha has more balls than you'll ever have." The Omega smiled proudly at his comment. Out of the corner of his eye, he noticed Bruce glancing back in surprise at him coming to Stephen's defense so quickly.

The Beta of the trio was the final one to chime in. He happily pointed at the "Pack Alpha" who was just emasculated by an Omega bar owner. "He's got you there, Siro!"

Siro flipped back his hair and picked up his drink. "Oh yeah? How do you figure?"

Before the Beta could respond, Alexander cut him off. "Because he's proudly working for an Omega and doesn't give two shits about what any Alpha thinks of him. *You,* on the other hand, can't seem to hold yourself together when an Omega and Beta barely question your manhood."

Siro knocked back his double shot. "There's nothing wrong with my manhood. I can prove it if you want." He licked his teeth while showing off a devilish grin.

The Omega raspberried. "No, thanks. Besides, already taken here." He passed the final completed drink to the Beta of the group.

"I don't suppose it's by another submissive Alpha?" Siro wondered as he gestured to his glass. "I'll do another."

Alexander furrowed his eyebrows. "Why are you so concerned over an Alpha working under an Omega? You don't come across as the type who is closed-minded about such things."

"Good intuition." Siro flexed his face. "You're right; I'm not bothered by it. I'm just curious to know what makes an Alpha do it."

Alexander held his composure. "Everyone has their reasons, I guess." He pivoted. "Is that cash or are we holding a card?"

Siro took a beat. "Yeah, a card is fine. Think we're gonna stick around. I like what you got here."

"First time?" Alexander asked. Siro nodded as he scanned the crowd. "May I ask how you heard of the place?"

The other Alpha slapped Siro on the back and jumped in. "Siro here wanted to know what made Matthew Whitmore so interested in this place."

"This bar doesn't read like Whitmore's M.O. I guess you could say curiosity took hold of me." Siro studied the bar like he was trying to crack a code or solve a puzzle.

Alexander nodded. "You a friend of his, then?"

Siro grimaced. "Hardly."

Out of the back, Stephen rushed up with a bottle as if it was a gift on the morning of Winter Solstice. "Sorry, had to rearrange some things back there."

"Thank Wolf-God!" Alexander exhaled. "I'm just glad we had it." Immediately, the Omega focused on finishing up the tray and handed it to Stephen, pointing him in the direction of the right customers. He then returned to the front of the bar, hoping to borrow extra time so he didn't have to ask Siro another question. But when he tried, he noticed the trio gone, lost somewhere in the crowd.

***

"Damn!" Stephen exhaled as he finally closed and locked the front door. "Is that what a normal Friday night looks like here?"

"Normal? No way." Alexander shook his head as he audited the night's transactions for the third time. "But with any luck, it will be!"

Stephen sat at the bar in front of the Omega-his arm supporting his head. He watched him continue to count several coins and exhale as the exhaustion overcame him. The Alpha wanted nothing more than to hold Alexander and lay his head on his chest to give him any reprieve. Since he knew that wasn't happening tonight, he offered his verbal comfort instead. "I thought things went well."

Alexander snorted at the overly generous statement. "By the skin of our teeth maybe." He sifted through several bills, writing down notes on the back of a receipt slip. When he was finally satisfied with the numbers, he looked up at the Alpha. "I'm sorry it was so hectic tonight," he confessed. "Knowing how tonight went, I have an idea in my head on how to prepare for what's going to happen for the rest of the week, not to mention for the fundraiser." He closed the till, tore off the final receipt and put it in the leather bag with several large bills. "I thought you did excellent on your first night under pressure."

That made Stephen smiled inside and out. "Thanks. I mean, it's not like it's saving lives like a doctor or even close to what you deal with each night."

"Even so," Alexander countered, "you'd be surprised at how many buckle under pressure, or even assume things are taken care of when really there's always more or the next step coming. There's a lot to anticipate, and you did a really good job. I'm just glad I didn't have to use you as a bouncer tonight ... which ... I must admit I may need to utilize you as in the future—if you don't mind?"

The Alpha stared him down. "I'll protect you from anything or anyone."

Alexander gulped. It took every bit of self-control he had not to comment back. Instead, he grabbed one of the equal piles of bills on the counter and dropped it in front of Stephen.

"Um. What's this?"

"Your tips," Alexander answered.

"*My* tips? I didn't bartend." The Alpha sat there perplexed.

"So? You worked the bar. That's how it works. Besides, I'm sure you will be bartending soon enough."

"Don't you think I should wait to get tips until then?"

Alexander hummed. "Some advice for you—when your boss gives you money you aren't expecting, you say, 'Thank you.'"

Stephen curled his lips. "Thank you." He counted the bills and then whispered to himself. "Damn!"

"Are you needing pay now or are you good until next Friday? That's when checks come in but obviously with you just starting..."

The offer was kind; but, at the same, Stephen couldn't help but take it as a reminder of where he was in life. To try and be the strongest Alpha for his potential mate, he tucked his tail and held in his pride. "I'll be fine until next Friday if tips keep coming in like this."

"Ha! Ain't that the truth." Stephen mused.

"Is there anything else you need from me?" the Alpha asked.

Alexander glanced at his watch, surprised it already said 3AM. "No. I just have one more thing I need to take care of here." He grabbed the leather money bag and the keys on the counter. "See you tomorrow?"

Stephen's heart felt full at the prospect. "See you tomorrow."

The taxi ride home for the night was pure bliss. Stephen knew the driver could see the plastered smile on his face every time he glanced back in the rearview mirror. Considering how late it was, he was sure the driver thought he was on something. Stephen didn't care what impression he gave off. The first night at work was more successful than he could have ever imagined. A week ago, never in his wild imagination did he expect to have a job he was proud to return to but also get to do it next to his Fated Mate.

That's when his face flushed red, and he had to confess that's what it really was all about. He could be working the most hated or demoralizing job in the city and it wouldn't change anything as long as Alexander was there. "Alex..." he found himself saying out loud. The taxi driver once again peered at him through the rearview mirror, making sure he wasn't missing an important direction. After a deep inhale, Stephen stared out the rear passenger window, declining to notice the last ten years of the city's development to grow and beautify downtown. None of the familiar nor new structures mattered; none of the classic nor modern lights caught his attention. It was all background to his mind's eye which replayed subtle yet memorable moments he wanted to cherish forever: the way Alexander lit up when he talked to customers, the unflappable confidence he displayed whenever a challenge arose, and even the few exchanges they were able to have when the Omega wasn't giving him a direction or an eventful story from the bar when a customer wasn't in earshot. It was the latter he transfixed himself on. In those instances, Alexander let his guard down the most to where his true scent pushed through—the deep pomegranate fragrance he wanted to be bathed in.

It was by pure luck that the taxi rolled up the driveway to the house right as the Alpha began thinking of his Fated Mate in *other* scenarios. The heavy concentration surely would have given his own scent off alerting the Beta driver he was sexually interested in him by mistake. After paying the charge, the Alpha stood tall and stretched as he watched the vehicle lead with its lights out of the driveway back to the heart of the city. Tonight, the brilliance of the moon kept the night from being pitch black. Everything was covered in a muted blue light, giving Stephen all the assistance he needed to get inside.

Before he even made it to the front door, a move he knew his Sur would hear in an instant, he considered his old method of sneaking into the house. He grinned as he dared to think it could even work; curiosity caught the better of him. His heart thumped with nerves and he instantly transformed back into the rogue teenager he once was as he made his way to the side of the house. Just like ten years ago, he irrationally thought even the excessive crunch of grass beneath his feet had the power to wake his parents from their slumber or set off the imaginary alarm system both he and his younger brother assumed existed. With that in mind, his steps were slow and calculated, like a bandit or a thief. Upon reaching the window of the guest bedroom, he felt his hands get warm and clammy. The sensation rushed throughout his body and caused a shiver to go up and down his back.

He first attempted to lift the archaic window with minimal effort, hoping it would give way. By no surprise it failed miserably, hardly causing a faint vibration much less any noise of progress. The Alpha told himself to grow a pair and used the courage to thrust an exorbitant amount of effort into an upward push. His whole body cringed when he heard the unnerving squeal of wood scraping against metal. He cursed himself instantly, wondering why he thought this was a better move or a smart one. Stephen only imagined the terror running through his parents' minds as they jolted awake in the middle of a night to the strange noise.

The next few seconds were followed by complete and utter silence. He even closed his eyes to make his hearing the only focus, to hopefully trace his ability all the way back to his Sur and Veo's bedroom. With a pulse throbbing in his head, he waited for what seemed like forever in anticipation. Shockingly, no one came to investigate. A flood of elation washed over him, and he contemplated his next move. Although he was still physically capable of hiking his body five feet up onto the window ledge like he was on a balance beam, he didn't consider his body's considerable mass. He was easily twice the size now compared to back then. The window however did not grow. As a joke, he concluded it actually shrunk. Stephen knew immediately his broad shoulders and larger waist size were going to cause issues. But giving up now meant the stress of what he did so far was pointless.

After one deep anticipated breath, he steadied his hands on the peeling paint of the old ledge and hoisted himself, suspending his lower half. The awkwardness of it all caught him by surprise— muscle tone apparently had no substitute for form and execution. In attempting to compensate, he lost his balance and felt his body involuntarily fall forward and worm itself into the opening. Every obnoxious hit and scratch down his back *really* reminded him he wasn't 19 anymore. And yet, after several grunts and uncomfortable body positions, he finally landed himself clumsily on the hardwood floor. His chest heaved as he stood up and looked at the motionless window, staring back at him like the perfect essence of innocence. The Alpha chuckled at himself, claiming he knew better. The only reprieve from the whole ordeal was the fact that, unlike when he was 19, the guest bedroom was his final destination. He no longer needed to carefully open the door, sneak down the hallway, and walk up several agonizing steps to get to his childhood bedroom.

Exhausted, the Alpha shed his shirt and pants and crawled under the covers, satisfied, and entertained by his own antics. They weren't all that different from the ones he and his brother used to pull. But after reflecting further, he realized most of those escapades were *his* doing and that Warren was there by proxy, sometimes by force. At the time, the Alpha only considered it favoritism in which his younger Omega brother only received a fraction of the punishment he ever did. Now, he looked back and realized it was rightfully justified. Then, there was the irrefutable understanding that, in the end, Warren paid the ultimate price, and Stephen himself only received a fraction of the punishment. *That* would be there as long as the Alpha lived.

When his tear ducts began to swell and eyes began to sting at the thought of his brother, he shook violently to get his mind in a different headspace. Frantically, he searched for another topic to save him from an emotional outpour he wasn't ready for. It was no surprise thoughts of Alexander came rushing back to save the day. The lingering emotion allowed the Alpha for the first time to really examine the predicament he was in. Was a mismatched Fate really a thing? It had to be. If not, why then did Wolf-God feel the need to show Stephen that Alexander was the one he should be with? It could have been anybody. The Alpha tried to remember any thoughts of this phenomenon being legitimized.

Unfortunately, prison for a decade removed him from applicable scenarios or exposure to the scientific part of social courting. There were no instances of an Alpha Fating another Alpha—at least—as far as he knew. That was something prison could have been the perfect experiment for considering there were two hundred Alphas confined to a small area with a majority of them still in their reasonable childbearing years. Throwing a fertile Omega into the fray was easily comparable to throwing an innocent lamb in the middle of pack of hungry pack of wolves. The results were obvious in that scenario. This, however, was not.

While gently massaging his arm, the only thoughts Stephen could remember was what he already feared the most. Alphas, and even desperate Omegas, weren't above the practice of trying to either fake a connection to imprint or regrettably staking a claim while highly intoxicated. It hurt Stephen even more to think Alexander was in one of the worst professions possible in regard to receiving such propositions, no doubt putting his own claim further into question.

But then his inner wolf considered the other side. Although Eric, Alexander's business partner, was the one who essentially hired Stephen, Alexander had full authority and control over how today went. If the Omega wanted to, he could have made the entire experience miserable, daring Stephen to make a mistake in action or word and be removed for it. Was the Omega *that* desperate to keep an Alpha as an employee who was also trying to court him as a Fate? Perhaps. The success of the night however proved to Stephen that Alexander didn't think of him as a lost cause, and right now, that was what he held onto.

A warm sensation flooded his chest as he anticipated getting to know the Omega over the next week. He felt like an adolescent wolf getting ready to announce he wanted to take his crush to the school dance complete with a rose in hand. The logical human side of him calmed and centered him back. Whether Stephen liked it or not, the success of one shift didn't mean mating contract. Alexander made it very clear the Alpha had to walk the line. Falling out of bounds wasn't an option. Therefore, he made a solemn vow he wasn't going to stick his nose into the Omega's business or personal life unless offered. Because he didn't know just how far loyalty stretched, he wasn't going to go behind Alexander's back and pump his employees for information neither. Whatever the Omega or his employees wanted to share, he'd take it, but until he was an official employee, there was no reason to chance it. After all, it wasn't as if he wanted to spill his own personal life. He knew however, that day would come.

Abruptly, the sound of a bird chirping pierced his ear. Looking out his open window, he realized the blue light of the moon was getting replaced with the blue light of incoming dawn. Shocked that the time was racing by, he told himself to cease the wheels constantly turning in his head and get some shut eye. For as fast as the night went, he suspected the next few days would go by even faster.

---

"Wolf-God, Daniel, did you get lost back there?" Alexander tried yelling over the crowds which filled the tavern to max capacity. Even with Eric, Bruce, Stephen, and himself manning the bar at all times, the insatiable thirst of the crowds were overwhelming. But the Omega held firm and steady as he stayed focused in his zone.

Sweat dripped down the tips of Daniel's red hair as he carried two large bottles back from the walk-in. The only regret he had was not staying there longer, feeling the only reprieve from the hot thick air pumping from the main room where he could barely see an open space now which wasn't occupied by a patron. "Hey, give me a break! It's not like I have this place memorized. Plus, I didn't know you had this much back there."

"Normally, we don't. But this is a *little* different," Alexander replied sarcastically.

"A little? You've never been this busy. I don't know if *any* bar has been this busy!" Daniel only received a facial acknowledgement from his friend. After he realized he wasn't doing Alexander any favors now, he once again took an empty tray and began making a round for empty shot glasses and tumblers. Luckily, following the same pattern allowed him to be much more efficient a couple hours in. He did a dance around several groups of men in business suits who were throwing back cocktails and drinks as if they were celebrating a political victory already, even though voting day wasn't nearly upon them. In the back half, he observed pockets of common folk who were slowly but surely warming up to the idea the bureaucrats were truly out to give them a voice in the day and age where Low-Types and Omegas were on the precipice of finally gaining equality that meant something. Having the event at Alexander's bar proved that. While getting lost in the train of thought, he almost smacked into James who was on the same mission.

"Whoa! Heads up, little buddy!" James said while barely missing scalping Daniel with his full tray of empties.

"Sorry!" Daniel huffed out. "Is it over yet?"

"Right?" James laughed. "I hate to tell you, but we've only been at this for two hours now."

"*That's it?*" Daniel gasped. James grinned in amusement. "Hey... come here..." James leaned down to give Daniel his waiting ear. "What does Alex think of Stephen?"

James nodded in consideration. "Doing good. He's behind the bar right next to Eric. That means something."

"It means he's a good bartender," Daniel confirmed.

The Beta shook his head. "No, not that." He paused. "Alex wouldn't be caught dead allowing another Alpha to man his bar unless Eric forced him to."

"Did Eric force him to?"

Once again James shook his head to help communicate above the bar noise. "No, I don't think so. I mean, look at them."

Daniel peered through the patrons to get a look at both Alexander and Stephen working side-by-side like they had been doing it for years and not a week. He then noticed Stephen whisper something into Alexander's ear, most likely also due to the deafening volume of the bar, which made the Omega laugh. The observation made Daniel smile, but it also made him think. "They work well together, don't they?"

"Yeah, I'll say," James confirmed. "Considering a week ago I almost expected to see Stephen's body chopped up in the dumpster out back... this is... this is a shock to me."

Daniel laughed. "That's funny! That's what Alex told me he feared would happen to *him*."

"Despite his sordid past, it's become a nonissue. It's almost as if Stephen never had a record. No dumpster crime scenes in the future I'll expect."

Then Daniel remembered himself. "Aw, shit, I forgot! I'm supposed to change out the trash cans." A sudden glance at the few bins around the bar made him curse himself again that he hadn't done it sooner. They were already full to the brim with throwaway plastic plates, napkins, silverware, and trash from the catering company who set-up adjacent to the bar and next to the "Meet and Greet" table of Jesse Minh, the man of the evening.

"You're never gonna be able to do that all yourself," James insisted.

"Thanks," Daniel replied, offended.

"Hey, we're a team tonight. We gotta keep it together. Get Stephen to help you."

The suggestion was illogical. "He's behind the bar."

"He and I are switching off every other hour. He's still our bar back. I'll bring this tray up there and tell him to help you out."

Daniel nodded as he handed James his empty tray who slid it under his. He surveyed the room to find the bins which weren't completely full yet, not wanting to admit James's assessment of him was right. After inconspicuously struggling with two separate bags, he tied them off and headed toward the back. By the time he got there, Stephen already had four bags double in size waiting at the door to the alleyway.

The Alpha surveyed Daniel. "You got those?"

"If you got the door."

"You got it!" Stephen held the door wide as Daniel carried, pushed, kicked, and used every strategy in the book to get the bags out the door. He held his tongue in making the effort to assist, not wanting to suggest the petite Omega couldn't do his job. Then, Stephen joined him as they threw several bags away, realizing they'd be doing this again before they knew it. "Whew! We did it."

"That we did," Daniel exhaled.

"You doing okay?" Stephen asked.

"Tired. But I'll live," Daniel answered honestly. "How about you?"

The Alpha answered back the same. "I'm doing good here."

"I'm not talking about the event." Daniel stood taller and crossed arms.

Stephen examined him cautiously, unsure of his angle. "Then what do you mean?"

"Alexander."

The Alpha held his face firm, but his instinct perked up. "What about him?"

"I see you," the Omega smarted.

"You see what?"

"The way you look at him." Daniel looked pleased with himself, like it was a secret he figured out all on his own.

Stephen tried to dismiss him. "I look at him like he's my boss."

"Right!" Daniel doubted. "I'm not stupid. I'm an Omega too, you know."

"Okay?"

"Give me a little credit that I know what it looks like when an Alpha looks at an Omega like he's waiting in the grass to pounce at the right moment." Daniel smirked.

The Alpha shifted his weight and cleared his throat. "I... uh..."

"Thought so."

The approach caught Stephen off his game. He rubbed both hands on his face. "I don't know what to say about it right now."

Daniel didn't anticipate Stephen to falter so quickly. He softened his stance. "Hey, it's all right."

"No, it's not," the Alpha clapped back.

"Why?"

"Because Alex is my boss and I just met you today? I don't know what I can or should say to you."

Even then, Stephen regretted saying as much as he did. The week of training did indeed go smoother than he anticipated. Every afternoon, evening, and night at the bar being around Alexander was a dream come true. Although they weren't mated or even dating, it was easy for the Alpha to pretend in his mind they were. The local and regular crowd coming in had finally gotten used to Stephen being a staple, and for that matter, so had Alexander. Minus a few nit-picky criticisms here and there, the working relationship was otherwise perfect.

On the other hand, coming home alone every morning frustrated he couldn't talk about being the Omega's Fate, let alone do anything about it was beginning to get to him. But he wasn't going to break one of Alexander's rules he promised to him on day one. Still, the irrational thoughts in his subconscious about another Alpha soaking his scent into Alexander's mating gland, stirred the wolf inside him. It made him want to claim the Omega every single time he saw him—just to get the biological need to calm down. Sexually, he was able to take care of the primal needs himself. However, a week later, even that was becoming ineffective.

The hardest for Stephen to admit was that tonight was not like all the other nights. Most of the clientele this evening were strangers— first-time patrons. Keeping the protective instincts buried inside of himself was difficult when he'd stare at an Alpha, or even a Beta, gazing upon Alexander with a targeted eye and salivating mouth. The wolf inside wanted him to snarl and give a warning shot to every man who did it. He had hoped trading off with James for the event would calm the frustration since he wasn't constantly face-to-face with the potential threats. But as he performed his job as bar back, he noticed himself continuously eyeing the bar, worried about what he couldn't see or hear. Now, to his right, he eyed the setting sun which whispered through the breeze that time was running out.

"Well, I have news for you. I'm Alex's best friend, so get used to the fact that I'm going to be around a lot."

Stephen looked back at the willful Omega. "That doesn't bother me."

Daniel squinted and once again used his calming voice. "Then what is?"

"I don't... I don't know how to deal with someone who doesn't want me back." Admitting the fault hurt his Alpha pride.

"Everybody has dealt with that before," Daniel dismissed.

"Not me!" Stephen barked back.

"Huh?" The Omega pushed his head back in disbelief.

The Alpha didn't want to go into the subject now; it wasn't the right time. Unfortunately, he felt backed into a corner. Dismissing his Fate's best friend on the first meeting wasn't a smart move. "I don't... do relationships. Or rather, I haven't been in one before. And I've never put myself out there or have cared enough to even consider someone as my mate."

"Oh." Daniel couldn't believe his ears. The handsome Alpha before him was clearly someone to stop and take notice of. Even after the brief recollection of his incarceration, Daniel knew Stephen wasn't in jail since birth, so he definitely had time to be in *some* sort of relationship. Still, he kept his judgments to himself, knowing his own track record wasn't anything to boast about.

"Sometimes, I worry that telling him was the worst thing I could have done," he finally admitted.

"He *knows*?" Daniel's eyes grew wide.

In the opposite way, Stephen's narrowed. "Yeah... of course he knows. How is it you don't? I thought you were his best friend?"

"I am!" Daniel defended.

"Then, how did you not hear about me telling him? Isn't that what best friends usually do?" The conclusion was a guess, as Stephen himself struggled to find someone who was legitimately that person for him.

Daniel snorted. "One thing you'll notice about Alexander, if you haven't already, is he's not a 'usual' person. He's a strong-willed Omega who feels he has to take on the world by himself because he thinks he's the only one he can count on. It's made him a very special, unique person to contend with."

Now Stephen was concerned. "Who in his life has made him feel that way?"

The Omega twitched his lips. "There's a few; I'll just say that." The awkwardness of the comment held the moment; a long pause set in.

"You're right though," Stephen commented.

"About what?"

"He is special; he is unique. I see that strength in him every day, but I also see that hurt you talk about. I think that's a barrier I'm going to have to work myself through somehow. But I'm willing to do that for someone I love."

"Whoa!" Daniel gasped.

Stephen's heart hitched in his throat. "I mean... I didn't mean—"

"No, I heard you," the Omega replied with a grin. "Okay. Damn. Now I know what we're dealing with." Daniel bit his bottom lip and tapped his foot on the torn-up concrete in the back alley. "If *that's* what you told him, now I *know* why he didn't tell me." He pivoted. "You've got a problem on your hands now." Daniel licked the inside of his cheek.

An unsettling feeling hit the pit of Stephen's stomach. "What do you—"

"Here you guys are!" Alexander yelled out from the rear door of the bar. "Are you two trying to give me an aneurysm? I've been trying to find you guys for like five minutes!" He walked up to the men ready to continue his onslaught, but as he neared, he studied their startled yet macabre faces. There wasn't any hint nor pheromone which gave away an idea of what Daniel had on his mind, and he didn't want to think about what was going through *Stephen's* mind. "What's going on?" he asked cautiously.

"Nothing," Daniel answered back first. "Just talking."

Once again, Alexander studied both men who clearly showed more than what they were willing to say. But now, there were more pressing issues at hand. "I'm completely out of ice in the bar, I need someone on dishwashing duty, that catering service is driving me *insane*! They think they're going to dictate orders to me. On top of that, I have everyone in there begging for a drink in their hand because Jesse Minh is about to give a speech! So, I need you guys there and 'on' at all times, okay?!" The stress poured out onto his forehead.

"Yes, sir," Stephen replied as he could barely look the Omega in the face, hiding his true intentions once more.

For a second, Alexander let his guard down. "I'm sorry, guys. We've never had a night like this since we've opened. I'm overwhelmed. Eric is overwhelmed. We all are. I know I'm asking a lot of you, and I appreciate both of you. Tonight, I'm going to be insane most likely until the last person is out of here, but just know, I'm grateful for everything you both are doing."

To Stephen, the voice alone was a soothing remedy. The words he spoke gave him the strength to press on and hold his insecurities for one more time as he was determined to be the rock the Omega needed, *his* Omega needed. "You can count on us. We've got your back."

"We got this!" Daniel assured.

Alexander smiled and sighed in relief. "Thanks. Now come on. I want to make sure I don't miss this speech!"

***

"Welcome, citizens of Tauris!" A proud Matthew Whitmore stood on a makeshift stage with a microphone enthusiastically catching his every breath. The bar cheered and roared at his words. Cameras, both professional and private, flashed and recorded every moment of his monumental presence. He flashed his white teeth and amused himself at the dedicated crowd. Without signaling for the need of a quiet audience, he knew they'd carry the chants and compliments till the morning sunrise. "Thank you, thank you. I want you all to know, I appreciate every bit of gratitude you have given me this evening. I've spoken to several of you already and hope to speak to many more of you before the night's out. One thing I've heard a few times now is that I, Matthew, have caused tonight to be the success it is. I said it to each person who said it to me, and I'll say it to you: I did nothing but announce when the event was, where it was going to be, and why we are here. *You. You* all are here. *You* all made this happen. And *that's* why tonight is and will continue to be a success!" Once again, the room erupted into a roar that could barely be contained by the walls of the establishment. Camera lights flashed like lightning and applause roared like thunder.

He continued, "Before we get to the main event, I do want to take a moment and recognize some very special individuals here tonight who indeed make this event possible. If you are working tonight's event, including the bar and catering staff, please let us recognize you now." Matthew scanned the floor around him and saw Alexander in the back, finishing up a customer. "Ah, there we are. Alex!" As he made the announcement, the patrons all turned and focused their attention on the Omega. "This man... this bar owner... this *Omega... this* is what we are here to do. We are here to show that society is not only thriving, but better when we have equal opportunities for Alphas, Betas, *and* Omegas to become whatever they want to be. And tonight, this fundraiser proves that Alphas professionally shunning their counterparts instead of walking hand-in-hand with them is a rhetoric long since dead and needs to be buried!"

As if he could do no wrong, everyone in the bar once again praised Matthew for his wisdom. "*I* believe that and so does Jesse Minh. And so, I sincerely hope, like both he and I, you are not only in awe of Alex's historic accomplishments, but also showing your gratitude to him and his staff, and that you not only enjoy yourselves here *tonight*, but many, many nights in the future! Here's to you and your staff!"

The entire room looked at the Omega with a proud respect rarely given to man of his accomplishment. But no one had that look more than Stephen, whose eyes sparkled as he saw Alexander bow his head in thanks and blush at the overwhelming reception. In the final seconds of the sun streaking across the tops of the buildings, the light hit the Omega's hair and skin beautifully, making him appear to Stephen like an angel. At that moment, he was perfect. Everything was perfect.

Suddenly, as if by some unspoken gesture, Alexander looked up and slowly turned his head toward him. For a moment, the two locked eyes in a way they hadn't yet. There was no hesitation, there was no animosity, and there was no sorrow. When the Omega slowly revealed a smile, a rush of pheromones exuded from the Alpha as he recorded every single minute moment of this perfection. Tonight, Stephen concluded, after the fundraiser finished, he was going to talk to the Omega once again about their future. And this time, he wasn't going to accept "No" as an answer.

Matthew continued his speech, but the words faded into the background as Stephen's gaze continued. Suddenly, his visual focus faltered as the light shining on his Omega was interrupted by a patron walking in from the outside, perfectly stepping in front of the heavenly beams and creating a shadow around him. It was then he noticed Alexander turn and recognize the man who came in. Quickly, the Omega turned toward Stephen and hurried past him, barely acknowledging him. The confusion set in further as he watched Alexander with a stuck smile round the corner and struggle through the maze of patrons still transfixed on Matthew Whitmore's speech. Finally, the Omega was able to reach the unknown patron and wrapped his entire body around his.

The embrace didn't make sense at first. A family member? A friend? A dedicated patron? No, none of those answers fit right. And then, the absolute wrong one did. In slow motion, he saw Alexander, *his* Omega, kiss the unknown man, then give him another full embrace. Everything flashed before Stephen's eyes. With every moment of the kiss taking center stage, memories of his Omega came crashing down upon him. He stumbled back for a moment and physically started to feel himself become ill. With nowhere else to go, he forced himself to the rear, past the walk-in and out in the now dark alleyway. His chest heaved and his blood boiled as he felt sparks go off in his mind. Like an automatic response, he felt his foot hurl into the giant dumpster, leaving a permanent impression into the unforgiving metal. The loud vibration of the dumpster hid the sound of the rear door opening once again, with Daniel there rushing toward him.

"Hey!" he yelled out as he rushed to the Alpha, full of concern. "Are you okay?"

"Who is that?!" Stephen roared.

Daniel immediately took in the Alpha's hormones and began to tremble at the sudden change, wondering if he had to fear for his own life. "Who?"

"The guy with Alex!" Stephen yelled out, frustrated he even had to clarify.

The Omega had to think for a second before realizing who he was talking about. "You mean Sean?"

"*Sean*?!"

The tone in Stephen's voice told Daniel he did not like where this was headed. "Yeah..."

"And who is Sean?" Loud thumps of boots struck the pavement as the Alpha knew but hoped against hope he wasn't right.

Daniel swallowed. "His boyfriend."

With his back turned, he stopped dead in his tracks. The confirmation did nothing to soothe Stephen in his catastrophe. He balled his fists as they shook with adrenaline. He turned. "You've got to be kidding me."

The petite Omega still had no idea how to interpret the situation. He almost wished he never came out to investigate. "No... why?"

"I have known him for *a week* and no one, not even Alex, has mentioned this guy. *Sean*? What the fuck?!"

"They've been together for two years." Daniel instantly regretted sharing the milestone.

Stephen growled at the comment. "You couldn't have told me this earlier when we were out here?"

"I tried!" Daniel insisted. "That was right when Alex came out to get us." Another growl erupted from the heated Alpha as he began pacing again. "Oh, come on. It's not like it's my responsibility to tell you anyway. Like you said, you didn't know the entire time you've been here."

"And why is that?" Stephen roared.

"I don't know!" Daniel yelled back, trying to figure out anyway to deescalate the situation before Alex, or worse, Sean came out to investigate two missing employees during a monumental night for the bar. "Alexander doesn't like people commenting about his personal life and that includes Sean." The answer didn't appease the Alpha. Daniel rubbed his forehead. "This doesn't make sense. You're telling me that when you confessed your feelings to Alex, his first response wasn't 'Sorry, I'm taken by my boyfriend of two years'?"

Somehow, Stephen was able to find humor in the logic. "No... not quite. But let me tell you, it would have been nice to know!"

"Why? What would it have changed?" Daniel posed.

Once again, the realization made Stephen stop his constant tramping in the small alley. "Nothing." His inner wolf whined as he let his shoulders fall. "It wouldn't have changed anything." With his mind repeating the calming mantra to himself, he non-threateningly approached Daniel. "Why do *you* think I haven't heard about him before now?" He held his breath.

The Omega inhaled the desperate pheromones from Stephen and sighed. "I know what you want me to say, and I don't think it's that."

"What's that?"

"That he's ashamed? That it's not working out? Am I close?" Stephen crossed his arms and scrunched his face. "Yeah, that's what I thought."

"It makes sense!" Stephen insisted. "Tell me another reason then."

"For starters, if Alex had any suspicion this is how you'd react, that's a good reason." The Alpha grunted in displeasure. "A relationship just isn't that big of a deal to Alex. He has so much else he's trying to accomplish in life, focusing on settling down really isn't an option for him right now. Even you can see that."

"Are you trying to tell me Sean is a relationship out of convenience?"

Daniel shrugged. "I couldn't speculate. What I *do* know is Sean is very easy going and isn't pushing Alex into anything. He's a strong Alpha who is stable and isn't causing drama in his life."

"Am I supposed to read in between the lines, there?" Stephen accused.

"It wasn't my main point but sure."

"You have quite the opinion of me, Omega. Not to mention, you have a lot of nerve talking to a Type 4 Alpha that way."

Daniel scoffed. "Yup. Make this all about Ranks and Types. *That's* the way to get to Alex's heart," he crooned sarcastically. "Meanwhile, over a hundred people from the city are packed inside the joint who support the erasure of all that backward rhetoric you just spouted. Oh, and let's not forget, Alex is being held by the arms of an Alpha who also supports the same."

Hearing the final part of Daniel's claim started the uncontrollable contractions in his arm and shoulder muscles. With a stern look on his face, he eyed the backdoor of the bar. "I'm gonna go talk to Sean," he muttered as he started down the path.

Daniel gasped as his instincts set off several alarms and whistles in his mind. "Oh, no you don't!" He chased after the Alpha and wrapped both hands around Stephen's solid fist, trying to pull him backward. The move was humorous—like a five-year-old trying to rip an immovable tombstone from the ground. After the futile attempt, it was enough for Stephen to stop and take notice of him pulling on his arm. Wolf's eyes glared down at the Omega and he realized now what he was doing. Coming back to his senses, he let go and remembered himself.

"Why not?"

Daniel had his hands on his waist as he struggled to catch his breath. "Because you have a face that says you're going to do a lot more than just 'talk' to Sean. Looks more like you're going to play 'Show-n-Tell' with the latest shiv you've made out of your toothbrush."

Stephen was getting tired of this unabashed attitude. "You're really going down a road you don't want to mess with, Daniel."

"Say, whatever you want, Stephen. You know I'm right. Everyone here knows you're an ex-con. You go in there and show any type of aggression, and you'll confirm all the irrational fears we have about you. If that's what you want to do—go for it. But I'll tell you right now, that's the one way to make sure you have a *zero* percent chance with Alex." Daniel's heart thumped in his chest like he was about to have a heart attack. He prayed to Wolf-God something he said got through to the Alpha.

After a long hard reflection, Stephen relaxed his pheromone expression and ended his threatening posture. "You're right," he confessed. "I'm sorry. I didn't mean to get angry with you. And I didn't mean to make stupid Rank or Type claims against you; I don't believe any of that either."

Daniel sighed in relief. "I know you don't."

"I was just angry and I didn't know what to say or do. I still don't."

"And I know that too."

"What do I do now, Daniel?" For the first time since meeting Alexander, the Alpha didn't know how to proceed on his journey in securing his Fated Mate. Now, the dream was floating farther and farther away, and he didn't know what to save or hold onto.

"Tonight? I don't think there is anything you can do. You need to be here for Alex and support him. He needs this and everything to be perfect. Right now, although you don't see it, you are a big part of that. You *have* to hold it together. That means avoiding Sean all together; hell, if you need to avoid both of them for the rest of the night, so be it. But you *cannot* do anything about it tonight. You know that, right?"

A breeze lifted scattered debris in the alleyway, and the sounds of dust and litter took the Alpha's mind off himself. Then, another joyous roar erupted from the bar inside. Jesse Minh had finished his speech. Stephen's time had run out.

***

"Alex!" A voice yelled out from the crowd as it made its way to the bar rail.

The Omega recognized the voice instantly but finished up the order he was working on and handed it off before gleefully acknowledging the man. "Jake! You made it! Did you just get in?"

"No, I got pulled in right before Matthew gave his speech. It's been a day's journey trying to get a drink and talk to you!"

"I know! I'm very sorry," Alexander stressed as he continued to gauge the growing crowd.

"No! Don't be! Everyone I've talked to so far has been impressed with the bar and the service tonight. You should be proud!"

"I am!" the Omega confirmed. "It's just we're getting maxed out … in space and in service. I hope we can hold the fort down so the dam doesn't break."

"Sounds to me like you have everything under control," Jake concluded.

"So far," Alexander replied cautiously. On cue, like a cruel reminder from Wolf-God himself, the sound of a glass shattering in the distance radiated off his ears. "Shit." Right behind him, as if he was anticipating it, the Omega grabbed a dustpan and broom, ready to locate the shards and liability on the floor. But even before he could move one step away from behind the bar, James grabbed both from his hands and went to do the task himself.

"See?" Jake smiled. "You got it."

Alexander returned the expression cautiously as he noticed two workers once again M.I.A. He scanned the room to find Daniel and Stephen but it was to no avail. "Is Dustin here with you?"

"He wanted to, but his son Drew had some event with school going on, so the entire family went to that."

"Aw. That sucks," Alexander deflated.

"Yeah, I know. I tried to convince him to just let Alec go so he could come here, but that wasn't an option I guess."

"Who?" The Omega lent an ear, trying to make sure he heard the name right.

"Alec." Jake understood the noise barrier and tried to enunciate better. "His mate."

"Oh, that's right. Alex. Alec." He gestured to himself then away. "Should have remembered that since our names are so similar."

"You should have!" Jake laughed. "How could you have forgotten that?"

"I guess my mind has been elsewhere?" He openly gestured to the tavern, as if he had to.

"Fair. That's fair. You know, if I'm not mistaken, their son, Mikaél, I think his middle name is Alexander as well."

The Omega rolled his eyes as he dried his hands on a bar towel. "With so many names in the world, you think the powers that be could come up with something different or more original."

"Names are important," Jake pointed out. "People are given them for a reason."

"Everything happens for a reason, right?" Alexander playfully patronized.

"Exactly." Jake nodded.

"Can I offer you your usual, Dr. Erricson?" the Omega offered politely.

"Alex, you are the last true bartender out there."

"And bar *owner*." He pointed with his finger and winked.

"I'll drink to that!" Jake affirmed.

Another voice sauntered in from the back and reached Jake's shoulder. "There you are! I have been trying to find you for the last ten minutes."

"Mr. Whitmore!" Jake embraced the man. "I've been trekking my way up here."

"I can see that!"

"You have this place packed, Matthew. It's great!" Jake complimented.

"I hope I didn't overdue it." The Alpha winced. "How are you doing, Alex?"

"We're keeping up just fine, Matthew. Don't you worry about us. You just make sure Jesse Minh gets elected," the Omega commented as he finished Jake's cocktail. "Are you having another of the same?"

Matthew glanced at his mostly empty glass. "Yeah. Keep it mixed, though. I have to play the part of a diplomat all night."

"Still, if you ask me, you should be playing the part of a political candidate," Alexander teased.

"Let's not start that again." Matthew beamed from the obvious compliment. "Besides, if tonight continues like this, no one will be able to beat Jesse."

"You don't think you could?" the Omega pressed.

The proud Alpha bowed his head in gratitude. "It doesn't matter. We have the same vision, and we have the same goal. Thank you for your support, Alex."

"No, thank you, Mr. Whitmore. What you have done for my place is something I don't think I could ever repay you for." Once again, Matthew put his hand on his chest and nodded. No part of his suit moved. No part of his hair fell out of place. He stood there as the model of perfection. Tonight, for Alexander, he *was* Wolf-God. As much as he wanted to bask in the glory, he felt James tug on his shirt, beckoning him to come to the side. "Sorry guys, duty calls! I hope you both enjoy yourselves." Even before hearing their responses, he felt his arm being pulled away.

After it appeared Alexander was preoccupied, Jake swiveled in his chair and held his glass up and clanked it against Matthew's. "Jesse's going to win, huh?"

"Oh, absolutely," Matthew replied without hesitation. "This is one success I have no doubts about."

Jake eyed his drink before slowly setting it on the bar. "You want to tell me what you're like when you do have doubts?"

Matthew turned and studied the Alpha. "Is this about Roman?" Jake nodded. "Have you talked to him about..." Jake nodded again. "And?"

"It was like talking to the wall." Jake hated every second of the confession.

"What?!" Matthew stressed in disbelief.

"He's wrapped up in this Fated Mate thing. I can't get him to shake it. He's so damn stubborn and content on waiting. I just... I don't know what to do anymore." Once again, Jake grabbed his glass, using it as his safety.

"You need to tell him the truth, Jake," Matthew insisted.

The words made Jake throw half of his cocktail down his throat. He swallowed hard and peered at the Alpha before him. He was the perfect businessman, the perfect mate, the perfect father, the perfect friend, and now, the perfect advice-giver. But Jake himself held his own Alpha pride, or stubborn personality, close to his chest. He wasn't sure which it was now. He deflected the comment. "Did you talk to Peyton?"

"I did."

"And?"

Matthew grinned and leaned in. "He likes Roman."

"Yeah?" Jake's expression lit up.

"A lot."

"Don't stop there!" Jake pleaded. "What did you say to him?"

Matthew knocked back the rest of his drink and set it down. "I just told him I noticed they talked briefly at the lab opening night. I asked him how it went, and he said it went well—brief—but well." He continued to see Jake catching and eating every word. "Then, Terrence and I started throwing around hints that we heard Roman was in the market for a potential mate. Boy, you should have seen his expression!" Matthew laughed. Jake enjoyed every minute of it. "Finally, I asked, hypothetically, if he'd ever consider having Roman be *his* mate if that opportunity came to be."

"He said 'Yes'?"

"That's putting it lightly. I think he was about ready to pack his bag and ask 'When and where?'" Matthew rubbed Jake's shoulder, hoping it continued to relieve the stress he was obviously carrying on his shoulders.

For Jake, the news was sent down from Wolf-God himself. But the elation was short-lived as reality rushed back in. "Now, if only I can get Roman to come around."

"Look, we said we weren't going to rush this. So, don't rush."

"You're right," Jake confirmed. "I just need to let this wave ride slowly. I'll do what you did... occasionally throw in comments and hypotheticals." Then he reflected. "That's so unlike me. When I see a solution to the problem, I want it done and over with."

"Then, consider this a *real* challenge for yourself," Matthew pointed out. "Your career hasn't always been easy. Navigate this like you would a proper discovery. Just because you think you've found the answer doesn't mean you close the books and claim you've done everything. You keep checking, trying new things, and do everything to make sure you aren't wrong. Treat this situation like that, and you'll have Roman begging for this contract."

Jake stared back in awe. "How on earth do I become an Alpha like you, Mr. Whitmore?"

Matthew smirked. "It's 'Matthew', Jake. And I'll let you in on a little secret, my friend. You already are." He winked. "Keep me posted?"

"You know I will. Congratulations tonight... Matthew!"

All Jake received in return was a gesture before Matthew disappeared back into the crowds, desperately grasping for his attention. The compliment from the Alpha stuck on Jake's face, but only for a moment. As he turned back toward the bar, he had another face looking at him with not so much enthusiasm. "What?" he asked Alexander.

The Omega eased in with a cautious look plastered all over his face. "What were you two talking about?"

Jake was quick to answer. "Nothing."

"This isn't about your sons going into a contract again, is it?" he concluded, already knowing the answer.

Jake grumbled in defeat. "You remember that?"

"I don't think this is a good idea, Jake." Alexander kept one ear open to Jake as he heard another customer list off an order.

The Alpha waited patiently for the customer to finish his demands before continuing. "It may not be 'good' but it's the best Roman's going to get out there. That's just the way it is for him."

Alexander doubted the claim. "Didn't we just have a conversation earlier about 'everything happens for a reason'?"

"That we did," Jake confirmed. "And because Roman can't—" he caught himself before uttering the shame, "—is different from other Alphas, *this* has to happen for a reason."

"Personally, I never find that parents meddling in the personal lives of their sons ever ends well. To counter that, I say, if Roman is waiting for someone special out there, Wolf-God has made his reason for *that* and not for this. He doesn't want you interfering with your son's mate, and I'm confident in that." Alexander finished the final pour and pushed them out to the customer waiting while accepting a large bill in return.

As good measure, the unknown customer gave Jake a look which told him to heed the bartender's words of wisdom. "Why do I get the feeling everyone else around me is smarter than me?"

"Because we're not parents," Alexander teased.

"Matthew's a parent!" Jake pointed out.

"Well yeah, but he's not Roman's parent. That makes all the difference."

"You're too smart to be a bartender, Alex."

The Omega leaned in. "And you're too smart to ignore that I'm right about this." He stared into the Alpha's eyes, making sure it stuck.

"Why aren't you mated yet?" Jake had the nerve to ask.

Alexander sighed. "I'm seeing someone. Does that count?"

Jake scoffed. "No. How long have you been with him?"

"Two years."

The Alpha furrowed his brows. "Then why aren't you in a mating contract with him?"

Finally for the first time since Matthew's speech, Alexander saw both Daniel and Stephen amongst the crowds, picking up empty glasses and cleaning off tables. Stephen glanced up only for a second and then went back to work as if he never saw him. "Because you're right..." He stared off.

After no conclusion was given, Jake gestured with his now empty glass. "Right about..."

"I am too smart." He broke his trance and noticed Jake's glass in front of him. "Another one?"

The Alpha wasn't entirely sure where he was going with the comment, but he had his own problems to drink away now. "One more wouldn't hurt."

"That's what I always say." Alexander laughed back.

[Daniel: Boy do I have a bone to pick with you!]

[Alexander: Shit... what happened? Did I forget to do something? If so, I'm sorry. I don't have a functioning brain right now. I'm surprised you're even up!]

[Daniel: I'm absolutely running on empty. Have been for the past few hours. And I'm absolutely furious with you! If I hadn't gotten paid in cash tonight, I would have left you on 'read' for a week.]

[Alexander: Why?!?! What happened?!]

[Daniel: When were you going to tell me about the whole Stephen thing?]

[Alexander: I did tell you about the Stephen thing. His past is his past. What else is there to say? ... Please tell me something didn't go down that I don't know about.]

[Daniel: Nice try. I'm talking about the fact this guy thinks you're his FATED MATE!!!!]

[Alexander: Did he tell you that? If so, he and I are going to have some words the next time I see him.]

[Daniel: When it comes to being your *Fate*, I had two people tonight tell me about it. Neither were him.]

[Alexander: Bruce and James need to keep their mouths shut.]

[Daniel: Hey! I didn't say it was them!]

[Alexander: Uh-huh. Anyway, I'm sorry for not telling you. My goal in not telling you is the same reason I don't talk to anyone about it. I don't want it to be a thing. I'm hoping after a while it will be like it never happened. Once again, I'm sorry. I should have told you. But I haven't told anyone that. The only ones who knew were the ones who were present that day when it happened. And I swore I had them bound to secrecy. It appears that isn't the case.]

[Daniel: Blame the booze. Haha! Wait. If you haven't told anyone... does that mean Sean doesn't know????]

[Alexander: Take a wild guess.]

[Daniel: No???]

[Alexander: Totally No!]

[Daniel: Hmm... wonder how that is going to turn out...]

[Alexander: * sigh * Is there something else I can help you with? I already told you I'm sorry. But I am literally texting you with one eye shut and a splitting headache, and all the light sneaking into the cracks of the window is telling me I should have been asleep forever ago.]

[Daniel: No. ☹ That's it. Sorry. Didn't mean to be so critical. I was just hurt I wasn't told. As far as being awake, I have other ... activities keeping me up.]

[Alexander: T.M.I.!!! I don't need to know about the private hobbies you do in your home.]

[Daniel: Who said I was home?]

[Alexander: ... where are you?]

[Daniel: At Bruce and James's place.]

[Alexander: WHAT?]

[Daniel: Talk to you later, friend!]

[Alexander: Uh, no! I wondered what was going on when I saw you and James talking constantly like you two were hiding some devious plan. I need an explanation, sir!]

[Alexander: Hello?]

[Alexander: Just wait until I see you next time, mister!]

"Jeez, did you forget how to unlock the door?" Kane criticized as he stared down his inconsiderate offspring. All he received in return was an inaudible remark. "What's wrong with you?" he asked defensively.

"Stephen?" Marlon tried, standing behind his mate near the front door. Once again, their son gave no indication he was even present at the moment. They saw their son hunched over, making a clear path to the guest bedroom.

Another quick inspection gave Kane all the clues he needed. "He's drunk."

"What?" Marlon gasped. "How did he even get home?' He ran to the door and searched for a possible vehicle, but by the time he reached the door, none were in sight.

"Taxi, I assume," Kane muttered.

"At this hour? I didn't know they even ran at this hour."

"Either that or someone dropped him off. It's not like he walked here." The Alpha paused as he saw his son for one final moment before he opened the bedroom door and vanished into the room. "At least, I don't think he did."

Marlon touched his chest in fear. "You don't think something happened…"

Kane picked up on the train of thought. "Don't know. Maybe. I bet that event had him completely wiped out. With so much that probably went on, it could be anything."

The Omega stared back at his mate, feeling hurt for his son and whatever he was going through. Fearing the worst, he reached out for the comfort of his Alpha, hoping the touch alone could prevent him from thinking any legal or moral issue occurred in which he'd lose his son again. But this morning, he wasn't going to get the answer he desperately craved.

The room and his surroundings were completely void of any disturbance or noise. Stephen's wolf howled deep inside him, a heartbreaking lullaby to a lost love. *Lost* love? No—a love he never had. All the alcohol in the Alpha's system couldn't deter his mind from making all the right connections on why Alexander dealt with the whole situation so easily. He was already mated. Contracted? He didn't know—didn't want to know. Without removing any piece of clothing from his body, he face-planted himself onto his bed and solidified like concrete.

Tears pushed out but the only sounds coming from his throat were those in frustration as he tightened his fist around the fabric of the comforter. *How could I be so stupid? How could I be so blind?* A million thoughts rushed through the Alpha's mind on all the stupid assumptions he made from false hope. Alexander was a beautiful creature—of course he had someone in his life. Stephen cursed himself for thinking that just because he had a daunting challenge being a bar owner it meant that he was also untouchable when it came to love. It was an insult he wouldn't accept for himself, yet there he was, putting it onto the one man who he supposedly held in the highest regard. He let out an emotional sigh. "I'm such a fucking idiot."

Memories of the past week flashed before him. All the camaraderie, all the smiles, the jokes, the teasing, and even little connections... they were nothing more than a show of Alexander's true character of humanity and kindness. None of it was for him being his potential mate. Stephen felt lost on exactly where he truly stood with the Omega. A rotten feeling hit his stomach as he dared to even consider how far he'd have to rewind to find out the real relationship they had and not the relationship he created in his mind. Or maybe his tolerance for alcohol had severely gone down and his body was revolting against him. After only a few more moments of his head spinning, he was certain it was the latter. Hardly able to lift himself up in time, opening the window even took too long. He aimed his head out the window, and whatever was in his stomach for the past six to eight hours was gone.

Unfortunately, there was no reprieve after his stomach finally ceased its horrible onslaught. His head throbbed and his heart throbbed harder. The sorrow he bathed in began to turn as he felt betrayed by everyone he worked with. *Alexander is mated?* He couldn't comprehend how something like that even went unnoticed. Once again, he reviewed all instances in which he could have missed a hint or reference to the Alpha who owned his mate. No, he couldn't think like that. The Alpha who was *with* his mate. He sighed to himself as he barely stopped himself from having to revisit the window.

An unwanted name suddenly flashed in. *Sean.* The name had been spoken before a few times. That's who it was. The tall, confident, and successful Alpha had been in the bar the entire time, and he didn't even know it. Not literally in person, but in spirit. That, of course, only sparked another question as to why he had never seen the Alpha before or why it wasn't ever specifically nor explicitly brought up.

Stephen growled to himself as he finally kicked off his shoes. They were the only articles of clothing he was willing to put effort into as far as undressing. Once again, he collapsed onto his bed, fully clothed in attire which carried a scent that continued to constantly throw him back into the bar. That was when it hit him. *The bar.* With everything that had happened tonight, it completely and utterly left him that tonight was his last probation night. That meant tomorrow started his first day of work as a true employee... or... his last day on the job entirely. Was that the punchline to the cruel joke of the night? Was Stephen nothing more than a simple pawn used until he wasn't needed anymore? Did Alexander secretly wait until tonight's fundraiser in order to bring Sean out on full display and let him know he was already taken? Once again, he felt his inner wolf and human fighting for the right conclusion. Jealousy and paranoia were human traits ... but protection and the incessant need for answers were pure wolf.

The event alone left him completely exhausted. The betrayal and heartache zapped any possible energy he had left to perpetuate the examination further. In one last conscious thought, his wolf gifted him just the lone memory of Alexander, his Fate, staring back at him, giving him every validation of why he existed and was put on this earth.

# EXHIBITING WOLF INSTINCTS IN HUMAN FORM

Stephen worked the late afternoon shift at South Street Tavern as he would any other day. Normally, he'd be conversing with the clientele, making light jokes with the regulars, and schmoozing newcomers but today... today he was a zombie. Both Bruce and James noticed it immediately when he arrived at work and took it as a cue to take over more than what they normally did. Each minute was agonizing as time refused to move. Cleaning the tables or the bar for the third time wasn't helping either.

"Just because Alex is sick doesn't mean he contaminated the place, Stephen. Why don't you come back up to the bar and socialize with some of the customers? Get your mind on something else for a while?" Bruce offered.

"I can't believe that on all days to be sick, *this* had to be the day?" the Alpha griped. Even though he experienced his own hell last night, worthy of keeping himself home, he still felt as if today was a cruel punishment. Wolf-God was clearly a vengeful animal, sparing no one, especially him.

"Would you rather he'd been sick for the fundraiser? He would have burnt the place down and we'd all be out of a job." Bruce received a dirty look for his poor choice of words. "Sorry"

Stephen continued to eye the Beta with a stern look. He knew he didn't mean anything by it. "It's okay." Regarding his question, he didn't want to admit out loud that yes, there was indeed a part of him that wished Alexander *had* been sick at the event. Perhaps certain events that night wouldn't have happened the way they did. But deep inside, his inner wolf bit back and shamed him for even thinking of wanting his Fated Mate in harm's way. "No, I don't want Alex to be sick. I just want to know for sure is all. Not knowing is driving me crazy!" He slapped down a saturated towel on a table, pulled out a chair, sat, and moped.

"You have nothing to worry about," Bruce assured him.

"Oh yeah? How do you know?"

"Because bars are gossip farms—cultivated and spread throughout the city as they were designed to be. And that goes for the employees too."

Stephen gave an awkward look. "What does that mean?"

"Neither James nor I have heard anything bad about you—not from a customer—not from Eric—and certainly not from Alex. If we had, we would have given you a heads up. Coming in today was the right decision. You're not going to get fired for keeping a normal schedule. It's *one* day. Besides, we're busy enough to where it warrants you being here."

"I just want to hear him *say* it." Stephen exhaled and bottomed out.

"What does he want?" James asked as he walked over, wondering what the conversation was about.

Bruce obliged. "He wants to know from Alex if he passed his probationary period and can be considered an official employee now."

"Of course, you are!" James replied.

Stephen's head lifted with hope. "I am? Alex told you?"

"No. But we would know by now if you weren't." The words did little to assure Stephen of anything.

Bruce lightly hit the side of the Alpha's arm. "See?! What'd I say?"

"Is that what this is all about?" James couldn't believe the situation had the Alpha in such disarray. "Or is this about something else?"

Stephen's eyebrows furrowed. "Like what?"

"Like..." James drew carefully, "how the second half of the night you became a completely different person?"

"I don't know what you're talking about," Stephen denied.

"Don't even try it," Bruce called out. "We all saw it."

"Hey! I could sure use another drink here!" a bar patron yelled to the back.

"What happened to the one I just gave you, Tom?" James yelled back.

"I drank it!" Tom slurred back.

James tilted in his head. "In two minutes?"

"The last one you gave me had a lot of foam," Tom innocently stated.

Stephen lifted his head and whispered, "He says that about all the taps."

James decided to use the line, yelling it back to the inebriated fool. "You say that about all the taps!" Stephen snorted and hid his face while Bruce chuckled into his fist.

"Yeah, yeah, it's true! If you want, I can get up and inspect the taps myself. I used to work in a bar before. Managed the whole thing by myself. I know what I'm doing."

"You get behind that bar, old man, the only thing you're going to be inspecting is a broom handle up your asshole!" James shouted back. Both Bruce and Stephen looked at him in awe.

"Damn, James. A little harsh, don't you think?" Stephen commented.

"...You got any olives?" Tom asked.

James shook his head and pulled at his hair like he was talking to a madman. "I can't believe this guy."

Bruce refocused. "You want to clue us in as to why you avoided Alex like the plague? We all noticed it, including him."

Stephen decided to bite the bullet. "What do you guys know about Sean?"

"Sean?" James asked. "Oh, *Sean*." Both brothers instantly concluded the issue at hand. "He's a good guy. Comes in occasionally, but otherwise, we don't see him."

"What does he do?" Stephen asked out of curiosity.

"Works for a bank," Bruce replied.

The thought reminded him of his not-so-welcome encounter at the bank he had weeks ago. It made Stephen cringe knowing Sean belonged to the affiliation. "How come I didn't know he existed before the event? I didn't even know Alex was taken, much less hear a name to even surmise he was with someone." The defense wasn't entirely true in retrospect, but right now, Stephen was desperate for any validation.

Both brothers shrugged. "It was probably the timing," James concluded. "You came right around the time we found out Matthew Whitmore asked about the place. Alex thought about nothing else other than getting you up to speed I suppose."

"Plus," Bruce interjected, "you made that Fated Mate claim on day one." James flexed his eyebrows as he replayed the moment in his head. "It doesn't make someone want to divulge their personal life, that's for sure."

Stephen found himself acting like a broken record. "Regardless of what I said, if someone was trying to court you, and you were taken, wouldn't that be your first response?"

"If someone declared me as their Fated Mate? Hell no," James rushed in. "Not that we'll ever know." He took one quick glance at his fellow Beta brother, an acknowledgement that neither of them would ever experience the highly sought-after connection. "The last thing I'd tell a stranger who wants to claim me is that there's someone else in their spot. Can only imagine what that'd be like."

"I guess you have a point there," Stephen begrudgingly confessed.

"But that's not a thing anymore, right?" Bruce asked. "I mean, he's not really your Fated Mate." Now the Alpha's eyes narrowed in as his pheromones told both Bruce and James all they needed to hear. "Oh," Bruce replied as he now understood the predicament.

"Last evening, there was a moment where everything was perfect," Stephen began. "He looked beautiful, he looked happy, he looked proud. Selfishly, I wanted to be a part of that. I had even told myself I was going to approach him and talk to him again about it."

"Damn—you were going to pull that out right then and there?" James asked.

"In hindsight, I get it. If it had invoked the same response he had last time, I'd be a hundred feet away from the building with a restraining order on me by now."

"So why risk it?" Bruce sat forward, studying the Alpha in his internal conflict.

"Because Alex *is* my Fate, guys. I know it, my inner wolf knows it, the feeling is unmistakable." He shook his head. "I don't know why Wolf-God is putting me into this position to be matched with someone who doesn't feel that connection back. But there is something inside me that's saying not to give up and I won't. Not now. Not ever." He observed both brothers give each other a look—one that told him the fight to get there was going to get worse before it got better. "If I think about it, the reason I was considering doing it last night was because I figured if I got Alex in a moment where his wall was down, maybe his mind and his heart, and his wolf would have been more receptive to me; maybe I'd find out I'm not going crazy and that he'd finally see what I saw all along."

"And then Sean came in last night," James concluded.

"Yeah. He did." Stephen's shoulders dropped as once again he was reminded of the "Alpha in his spot" as James put it. Hearing it and being reminded of it was never going to get easier.

"James!" Tom yelled. "Where's my beer? Ethan needs one too!"

"I'm coming, Thomas! I'm coming!" the Beta gruffed as he walked back to his post.

"Do Betas even do that?" Tom snickered.

"When you decide to pay one to sleep with you, you might find out," James clapped back.

Both Bruce and Stephen snorted at the retort. Then Bruce laid his hand on the Alpha's shoulder. "Hey. We have your back here, you know that. Just get through today and you'll know more answers by tomorrow. I promise."

Stephen nodded in defeat and lifted his heavy body off the chair, throwing the bar towel across his shoulder as he trekked his way back up.

"Hello?" a voice called from the entrance, carrying a bottle of champagne and some flowers. His sleek charcoal gray shirt set off every muscular curve in his chest and arms while his petite waist was snuck in black slacks and a belt with a gold buckle. "I don't suppose Alex is here, is he?"

"Sorry Sean, he's taking a sick day." Bruce spoke as he finished up an order.

"Ah. That must be why I can't get ahold of him." Sean surrendered his objective and took a seat at the bar, setting the flowers and champagne on the rail.

"You can't get ahold of him?" Stephen blurted out.

"I imagine he's been sleeping—worn out like crazy. He probably has his phone off." As he got himself comfortable, he noticed the Alpha working behind the bar. Studying the man, Sean was able to assess he was physically equal in his stature. He could also scent the simmering pheromones coming off him. "Sean Crenshaw," he offered.

The Alpha restrained his instinctual urges and relied heavily on his human ones as he politely held out his hand for a greeting. "Stephen Matheson. You must be Alex's boyfriend."

"Boyfriend?" Sean snorted. "I suppose that's what kids in school or newly coupled pairs call themselves. We've been together for two years now. I like to think of him as my mate—makes it more *permanent* that way."

Bruce and James glanced over, waiting for Stephen's response. It didn't disappoint—albeit—it didn't help either.

"Oh, I'm sorry. I didn't mean anything disrespectful by it. I was just going off what Alex told me." Stephen casually let the words flow from his tongue. His face stayed neutral but his tone carried a sense of accomplishment.

Sean used his eyes to size the bartender up and down and he smiled in satisfaction. "How long have you been here? I hear you're new?"

"Yes, sir. One week now."

"Enjoying it here?" Sean continued.

"Love it here," Stephen answered without hesitation. "Feels like home." Sean's face fell slightly at the comment. "I'm sorry—I didn't ask you what you wanted to drink."

"Bruce—you mind getting my order?" Sean beckoned to him behind Stephen.

The Beta walked up to his fellow co-worker and spoke under his breath. "He likes Trailblazer #4 on tap. I can get his order and keep him company if wanna switch sides."

"No, no," Stephen insisted. "Simple order. Nothing I can't handle." The Alpha intentionally blew off the offer. He wasn't backing down from this. After filling the order perfectly, he set it gently in front of Sean. "Are we paying cash or holding a card?" Bruce cleared his throat and shook his head. "Oh."

Sean smirked. "Just one of the many benefits I get from my mate." Stephen tightened his mouth and nodded as he casually inspected the garnishing box. "So, just a week, you said? Where were you before that? Another bar in the area perhaps?"

Stephen shut the garnishing box lid with a thud. The trap had been set and he walked right in. He now realized this was the goal all along. The options before him at this point were few. He either tucked his tail and skirted the issue like a submissive Alpha or faced it head-on and fearless like a dominant one. "Incarcerated for ten years."

The look on Sean's face showed its satisfaction, especially as a few other bar patrons caught wind of it and started whispering amongst themselves. "Oh, that's right," the Alpha drew out nice and slow. "I remember now."

Stephen's eyebrows furrowed. "You remember?"

"Stephen Matheson? Of course! The fallen son of Kane Matheson, the once well-respected authority in this town."

Bruce stepped over to the brewing Alpha standoff. "Hey, Sean, the flowers and champagne look great. Is that to congratulate Alex on the success of last night?"

"My mate just made history with this place. I was hoping to celebrate with him, yes."

Stephen's wolf growled inside him—hating the fact Bruce usurped the primal need to defend himself and his family. He wasn't going to let it end this way. "I'm not fallen. And my father is still respected in this community."

Tom's ears perked up. "Whoa. The wild wolf has a past! Let's hear it."

James intercepted the inquiry, "No, no. We don't need to go into that. You said yourself, Tom. It's the past. Let's leave it there."

"I'm sure the Alpha doesn't mind sharing. Clearly, he's not ashamed it," Sean egged on. He used his index finger and thumb and outlined his lips, relishing the moment.

Stephen's skin heated as the adrenaline rushed through him. "I had a history of drugs. And, by proxy—"

"Come on, Stephen. You don't have to do this," James pleaded.

The insistence fell upon deaf ears. The Alpha held his breath. "I was held responsible for the death of a minor who found and used my stash." Stephen locked his gaze onto Sean, never wavering in his stance nor pheromone palate.

Bar patrons murmured as Tom rubbed his neck. "Uh... shit." He stood up to his bar stool and grabbed his glass. After giving Stephen one quick glance, he looked at the Beta brothers. Sliding to his right, he found an open chair next to a couple other patrons who welcomed him in their circle of unease.

Even though Sean marveled in his ability to play the fellow Alpha like a puppet, there was unsettling miscalculation in Stephen's resolve. The goal he was trying to accomplish didn't pan out the way he wanted. It was evident Stephen was a force to be reckoned with, and he wasn't going away anytime soon. However, that wasn't going to stop Sean from trying to speed up the process. "That's quite the burden to carry on your shoulders."

"You don't know the half of it."

"It's also quite the burden to put on this place."

Stephen quickly scanned the members of the bar before coming back to the Alpha. "*This* place?"

"Absolutely. Bars play a role in society that judge and synthesize how the real-world works. But before they can be that safe and successful space for the public to exercise that need, bars first must go through their own purgatory and judgement. They're bound to the spirit of the patrons who come in and the people who serve them. At first, anyone would think this standard to be fair, one that every single business is rightfully subjected to. But bars, breweries, taverns? They pay the ultimate price. No other business, one that's legal anyway, allows the social norms of its patrons and workers to be broken in order to establish a comfort level that says with each drink you take, and dollar that's exchanged, you are creating a *new* social norm which has *new* rules. The goal of every bar is to make sure you are comfortable doing it here, at *this* place, so you won't want to go and do it anywhere else."

Stephen rolled his eyes. "What the hell is your point?"

"My point is: South Street has had a sordid past that stretches beyond even you and me. My mate had to work hard to get his foot into this place. I'm very proud to be a part of that legacy considering we met when he was just starting to petition the city for the license. Since that first day, he has had to create a reputation that not only says it's safe for traditional customers to come back here, but to usher in a whole new underserved population as well. And last night's political rally here will help propel South Street to a level of notoriety most establishments will never see in their entire lifetime. But here you are, Stephen Matheson, selfishly pushing your way in here and deciding it's worth my mate to gamble that entire reputation and his entire career, and the career of everyone else who works here, on making sure you have a job."

Stephen swallowed hard. The words were meant to hurt—that was the easy part. The hard part was the logic. Spinning the future potential of the tavern while placing *him* as the main obstacle was hard to ignore. He fought in his mind to level out what was fact and what was conjecture. Shaking it off, he held his own. "I didn't do that. Alex made that call—not me. It was his prerogative. He decided I was worth it."

"Hmph," Sean scoffed. "What I heard was Eric made that decision and Alex was against it from moment one. Or do I have it wrong?"

Stephen held the moment. "No, it's not wrong." The urge to pounce was teetering on the point of no return.

"Sean, Stephen has been a great addition here. He's a hard worker and he's great with the customers. That's all that matters. You're making something out of nothing. It's not a big deal," Bruce defended.

"Well," Stephen paused as he turned slightly in his swivel chair, "let's ask those precious customers what they think." Continuing his bravado, he addressed Tom and the few others he joined. "Tom, what's it like knowing you're getting served daily by a man who's been convicted in the death of a child?"

All three bartenders stood there in shock. Bruce, James, nor Stephen could believe Sean had the nerve to be so flagrant while also carrying the tone which said he didn't care two cents worth for anyone's comfort at this point—and it showed.

Tom's forehead creased as he realized what was going on. With all eyes on him, he only had one option. After a deep breath, he finished off the last quarter of his beer and firmly placed it back on the bar. He licked his lips and nodded to his fellow patrons on his right. It took the half-inebriated man a moment to find his balance as he stood and stretched his arms. He pulled his wallet from his back pocket and sifted through several bills. The expression on his face said he was calculating ... or contemplating. Either way, he settled on one large bill, folded it in his hand and carefully set it next to the empty glass. He creased his lips into a neutral smile, tilted his head forward, and made his way toward the exit.

The sight was a black eye on not only Stephen, but the entire bar as well. Mere seconds later, in the hushed silence, the remaining members also found themselves repeating, almost perfectly, the same gestures and routine the former patron had before processioning out one by one.

"Hmph." Sean tapped his fingers on the bar like he was an innocent bystander observing it all play out. "Guess that answers that question." Slowly, he lifted his glass and felt the brewed ale go down his throat like a victory lap. Having the employees all carry an expression like death was the cherry on top.

Bruce could feel the pheromones coming off Stephen which indicated only the worst possible outcomes. He pulled the Alpha back and attempted to center him. "Why don't you take a break? Take a walk." he offered, unsure if the suggestion even cracked the surface of the much-needed repair.

"How about you take the rest of the day off?" James added. "Bruce and I can take care of this. Eric's going to be here soon, anyway." Stephen was lost in a trance he couldn't comprehend. The haze stuck to him, and he didn't know how to react. Right now, he couldn't tell if his anger management had kicked in automatically to save Sean from having his lungs ripped out, or he was truly in a state of mental breakdown. Perhaps in only to give a customary or automatic response, he nodded his head in agreement. But fate had other plans.

Unable and unwilling to let the addiction of satisfaction subside, Sean once again found himself speaking like a slithery serpent. "Come on, we're just getting started!"

Bruce and James both reacted in their own subtle way which read they couldn't believe what was going down today. But both knew they were stuck in a position which didn't favor them either. Kicking a High-Type Alpha out of any establishment without a severe law violation to back it up alone came with ramifications depending on their social status. Unfortunately, Sean possessed all those qualities and privileges. Even more so, meddling in Alexander's personal life by banning his boyfriend, or mate, whatever he was for the day, brought Sean to a whole new level of immunity neither Beta wanted to risk.

Stephen, on the other hand, had no rules. "What on earth would you want to continue here? Didn't you already accomplish your goal?"

"You're still working here... so, no," Sean replied aptly.

"And I already told you, that isn't changing. I'm only leaving when Alex tells me to and he's not going to. He *wants* me here." The words came out faster than he could process in his mind. If the message itself wasn't enough for Sean to press the issue, the look on Stephen's face was.

In a similar way, Sean's face reacted, and pheromones released at the utterance of the claim. "You wanna clue me in to what makes you so Wolf-God-damned special?"

Without even looking behind him, Stephen could sense both Bruce and James shaking with trepidation, wondering if he was going to reveal the seemingly Fated Star-Crossed claim he was incessant on. The Alpha himself pondered the effects of revealing the truth. Doing so would validate his position, not only in the tavern, but to Alexander as well. Sean viscerally would be removed as the Alpha Wolf and lose his status with the Omega professionally and personally, leaving all the room for Stephen to take his rightful place. At this point, it was now or never. He felt his heartbeat in his chest and in his head. He took a deep breath in and sighed. "Nothing. Nothing makes me special."

The instinctual worry Sean held internally melted away to a shallow laugh and entertained expression. He eyed both Betas who shared an equally perplexed look. "I don't know where you boys found this one, but damn, you got one hilarious mutt on your hands." Sean knocked back the rest of his glass and sighed in satisfaction. "Ahhh," he crooned.

"Will that be all for you?" Stephen asked deflated.

Once again, Sean couldn't help himself. "You know what, I think I'll have another before I step out. If you don't mind." He winked as if there was any other option.

Stephen rustled up a clean glass and filled it properly. "Yes, sir." He walked it back with a subtle expression on his face.

"See?!" Sean smiled with glee. "The Alpha even knows his place! Man, I love it here. I should come by more—" In an instant, the entire beer glass shot off the bar and landed right in Sean's lap. Golden ale splashed up and immediately soaked into the expensive shirt, while the black pants only left the results up to the imagination. The Alpha growled from the throat as his body involuntarily jumped up, futilely avoiding every drop possible. In the final second, the now perfectly emptied glass rolled off the top of his thigh and smashed on the floor below. Sean stood next to his chair, flabbergasted. "You stupid fuck!"

Bruce acted immediately like it was programmed into him. He grabbed a bar towel and rushed to the outside and around again, not even looking at Stephen or breaking face as he instinctively went into clean-up and damage control.

James's reaction, however, couldn't have been more opposite. With both hands cupping his mouth, he struggled to keep a straight face and attempted to hide the sounds of uncontrollable snorting as he became glued to the scene unfolding before him. That moment alone instantly cemented itself into his permanent memory bank. He already knew the snide comments and stories which were undoubtedly going to come from this.

At first, Stephen stood there, frozen like a statue, unsure of what even transpired. It took more brain power to comprehend that he had even done it. He had to replay the scene over and over in his head to figure out if he knowingly did it or if his subconscious had taken over and done it for him. A ball of nerves exploded throughout his body. But before he could try going down a path of catastrophe, he heard James still struggling to stifle his entertained reaction. It was then Stephen broke into a slight smirk and decided he wasn't bothered by the turn of events. The enjoyment was short-lived, however, as Sean's rant and Bruce's apology began filling his ears. "I'm so sorry." The reply was automatic, and he struggled to find the correct tone of sincerity.

"Shut up!" Sean blurted out as he attempted to recover. He reached over and lifted several cocktail napkins off the bar and desperately tried to soak up the excess in his leg and torso area. But every time he pressed the paper into his fabric, the cold and wet sensation made his skin crawl, and he gritted his teeth.

To add insult, Bruce in his own attempts, crouched down and found himself constantly rubbing the white cloth into the Alpha's crotch area to desaturate where most of the spill occurred.

"It—it was an accident." Stephen found himself repeating sentiments like they were tape recorded.

"The hell it was! You did it on purpose," Sean roared back.

Bruce stepped in as he vigorously rubbed a towel into Sean's inner thigh. "I saw it, Sean. He didn't do it on purpose."

"Yeah, it was an accident," James chimed in, able to finally gather himself up.

Fed up with the lone point of view, Sean huffed as he realized there was only so much he could do in the bar as far as clean-up. Besides the questionable future of his outfit, he knew the sticky sensation and smell was only going to get worse as the minutes ticked by. Finally, he was completely over Bruce constantly rubbing his crotch like he was using a scouring pad. "Dude! Just stop!" Sean held up his arms and backed away, breaking the Beta's uncomfortable concentration.

"I got most of it!" Bruce tried. "I can finish if you want. There's just that one area to the left of—"

"No!" Sean cut the Beta off and shut his eyes. "You people are lousy! You choose shitty people who give even shittier service and give the shittiest apologies! With the amount of beer I'm now *layered* in, there's no amount of rubbing that's going to get all this out."

Bruce's shoulders fell as he folded the soaked towel in defeat. "I don't know about that. I mean, it doesn't feel like you have a lot down there for it to soak into."

At that point, James couldn't hold himself back. The hard-hitting laughter put him into a coughing fit.

Sean eyed both Betas with disdain, but it was Stephen he narrowed in on. "You think this is funny?"

Stephen's voice straightened out. "No. Not at all."

Stealing the damp bar towel from Bruce, Sean made a pointless attempt at drying his hands as he spewed the first thought running through his mind. "Yeah, well, maybe if your dead brother was here, you would," he muttered.

An emotional barricade breached instantly within Stephen as he bared his teeth. "What did you say?"

Sean, proud of himself for hitting a nerve, balled the soiled towel and threw it toward the Alpha's head. "You heard me."

The words spoken rattled into Stephen's mind and prevented him from completing an easy catch. The towel side-swiped his face, leaving a faint scent of sour beer as it hit the floor with a thud. Instead of guiding him to years of rehearsed de-escalation tactics, his inner wolf stood every single hair on its coat to attention and revved back on its hind legs, ready to spring into action. With a blood-thirsty howl protruding out of razor-sharp teeth, he gave Stephen permission to defend his brother's honor. "Why, you son of a—" Even before finishing the statement, the Alpha found his arm jetting out and grabbing Sean by the collar. His animal instincts roared as he cranked his free arm back with a closed fist ready to show Sean what he was really capable of.

A slight turn of a handle and click of a door revealed two individuals lost in their own conversation. The familiar voice spoke first. "You wouldn't believe the number of positive reviews online flooding in. I had to shut off my notifications so I could sleep-in this morning." Eric's high came to a screeching halt as he observed the altercation reaching a point of no return. "Stephen! What the hell are you doing?" He instantly grabbed both sides of his head as panic set in.

"Oh, shit," James uttered as he realized who was right beside Eric, holding a clipboard, wearing an official badge, and sporting a very concerned look on his face.

The numbing sensation of being caught in the act allowed Sean to jerk his body backward as Stephen found himself at a loss for words. "Eric! I—"

"About time someone who isn't psycho comes in to run this place!" Sean adjusted his shirt, trying to hide the obvious disheveled state he was in.

Eric hastily stepped forward with his finger aimed directly toward Stephen. He lowered his voice as best as he could in present company, but it was far from soothing or relaxing. "Not today. Out of all the days—" His concentration broke briefly as he heard and felt shards of glass crumble beneath his boot. He looked back up toward the Alpha bartender in disdain. "I needed this day to go perfect. *We* needed this to go perfect!" he rambled. "I've got the entire city shining a spotlight on our place with a city inspector attached to my hip because of the success last night. Are you trying to ruin everything?!"

The city inspector cleared his throat and made a wide turn to avoid any potential run-in with the current company or scattered shards on the floor. "I'll just check the back really quick."

Eric's face pained as he saw the inspector walk off on his own. Then he returned to Stephen. "You want to tell me what on earth possesses *you* of all people to put your hands on a customer? Give me one good reason why I shouldn't throw you out and can your ass?"

"It wasn't his fault," James spoke out.

"You bold-faced liar!" Sean uttered.

"It's true." Bruce walked up to Eric who was mere inches away from Stephen's face. He beckoned his boss to relax. "Sean stirred up drama and caused a ruckus."

Unimpressed, Eric scoffed. "I don't really care. Tell me he put his hands on Stephen first and maybe I'll reconsider my position. But I doubt Sean would attempt to outright challenge a brick wall— unless you wanna tell me otherwise?"

Sean grimaced in disgust at the backhanded compliment. But right now, he couldn't be deterred from his focus. "Didn't lay a finger on the psycho. Personally, I think a good report on Attempted Assault is in order. The brute doesn't know how to act in public anymore. I think the slammer is more his home anyway."

"You threw something at him!" James pointed out, crossing his arms. "Talk about assault."

"Oh, that's preposterous!" Sean waved off.

"It's not if it's true." Bruce stood taller, also crossing his arms, showing Sean he was about to be defeated in his own game.

"You don't actually believe that, do you, Eric?" Sean invoked his golden parachute with a warning glance.

"Well, thanks to the cameras we got installed after the storefront window was hit, I don't have to take anyone's words. But if you want to fill me in on anything that's missing, I'd appreciate it." Eric gave a look back which said he wasn't in the mood to play politics. His eyes still fumed from the potential debauchery of the inspection still in progress.

When no response came in his favor, his arms fell to his side, giving Stephen one last stare down. Then he hiked his shoulders and sneered at Eric. "I'm outta here." Behind him, the door shut hard, leaving everyone once again in an overwhelming state.

Eric was about to continue his tirade when the inspector walked out from the back, scribbling several notes on his pad. "Well, I think that will do it." He ran his pen down the side of the form, making sure he checked all his boxes.

Eric's disposition fell to that of a submissive Omega's. "Wait... that's it? You're done?"

"Mhmm," the inspector replied while signing the bottom portion. "No blue ribbon I'm afraid. You might have to save that flying colors inspection review on your webpage for next month." The edges of the form tore off slow and agonizing like a fickle checkbook. He somberly handed Eric the results.

The bar owner gasped. "A red line violation? For what?"

"You have an unsafe atmosphere here, Eric. It harkens back to what got this place shut down years ago." The inspector clicked his pen and put it in his breast pocket.

"What do you mean?" Eric doubted the claim. "We fixed all the major codes when we bought the place."

"You have employees who are physically antagonizing, a customer who wasn't properly assessed for injury, no report recorded, a wet floor, and broken glass scattered everywhere."

"Oh, now, come on. We walked in together. I'll review the footage and make a report myself. The wet floor and the glass— that just happened."

The inspector adjusted his glasses. "You and I have been here for a significant amount of time now, and none of the four men who work here have even attempted to clean it up yet. I don't even see a broom, a mop, or bucket in sight."

Eric groaned at the nit-picky observations. "All those are tertiary violations, Patrick. It doesn't warrant *this*." As his hand touched the report, he noticed the fine attached, and underscored. "$500?! For what?"

"Fire code violation. You're blocking your back exit with too much inventory."

"But I was here last night. That inventory wasn't there." Eric shot a look at his three employees, who immediately felt blamed for the situation.

"It's there now. Take care of it."

"Patrick, come on. Don't you think you're being a bit harsh here? It takes thirty seconds to move that stuff." He once again glanced at his failed employees, repeating the statement with a snarl in his voice. "It takes thirty seconds to move that stuff!"

"That's thirty seconds too long for someone struggling to breathe from smoke, toxic fumes, or a potential gas leak—not to mention a fire. You wanted to take on a business, Eric. That means you have to take this seriously. My license is on the line every day, and I'm not going to have anyone audit my report to find out I went easy on you just because you work for the city." He reached out and patted his shoulder. "Welcome to the other side, my friend."

"Patrick!" Eric's attempts fell on deaf ears as once again the door slammed. Immediately, he targeted the three employees who still looked like shamed pups. If only they knew the whipping they were *about* to get. James was on his radar first. "You're going to mop this up and the entire floor. If this doesn't happen from now on at least twice a shift to where I could eat off it, you and I are going to have problems. You got it?"

"What about the customers? You can't have that liability—that's what the inspector just said."

"Do you *see* any customers in here now?!" Eric yelled. His face gave a warning it wasn't going to be pretty if it didn't stay rhetorical. Bruce was next on his list. "I don't know how the fuck all that inventory got in that hallway up against that door, but obviously, there's not enough to do around here."

Bruce tried to plead his case. "I was doing that because—"

"Nope. Don't want to hear it right now." Eric gave an immediate cease and desist. "Clearly, the weekly inventory isn't enough, so when you're done with that, you can work on the yearly one." Finally, his sights were on Stephen. "And you: Out. Now."

Both Bruce and James stopped midway on their own orders as they watched Stephen stand there—lost in his thoughts. Having the strength to step in and rightfully defend the Alpha was easy on any other day. However, both men of stature were reduced to dust by their boss, and this was only one of them. Surely, Alexander's wrath wasn't going to be any less when he found out about what transpired today. What could be waiting for Stephen as a result of pissing off Sean went wild in both brothers' minds. Perhaps, this was the easiest exit.

Without any dissent physically or verbally, Stephen felt his wolf concede and he walked out of South Street Tavern and shut the door behind him.

# CHAPTER 09:

# PLAYING THE FAMILY MAN IN ALL THE WRONG PLACES

Two hot and heavy breaths were inhaled and exhaled out in regular intervals: one lighter and one deeper. The lighter of the two voices was muffled by a soft pillow. Occasionally, the lighter voice missed the fabric entirely, and the raw ecstasy vibrated off the walls and into the ears of the deeper voice, encouraging longer and harder thrusts. Flawless, unlabored hands grasped at the sheets barely able to hold onto the bed from the sheer intensity forced upon it. However, the balled-up fists of the young Omega weren't clasped tightly in pleasure; they were clasped tightly in prayer.

"Fuck! Yes, Alpha daddy! Put a pup in me, now! I want it—I need it!" The pleas were whimpered and moaned from the depths of his lungs as his body continued to receive the onslaught of pleasure from the older Alpha mounting him from behind.

"You want it, boy? I'll give it to you." Robert studied the wet shaggy dark brown hair of the young Omega bouncing and vibrating off the back of his neck. A few drops of sweat skidded down the center of the boy's back, going down the defined center indention and pooling in the small of his back just above his naturally smooth and unblemished ass.

The mental image of the passion in order to have Carey that wet inside and out was on the verge of sending the Alpha over the edge, forcing his instinctual sexual reproductive organs to push out a large, bulbous knot at the base of his man-sized cock locking the two together. From there, they'd both relax in victory as they waited for Robert's seed to jet out in several spurts, rushing out to implant in Carey's womb and make the two into a family.

But the visual image of the profuse sweat on them both reminded him just how long their session had been taking place. As he wiped the sweat out of his own salt and pepper hair, the effects of the physical onslaught set in. He turned his neck and caught the image of himself in the dresser mirror, mechanically humping his large frame onto the petite body as he had done time and time again. The harsh truth of his worn-out upper chest and rounder less fit belly took all the sexual pleasure away in instant. All that he had remaining was the deafening sound of an overt Omega writhing in pleasure without cause, since Robert had lost his erection a minute ago and was merely stagnant inside the boy. Exhaling, the Alpha pulled himself out in defeat.

"No! No!" Carey begged as he hit his fist on the bed. "I felt it! It was going to happen that time."

"It wasn't even close," Robert admitted in an annoyed tone. His large body collapsed next to the Omega's as he stared at the ceiling fan, convinced it was judging every unfaithful act which took place. "Just like every other time. I don't know why you always say that! It just puts more and more pressure on me that I can't handle!"

"It will happen; I can sense it." Carey turned his body around and landed on his back, realizing the presentation position wasn't getting anywhere anymore. His blue eyes studied the older Alpha who was caught in a trance elsewhere. He desperately looked for anything he could say to get Robert back in the mood and on top of him. "You know, my heat is coming up soon." No response. "When that happens, you should be able to sense my pheromones. The wolf inside you will want to mount me and not stop until I'm pregnant." Once again, Carey found himself talking to a mannequin who laid there, staring at the ceiling. He turned on his side and lifted his body up. "Robert? ... Robert!"

Finally, a reaction brought life back to the Alpha and he turned his head. "Yeah?"

"I said, 'my heat is coming up soon.'" Carey repeated, hoping for an ounce of the same enthusiasm in return.

"Let me know. We'll need to coordinate schedules. I'm not sure I'm going to be able to get away at a moment's notice, not to mention the time we'll need to get you through it." Robert scratched his arm, the long dark hair misted in a layer of sweat.

Carey's voice turned cold. "Do you want to have this pup or not?"

Robert sighed. "Of course, I do."

"Really? Because ever since I started showing enthusiasm for it, you have been completely vacant. It's like you're not even here."

The Alpha continued, looking everywhere but directly at his lover. "What do you mean? It's not like that!"

"A year ago, you were *begging* me to go off suppressants. You couldn't stop moaning into my ear about how you wanted to put your pup inside me every single time you even thought about sex. It took six months to get me on board. Now I feel like I'm the only one championing this at all!" The Omega's skin flushed red, and he bounced back to lay his head on the pillow, crossing his arms and pouting, feeling like nothing but a fool.

This time, Robert turned to give his full attention. "I'm sorry you've felt that way." He began to rub the young Omega's barren stomach. "There's just been a lot going on lately, that's all."

Suddenly, Carey started getting a knotty feeling inside him, and not the kind he wanted. "Is this about Nathan? Does he suspect something?" Now, the Omega sat up again, matching his lover's position.

Robert rubbed his eyebrow. "No. No, I don't think so. But anyway, it's not Nathan I'm worried about."

"Don't tell me that son of yours is snooping in places it doesn't belong." Carey's attitude gave him the strength to get out of bed and find his underwear, the one he specifically wore for Robert to get him in the mood. Putting them back on was never an enjoyable moment. The number of times he had to put them back on in frustration were beginning to outnumber the good times.

"That's just his personality!" Robert defended. "He's always been like that—ever since I can remember. It's like he was born with that natural sense of curiosity."

"And suspicion," Carey added.

"That too."

The Omega snorted. "I'm sure the constant tales of his Alpha father sowing his wild oats had nothing to do with it." Once again, he found himself folding his arms up in a defensive posture.

Robert squinted and targeted the willful sprite. "Come here."

After swaying back and forth, Carey dropped his arms, and crawled on the bed, sticking his rear up perfectly in the way Robert insisted he always do. He bit his lip and grinned, waiting for his punishment.

The Alpha bear hugged and then clamped down on the Omega, imprisoning him. "You are an unruly smart-mouthed little pup, aren't you?"

"Mhmm," Carey moaned.

"Little boys like you need to get taught their place." Robert warned with a finger as it glided down the Omega's taut back.

"Please teach me a lesson, daddy," the Omega sang. One hard slap bounced off the small curves of his underwear. He moaned out in ecstasy. "I'm sorry! I won't say it again!"

"Yeah?" Robert's voice was low. "I'm gonna make sure of that."

Another hard slap hit Carey's ass. And then another. The Omega started thrusting his body back and forth on the Alpha, begging for another swift corrective action. Finally, he couldn't take it anymore. "Oh Alpha daddy, I want you inside me again. Fuck me!"

Robert's eyes dimmed and his jolly face faded to nothing. His arms also relaxed as his hand stopped mid-motion for another onslaught. A couple beats later, he blindly grabbed for the night-stand and reached his glasses. After placing them back on, he examined the bedside clock. "Shit!" He sprang out of bed, sending Carey off to the side. "We needed to be dressed fifteen minutes ago."

"Why?!" Carey exclaimed as he rushed to find and put his own clothes back on.

"Because Alex is going to be back from the pharmacy any second now. We were on borrowed time as it was." Running to the bathroom, he splashed cold water all over his face and hair and vigorously rubbed a bathroom towel over himself to dry off. He frantically put on his button-down shirt, trying to clasp each one as efficiently as he could, wishing he had a time machine to go back and fix his mistake. How far back he needed to go, he wasn't sure.

"Why the fuck did you invite me over then if you felt we were going to be so crunched for time?" Carey thrust his belt back through the loops of his jeans as he himself cursed the potential of being caught.

The Alpha felt at ease finally with them both dressed and presentable, only minutes away from departing and hiding their affair once more. He smiled. "Because I wanted you so bad. I couldn't resist you, baby." He stared into Carey's hypnotized eyes and kissed his velvet lips. The boy's moan was music to his ears. "I'm sorry this didn't go quite as planned. I'm excited for your heat, though. I think you're right—that's when it will happen. Till then, we'll just practice to make sure we're ready for the big one."

Carey's eyes began to water as he embraced Robert, fully elated he was getting the Alpha back. The moment was short-lived as he felt an undeniable push, indicating the Alpha was serious about him leaving, like yesterday. With a slight fall of his shoulders and a content expression remaining, Carey slipped on his shoes and found his bag near the front entrance. "You know—if we really want this to happen—you should consider going to fertility with me."

Robert's Alpha wolf growled. "I wouldn't be caught dead in that place."

"Well, calling me 'boy' is hot and all, but I'm basically the same age as your son Alex. I'm not going to be fertile forever. So, either shoot in a cup and give me a turkey baster or consider going to the clinic with me." He glanced at Robert, taking in his reaction. "See ya."

"Bye," Robert replied automatically. He watched Carey get into his sleek car and don a pair of shades. Then, the vibrant Omega sped away, showing little sign he ever existed in the Alpha's life.

***

"Hey... I'm home," Alexander announced while carrying in a couple grocery bags.

Robert stayed in the kitchen, casually glancing at the mail as if he hadn't looked at it twenty times over already. "Did you get what I asked for?" he yelled back.

"Yes." Alexander barely spoke aloud before entering the kitchen. After setting the bags on the counter, he searched through and picked out a pill bottle and handed it to him.

Robert adjusted his glasses and read the label. "I said to get the ones with the vitamin boost," he criticized.

"They didn't have any there. Otherwise, I would have. I figured you would have wanted these versus nothing." Alexander sighed in the same way he had for the last ten years whenever his father showed his obvious discontent in his Omega son's attempts. Searching through the grocery bag, he found his own prescriptions and began measuring out his own daily doses.

"I would have rather you'd gone to a different pharmacy to get what I wanted." Robert shook his head while he weighed his options.

He reluctantly settled on the bottle in his hands and opened it. The directions on the supplements said to take two—so he measured out four and swallowed them whole before gulping down a half glass of water.

"Don't start with me," Alexander clapped back. "That's where my prescription was getting filled. I waited an hour for the doctor's visit and then another hour in the pharmacy waiting for the meds. I'm not in the mood." The Omega pulled out a new container of orange juice, filled and drank it after popping a few various pills of his own.

"You sound better," Robert pointed out. He glided his fingers through the natural part of his hair, which was now showing obvious signs of receding.

"Don't let that fool you; I feel like shit. My body just collapsed after last night." The many successful memories of the night came flooding back. He wanted to smile at the thought of them, but then he remembered his body aching once the final customer reluctantly left the tavern, as if Alexander didn't have a life outside listening to the first-time patron's life woes. After a reflection, he realized he didn't actually have much of a life outside the tavern, but that didn't mean his customers were entitled to it.

"What did the doctor say?" Robert kept the casual conversation going, hoping to bring normalcy back into the house.

Alexander grunted. "I don't know why you insisted I go to the doctor so badly. In twenty years, I think this is the first time in my life where you cared enough about my health to advocate for me getting medical attention." He rested his chin on his arm as he waited for his spiritually absent father to respond.

"That's not true! I've always taken note of you and your brother. You both just grew up with solid constitutions, never felt there was a reason for either of you to go. I'd never ignore a person who needed medical assistance. When have I ever ignored your need for medical attention?" Robert ignorantly questioned.

The answer was immediate. "How about when we were down at Dillon's farm and their horse kicked me in the leg?"

The Alpha moaned. "Not the horse story again..."

Alexander continued, as if reciting a poem or famous story, "Then there was the time the school nurse insisted I go to the doctor for my fever spike, and you literally told a medical professional to their face you thought their equipment was broken or that I had somehow, right in front of him, stuck the thermometer up against the heat lamp."

"I get it," Robert admitted.

"How about the time Jin opened the car door and the corner of it sliced into my eyebrow? You said as long as it stopped bleeding, I was fine. Then, Veo secretly took me in anyway the next day, and I ended up getting five stitches. And you should have seen the look on the doctor's face when he heard *that* story."

"Enough, Alex!" Robert's tone shifted.

"I at least can give you credit for getting me help with my fertility issue, or rather, *non-fertility* issue."

Robert scanned the bags. "Did they refill your prescription?"

"Yes, Sur," he replied in annoyance. "Guess that's one good thing about having a doctor for a dad. Until he doesn't want to write you a prescription for simple symptom reducers."

"Oh, sure, have it both ways. Resent me for not doing more and then criticize me for caring. You looked like you needed to go, so I encouraged it. And I'm not going to prescribe you meds when I don't know what's wrong; it's not my field." The Alpha shook his head as he tapped useless junk mail on the counter before turning around and tossing them into the trash.

Alexander considered the logical statement—but his Omega wolf told him something else was afoot. Then, he looked around suspiciously. "Where's Veo and Jin?"

Robert casually looked down on the counter as he centered his thoughts. "Out."

"Okay... out where?"

"Planning for his great escape, I guess. I think your Veo is getting him luggage along with some other stuff." He knocked his fist on the counter while looking out the window.

Alexander rolled his eyes. "'Great escape,'" he muttered. "I'd rather not call it that." Several emotions ran through his mind as he remembered failing to convince his brother to stay in the territory, or better yet, within Tauris City. "When did they leave?"

"Not too long after you did."

The Omega intuition sent off bells and whistles in his mind. It was the last thing he wanted to surmise but the first and only conclusion he could think of. "You can't be serious." He eyed his father with disdain.

"What?" the Alpha tried. Alexander just turned around, ignoring him completely and targeted his location. "Where are you going?" A panic flushed over him as he followed his son, making various comments to somehow delay the inevitable. It was no use, however. By the time he reached the guest bedroom, Alexander had already sensed enough.

An overwhelming scent of perfume hit Alexander immediately. "Wolf-God, dad!" He coughed as he waved his hand back and forth. "Did you spray the entire room?"

"Spray?"

"Come on, Dad. I mean..." he walked over to the dresser and ran his finger across the slick wood, "it's still wet!" One more deep inhale near the bed told him what he feared the most was true. "And it doesn't cover up *that*." He pointed to the bed, where he hated imagining what happened.

"I... I don't know what you mean."

"The fuck you don't," Alexander muttered. "When are you going to stop doing this?" When no reply came, he shook his head in disgust.

"Don't pretend you get to dictate my life, because you don't." Robert stood firm. "I am a man, and I am an Alpha. And I am your father, which means I will always have authority over my life and yours. You are in no position to criticize me, and I demand respect!"

Alexander scoffed as he left the bedroom. "Respect goes to those who deserve it, asshole."

The Alpha growled, "What did you say, boy?"

"Don't call me that!" Even without looking at his father, as he continued down the hallway back to the kitchen, the word pierced his mind. It crawled beneath the Omega's skin like a perversion infiltrating him.

"You're my boy and don't you forget it!" Robert continued.

"I said, 'stop it!'" Alexander reached for the safety of the kitchen island, but it gave no reprieve as several thoughts played like still images in his mind.

"When you are in my home, I get to say and do what I want. You got it, boy?"

"STOP IT!" Alexander screamed at the top of his lungs. He didn't realize just how loud it was until he saw his Sur's expression change in an instant. It startled him and caused him to take a step back. Only then did Robert's commanding onslaught cease. As Alexander's heated face came to a boiling point, a tear escaped his eye and glistened down his cheek.

Robert's pheromones smoldered to nothing as he truly sensed his Omega son getting pushed to the brink of no return. In the raw release, he wasn't sure what his son was capable of, so he didn't push him further. Instead, he wanted to switch his tactics and come to some mutual agreement of the situation at hand. As he cleared his throat and began his peace treaty, the front door opened and in walked the rest of the Daventry family.

Both Nathan and Jin came in with several bags from various stores. Both of their expressions were cautious and perplexed. The scene in front of them looked and smelled dangerous, yet neither of them knew how to start the conversation.

Alexander stared at his Veo. Like his Sur, Nathan's face showed its years. But that was the only trait they shared. Nathan wasn't as tall nor muscular, but he was lean in his body frame. A full head of dark hair had several wisps of gray and his eyes displayed years of kindness, submission, and torment. Below his strong nose was a well-kept and trimmed beard and mustache which matched the salt and pepper look of his hair. Against all hope, Alexander wanted nothing more than his Veo to pull the memories of the past and present out of him and take them as his own. But the cruelty of such a wish wasn't anything he wanted someone else to bear, especially his loving Veo. Thus, he quickly looked at Jin's equally perplexed look and then stared off into the distance.

"What's going on?" Nathan asked, breaking the long silence. When his son refused to answer, he turned to his mate. "Robert?" Once again, no direct response came at first.

"Nothing," the Alpha muttered as he retreated down the hallway, leaving the three remaining members behind.

"You two have another fight?" Jin asked, already knowing the answer.

"What do you think?" Alexander spat back.

"Come on, you two. Don't start," Nathan warned softly. "As for you," Nathan looked directly at his Omega son, "I wish you two would stop trying to get on each other's bad side." Noticing the kitchen island being partially used already, he led his Alpha son to the kitchen table to unpack their shopping spree.

"What makes you think I started it?" Alexander posed.

Nathan laughed to himself. "Twenty-eight years of experience, how about that?"

Alexander shrugged. "Well, it's not hard to always be the problem when you feel even your birth was a problem. Right, Jin?"

Jin set down his plastic cup, left over from the fast-food restaurant he and his adoptive Veo visited before coming home. "Fuck. You."

"Alex! Enough," Nathan stressed.

The Omega was wounded. "I didn't mean that as an insult. I was using it as 'me too' reference point. Wolf-God, is everything I say in this house a personal attack on everyone?" Jin and Nathan glanced at each other without speaking. "Thanks. Thanks a lot."

"That's not fair," Jin defended.

"Oh? Care to explain any, and I do mean *any,* evidence to back that up?"

"Sure!" Jin responded, knowing the challenge was way too simple. "How about what you said when you finally left here and got your own apartment? I think that's enough evidence on its own."

"What did I say?" Alexander asked, offended if there was any proof in his example.

Nathan stepped in as he casually searched for receipts left behind in various bags. "You weren't shy about letting all three of us know exactly what you thought about us when you left. The distinct 'us' versus 'you' still haunts me if I'm to be frank." The lack of response told him his son understood his point of view, no matter how "in the moment" the criticisms were at the time. "So, do we get to hear what has your father brooding on the other side of the house?" Once again, the outspoken Omega chose to keep silent regarding the family matter. "I see."

"It was nothing, Veo, really. I promise." The hurt bled through the coverup.

"The problem with the word 'nothing' is when it is used by you or your father. That's when I know it means 'everything.'"

Jin nodded. "I agree."

"Stay out of it," Alexander criticized.

"The boy is right," Robert chimed in as he walked in casually, smiling to himself like he was proud of an accomplishment. "Nothing is wrong." He nodded at his Alpha son before embracing his mate and kissing him on the cheek.

Nathan once again looked at his Omega son, standing there, completely uncomfortable, with his mate acting as if *he* was the one out of place. "One day, maybe one of you will tell me the truth." The response carried a hint of attitude as he folded up branded paper bags and set them in the hallway closet with the others he collected. "Are you sticking around for dinner?"

"No, thanks," Alexander sighed. "I'm going to go out and grab something for lunch anyway. I'll just head home after that."

"We ate, but I can make you something here. Robert, did you find something to eat?"

The Alpha coughed. "No, I haven't eaten yet."

"I'm gonna go." Before his Veo could protest again, he wrapped his arms around him and whispered in his ear, "I love you." After letting go of the desperate embrace, he gave a casual hug to his brother and a mechanical one to his Sur. Continuing his robotic actions, he left his childhood home once again, regretting he ever stepped foot back into it.

*Later that day...*

[Bruce: Did Eric get ahold of you yet?]

[Alex: Haven't heard from him all day. Why?]

[ Bruce: Before I tell you, can I ask if you have decided on whether or not you were keeping Stephen?]

[ Alex: Is that what Eric wants to talk to me about?]

[ Bruce: It's related. What did you decide?]

[ Alex: Overall I like him. Can't think of a reason not to keep him ... unless there's something I should know?]

[ Bruce: Rough day today. You might want to get a hold of Eric.]

A loud ringtone filled Stephen's ears, jolting him upright. Considering he didn't have many contacts in his phone yet, his stomach did a somersault as he feared who it could be. Another somersault ensued as he read the Caller ID—confirming it. After one deep breath, he took the call, voice tepid. "Hello?"

"You better start talking, now!" the Omega's voice held nothing back as he huffed into the phone.

"Alex—just please let me tell you what happened before you say anything." With his free hand, he gestured out palm down as if his boss was right there in front of him, hoping it would assist in his damage control. But without the Omega there, it was more for him.

"Oh, I already heard. Eric told me all about it. I chewed him out for not telling me about it right away."

Stephen paused. "You just found out?"

"Not that it matters, but I guess he was giving me the courtesy of getting better before he dropped this on me." He let out a long, frustrated groan.

For Stephen, the thought of Alexander already in a bad way hurt. In an ideal world, he'd be there to assume his role as Alpha-caregiver to his mate. However, he was sitting on a couch in a rural home completely at the opposite end of the city, and that wasn't even the worst part. On top of the Fated Mate anomaly, here he was being the entire reason for the Omega's hurt and frustration. Well, that's not how Stephen viewed it. To him, this was nothing more than a provocation, an intentional one at that. "I've had a full week to prove to you I wasn't a screw up. Unless you can say otherwise, I think I did a damn good job." No response came through the phone—just an uncomfortable silence. "Everything was fine until earlier today."

"Oh, was it?" Alexander highly doubted.

Stephen couldn't place the skepticism at first. "Um. Yes?"

"If you ask me, this started the night before."

"When?" Immediately after saying it, other unwanted memories flooded back.

"I—I hate to be shallow about it," Alexander stuttered, "but to me, after Sean arrived at the fundraiser, you became a different person. That's mostly a conclusion I made considering you were scarce after that."

"Scarce?" The criticism hit Stephen harder than he wanted to admit, but his natural Alpha instinct kicked in and with it came a stubbornness many have perfected over the years. "It's a bar; it's not like I can hide much. Where did you think I hid exactly? Under the pool table?"

"Hey! Listen, smart ass! I have had to deal with a lot in the last 48 hours, so let's cut the attitude. It's not the best way to speak to your boss," Alexander snarled.

Stephen tucked his tail. "Sorry," he murmured. Deep inside he couldn't help but notice the Omega used present tense to make a claim on such authority over him. He prayed the word "former" would never be placed before "employee" or "boss" in the onslaught he knew was coming.

"The fact of the matter is, it was obvious that after Sean showed up, you essentially disappeared. The entire first half, you were there, by my side, being a team player. The second half, it was as if you were finding any reason to be anywhere besides behind the bar." In Alex's voice, a pain started to surface, like he was abandoned or betrayed. His head jerked as the emotions caught him off-guard.

"I did my job non-stop last night. Daniel was getting swamped. We needed all the bar and shot glasses we could get our hands on and clear off any table at the first possible chance."

"You mean when you two weren't in a rendezvous out by the back dumpsters?" Now it was Alexander's turn to push an attitude. Once again, he heard his own tone of voice, wondering why he sounded so bitter, or dare he say, jealous. "Frankly, I was worried then what shady business was going on between you two. Luckily, I can trust Daniel."

Stephen grunted. "And you can trust me!"

"Well, I *thought* so!" Alexander retorted. "Then Bruce sends me a cryptic text, and I have to track down Eric. I cannot believe the conduct you pulled, and then the city inspector having to walk right into it. The slap in the face to it all is knowing the whole ordeal involved Sean!"

The Alpha growled at the slightest mention of his name. "What happened between us was not my doing. I did my best to stay neutral—even though he was constantly trying to get under my skin." He pivoted. "I know my past history makes it easy to assume I don't have any skills or that I'm inept, but I'm not."

"What the hell was the issue anyway?"

"Sean didn't tell you?"

"Yes, he told me. Now I want *you* to tell me."

Stephen once again found himself hitting the play button in his brain to recount everything he remembered, exactly how it happened.

"This doesn't make sense to me," Alexander replied to Stephen's account. "Why would Sean just walk in and want to pick a fight with you?"

The Alpha lifted his head as he searched for a quick answer. Even though he'd had a few hours to reflect on the whole scenario, several times in fact, the events played out in his head in real time. He absolutely remembered everything Sean told him—that was burned into his memory for life—the incident afterward too. But with all that, along with the condescending snake-like expression, Stephen didn't devote a lot of time to why Sean was on the offensive from the start. "I-I guess … he felt threatened by me." The silence on the phone was uncomfortable. For a quick second, Stephen looked at his phone to make sure the call didn't disconnect. "Hello?"

"Sorry. I'm here." The Omega's head began to pound along with the stressed beats of his heart. "This is just weird." The words came out involuntarily laced with the frustration he had all day ever since Bruce texted him.

"I don't suppose Sean told you the same story about what took place?" The tone was already defeated.

"He had some minor differences," Alexander revealed. "Ironically," he chuckled, "he said the same thing about you—that you were threatened by him."

"You've got to be kidding. What does he claim I said?"

"He's making the claim you were rude and antagonizing. There were no specifics on what was said."

"You don't actually believe that, do you?" Stephen asked, flabbergasted.

Alexander pinched the bridge of his nose. "I don't know what to believe, Stephen. The fact is, you engaged with a customer when you should have done the exact opposite. Whether or not you spilling the beer on him was an accident, the whole thing culminating in the inspector slapping on an egregious fine for safety violations is a black eye on the place I can't handle right now. And it absolutely sucks it happened right after the success of the event yesterday. The fire code I will at least put a lot more weight on Bruce and James. But both Eric and Sean say that the altercation was still in progress when the inspector got there, and that no employee was in any hurry to locate anything to clean up shards of splattered glass. Not unless you want to tell me otherwise."

"No," Stephen sighed. "I can't." The writing was on the wall. Stephen merely waited for the final blow to seal his official pink slip. It was because of that he found the nerve to finally ask what he wanted to for the last 24 hours. "Why didn't you tell me?"

"Tell you what?"

"About Sean. Why didn't you tell me you had a boyfriend?"

"Because it's none of your business."

Stephen refused to accept the answer. "Even if that's the approach you want to take, it's strange, Alex. You want to talk about something that doesn't make sense? It's that."

"I'm not particularly interested in having this conversation with you. Once again, it's not any of your business."

Stephen's annoyance grew with every response. "I've worked a week's worth of shifts with you. In addition to not declaring it to me, there were no off-the-cuff discussions nor comments. It's like he didn't exist or that you don't want him to."

"The nerve you have to even say that to me! You know nothing about my relationship with him; it's not yours to comment on."

"Why. Didn't. You. Tell. Me?" Stephen punctuated.

"I won't let you hold me responsible for this—no way. You put me in the most uncomfortable position imaginable by telling me, in public at my job no less, that I was your Fated Mate. Do you have any idea how hard it is to share anything with you regarding my love life?"

Stephen's voice began to tremble "There isn't enough I could say to apologize for the position I put you in—especially if it's hurting you. But I know what I feel, Alex. I've felt it from day one and it hasn't gone away since. I know it's you, and I know it's real. I'm not some messed up freak who has brain damage or is crazy. This is an instinct that we're all programmed to know—it's unmistakable." He swallowed hard. "I have been put on this earth to be your mate, and it fucking sucks that you are keeping me from doing what I was born to do. You're keeping me at a distance when I should be there to take care of you and protect you."

"Protect me from who?" Alexander asked incredulously. "I'm not in danger. But don't think for one second I haven't thought about how you would have reacted had I told you about Sean from the beginning. Because I have to be honest, Stephen, you being incarcerated does make me worry about your behavior even though you weren't put away for being violent. It's unfair to you, but that's just the way it is. And it's not like it's without cause. I fucking walk back into my bar on day one of meeting you and you have one of my customers wailing in pain on the floor. Sean can handle himself, but that doesn't mean I want anything to happen—especially in my bar. If there's one thing I do know about an Alpha who is a Fated Mate, it's that most won't hesitate to demonstrate their dominance to another Alpha who creeps in on their territory. It's usually with fists first and words second."

"You have a Fated Mate and it's me, damn it!" Stephen blurted.

"Stop saying that!" Alexander broke down, wiping away his tears. "I'm sorry you are going through this, Stephen. I really am. But you are going to have to let this go. We're not a Fated pair, and you're not my boyfriend." After a couple of deep breaths, he relaxed his tone. "When I hired you, I told you I didn't want to hear about this anymore. Obviously, it's not something you are able to do right now, and your head is in a different mindset right now. I think it's best if you don't come to the bar for a while."

There it was—the statement Stephen was dreading. Knowing it was coming didn't ease the pain from hearing it. "Okay." The word slipped out in surrender. "Do you want to meet someplace else to give me my last pay since you don't want me at your bar anymore?" The Alpha shut his eyes tight, hoping to cut off his tear ducts.

"I didn't say that," Alexander corrected. "I said don't come by for a while. Come back on Friday."

"Friday? Why Friday?"

For Alexander, the answer was obvious. "Because that's the busiest night of the week and I need you there."

Stephen shifted his tone back to resentment. "What? As a favor?"

"No... as my employee. As my bartender." Part of the Omega was excited to say the words, but the other part was in disbelief he was even offering Stephen the opportunity, thereby indirectly accepting the fact he was going to further subject himself to the Alpha's unpredictability.

The thought process was no different for Stephen. He couldn't believe Alexander wasn't shutting him out completely—especially after once again letting him know his true feelings were alive and well. The doused flame flickered back to life. "Does this mean you are hiring me ... officially?" he asked for clarification—not wanting to be wrong.

"Yes," Alexander confirmed. "I think you've earned it. I want to chalk up today's incident as an unfortunate mishap that I'm sure won't happen again, right?"

"Absolutely. You can trust me on that," the Alpha's voice was solid.

"I hope so. Because believe me, any city violation or issue with the law that directly can be traced back to your involvement or negligence, don't even ask me if you have a job anymore. You know the answer."

"Understood and ... thank you."

If Stephen could see the Omega now, he'd see the gentle curve of his lips as he softly smiled. "You're welcome."

"So... what about Sean? How's that going to play out?"

"I'll take care of it. He really doesn't come by the bar ever—just every now and then for notable things like last night. Hopefully he'll cool off and let bygones be bygones."

"Alex, you know this means everything to me, right?" As much as he enjoyed being able to say it, he hoped he didn't jinx his new job offer already by doing so.

"I know, Stephen. Don't make me regret this. Please."

# CHAPTER 10:

# HEARING THE CALL OF TEMPTATION

In a dark alleyway, deep within Tauris, the safe sounds of the city hushed to an eerie silence. All that was left was an occasional scratching noise from street shoes gliding across the worn-out pavement. The moon desperately tried to show its glow down the long ominous open tunnel, but the tall buildings surrounding it gave no chance to the brilliant light. Every so often, a lone streetlight, barely clinging to life, flickered to reveal scattered trash, wooden pallets, beat up dumpsters and trash bins, and graffiti plastered on brick siding. If anyone dared to stop to look and decipher the intricate words done up in spray paint, along with the unwanted artistic graphics, they'd see a museum of work immortalized like an art gallery. But most avoided these alleyways, much less stopped to take in the underappreciated sights. If a person ever did halt their steady pace, it meant they were looking for something or someone—or just downright ignorant of what lay in the shadows.

A teenage Stephen with an unshaven face, complete with ill-fitting jeans and an oversized zip-up sweatshirt, feared nothing in this underground realm. In some aspects, it felt more like home than the home he grew up in. At first glance, an innocent bystander would wonder why the Alpha wanted to be in such a lonesome and desolate place. Any depraved individual knew exactly what the rogue wolf was after: trouble. Stepping deeper into the center of the alley, Stephen stopped short of the boundary which gave another small patch of light from the high lamp stretching out from a warehouse building. The hesitation to go farther asked for an invitation, and that was exactly what the tainted soul received.

A striking sound of metal gears forced to spark by a calloused thumb hit the young Alpha's ear instantly, cutting through the silence. To his right, the bright glow of a flame lit a cigarette and a partial view of a face long since dead before Stephen lost his own innocence. The man also wore heavy clothes, most of his identifiable features covered in a hood. After a quick surveillance around, Stephen only gestured with his head. The man in the darkness, barely visible from the burn of the cigarette, exhaled a cloud of smoke and turned into another corner. Stephen knew this as a welcoming sign to follow and joined the man in a maze of backstreets connected by a thin path of bricks which hadn't seen the care it deserved in decades.

Nerves and excitement washed over the Alpha as he anticipated what was to come. Although the night being colder than expected, a few beads of sweat drained down his thin arms and soaked into the fabric of his sweatshirt. The smells of wet pavement mixed with rot and decay. Then, the essence of the cigarette drew into his nostrils along with the stranger's scent. A Beta, Stephen concluded silently. Because he was a Beta, the man didn't possess any luring or note-worthy scent which cemented individuality and attraction pheromones. It made Stephen wish the man possessed an alluring scent since the years of cigarettes and body odor were nauseating to take in.

The silence was a double-edged sword. On one hand, it gave no chance for either party to say anything wrong or be misinterpreted. Pheromone and facial expressions communicated louder than words in these parts. Unfortunately, it also led the Alpha to think about several different scenarios going through the Beta's mind—most of them *threatening. Stephen had enough cash in his pocket to kill for. If the unknown dealer didn't end his life, Stephen was content if the drugs did. Once the destination came into view, the man threw back his hood, revealing straggly, poorly styled hair. Whatever strange hair color the man possessed, it wasn't natural. Even more noticeable than the color and horrific cut was a long rat's tail braided down his neck and tucked into his shirt. The man put the half-used cigarette into his mouth and steadied it with his lips. Then, he used his dominant hand to pound hard on a metal door revealing no possible entry from the outside. No answer. Once again, the man tried the door, pounding even harder than last time. No answer.*

*Fed up with the man's inability to promote progress, Stephen walked up to the metal door himself. He opted to knock methodically on the square glass pane centered high up on the entry. Instead of the harsh vibration of the metal, a soft yet firm sound echoed off the small glass. Like the vagabond's attempt, Stephen's didn't elicit anything different. The Alpha's frustration grew as he feared he'd been led down a bogus venture, getting his hopes up for nothing. The patience he had, anticipating his fix to be quelled, drained off his body as his pheromones began to grow with his frustration, ready to attack the foolish stranger, making him pay for prolonging the agony he already felt. But Stephen really wanted what he came for. In one last ditch effort, he continued the pattern of knocking on the glass incessantly. The noise rang into his ears to the point of annoyance. It was then he realized the only way to end the excruciating sound ... was to wake up.*

As he opened his eyes, the Alpha's head immediately jerked off the soft pillow. A bright light from the room and the sun shining in hit his eyes as he struggled to focus in on a figure standing at the window. Once again, the never-ending sound of a fist knocking on the glass continued to assault his ears. After a few moments, the blurry vision revealed a man from his past he wasn't sure he recognized. Stephen couldn't fathom the truth his brain forced him to believe about who was there. Perhaps another dream was running its course and he'd wake up once again to the peace and quiet he was getting used to over the past few days. But as soon as he threw back the covers and apathetically moved his legs off the bed and to the floor, he understood this wasn't a dream.

"Okay! Okay!" Stephen finally blurted out. He yawned and considered the physical state he was in. It only took another moment for the Alpha to determine the man at the window had seen a lot worse than him only in his underwear. He casually walked to the window, unlocked the side latches, and pushed the window all the way up. Without the morning's disorientation and the glare of the sun off the glass, the visual was clear and unmistakable. Worse yet, the harsh memory of cigarette and body odor seeped into his nose, confirming his suspicions. "What the hell are you doing here?" Stephen asked in disbelief.

"Well, well, well," the Beta marveled. "As I live and breathe... and I never thought I'd see your pretty face again."

"I didn't think I'd see your sorry ass again, either," the Alpha replied coldly.

"Ouch." The Beta took it in stride. "That's not the greeting I expected."

"*I* didn't expect to see you at all! Especially here! Are you crazy?" Stephen stuck his head out the window to reveal a beat-up car from yesteryear painfully sitting in the long driveway. He heightened his hearing, wondering where and if his parents knew the solicitor was there, creepily standing at the window.

"They're gone; I already checked," the Beta replied, proud of himself.

Stephen narrowed his eyes. "What do you want, Rat?"

"Hey, hey! Let's ease up on the name-calling. I can't have that moniker be said out loud so freely these days." He flapped his jacket.

"Gets me into too much trouble. It's 'Raymond' or 'Ray' will do just fine."

"You *are* trouble, Ray. And what makes you think that a different name is going to protect you from your reputation? You are 'Rat' and everyone knows you as 'Rat.' Hell, you even have a rat tail as your signature."

"Nah-uh!" Raymond waved his finger and then turned on his heels to reveal the back of his head. "Not anymore." He smiled, revealing his crooked yellow teeth. "I'm a whole new man these days."

Stephen studied the man carefully. Although he had to applaud the older man for revealing his natural brown hair and fitting himself into presentable jeans and a button-down shirt, his exhausted pale face said otherwise. The man appeared more feeble and less statuesque as he remembered; no doubt weight loss played a major factor over the years. The Alpha concluded liquid dinners from glass bottles and desserts taken in by snorting or injecting were his daily routine, or at least, weekly. Any doubt washed away quickly when again he noticed the eyesore sitting in the driveway.

"Does that mean you've settled into a new lifestyle, or are you still 'dealing' with old habits?" Stephen threw out tongue-in-cheek.

"You know what they say: old habits die hard." Raymond smiled once again. "Things have changed for me, though."

Stephen wasn't particularly interested, but he decided to entertain the conversation a bit longer. "Oh?"

"I'm out of the streets and facing Tauris head-on. I'm done with the riffraff. Can't make a living off trading W.S. for blowjobs from desperate souls only steps away from death's door." Stephen cringed and turned away at the vivid image. "Oh, don't get me wrong. It's still nice to visit my old stomping grounds once in a while." He slithered his tongue.

"That's disgusting," Stephen replied condescendingly.

"What the hell is wrong with you? You weren't like this before."

The Alpha crossed his arms. "I don't suppose you happen to remember the last time it was when you saw me?"

Raymond twitched his lips as he concentrated on his thoughts. "Summer Solstice?"

Stephen snorted. "Yeah? In which year?"

"Uh..."

"Exactly. Try ten years. I was locked away for ten years. That's plenty of time to change a person, Rat."

"Hey!"

Stephen grunted. "Sorry. *Ray*." He paused. "You look different, you sound different, but you're living the same life. That's what it looks like to me."

"Don't get cocky," Raymond warned. "What do you think makes you so much better?"

"I'm living the straight life. I've been clean for a decade, worked through most of my issues, focused on my health, and am now investing in a brighter future."

Raymond chuckled. "A 'brighter future'? Your reputation precedes you." The look he received back from the Alpha was a warning shot, causing him to change his tone. "Okay... so... let's hear it. What is this 'future' you are so optimistic about?"

"I have a Fated Mate."

The Beta's eyes grew wide. "Whoa, really? Sweet! Congrats, man." Suddenly, he panicked. "Oh shit, is he here?" Frantically, he peered into the room and scanned it to see if indeed anyone else was there.

"No, he's not here."

"Oh. At work, I suppose."

"I don't know. Maybe?"

The older man cocked his head. "You don't know where your Fated Mate is?"

Stephen shifted his weight and rubbed his eyebrow. "It's complicated."

"Ah," Raymond sang. "I'm not good with drama; I like to keep things nice and simple." He gestured his hand out like a surfer riding a wave.

"Well, I'm not good with it either," Stephen remarked. "Which is why I need you to leave."

Raymond's entire "nice and easy" pantomime record-scratched to a halt. He straightened up and looked back in disbelief. "Leave? Why?"

"Because I told you already: I'm changing my life. That means letting the past be the past and not reliving my transgressions. And I'm sorry Ray, but that includes you too."

The Beta leaned into the comment for a second before balancing back, using the moment to absorb the new information. This wasn't the reunion he was expecting. Even if he could have seen this scenario, he didn't anticipate Stephen tossing him out and drawing a clear line between who they each were. And it was evident that Raymond was on the losing side.

"Hmph. Okay." His face changed from disappointment into a courtesy smile he relegated to customer service. "You need time; you need space. I respect that. I know me being here probably triggers a lot of unsightly memories; that's fair." Stephen's face twitched in confusion, but he continued reciting his rehearsed monologue. "I care a lot about you, my old friend. Just know, I'm always here for you. Give me a call when you're ready. I'll be around waiting. And if you need anything, and I mean *anything,* you just let me know."

"Thanks, but I have things under control. I don't have your number, so don't anticipate me reaching out to—" Before he could finish his sentence, he saw Raymond fetch his wallet from his back pocket, pull out a business card and slap it on the windowsill. He picked it up and examined the professional name and number as if he was an accredited lawyer or experienced car salesman. "A business card? You're *that* visible these days? Isn't that ... risky?"

Raymond smiled, entertained by the caution as he walked back to his car. "I told you; things are different for me now. I'm not the rat in the dark alley anymore." Once he opened his car door, he took one more look at the Alpha. "People don't change Stephen, especially people like us. We either get smarter or dumber—those are the only paths. Hopefully, you'll follow me in my good fortune." He winked. "Have a good one, my friend. See you soon."

Waiting the rest of the week to return to work was torture. Although Stephen was never told specifically to avoid talking to any employee from the bar, including Alexander, the lack of invitation and the noticeable absence of anyone reaching out for a welfare check spoke volumes. That is why it was easy to focus all his attention on Crusher. With the heavy payout in tips from the fundraiser, he was able to set aside some of it for repairs and touch-ups. The pride he felt in securing a job and being responsible for money filled him with pride. The attempt before incarceration was dismal when compared to the effort he put in now—another reason why the thought of losing it frightened him. In addition to the feeling of true pride, the amount of anxiety he developed over his Fated Mate was also new. Of course, this was a much less welcomed emotion. Not even his sentencing hearing invoked the stressful feelings he had now. Being numb had its advantages back then. But feeling alive now had even more— despite the consequences of allowing emotional vulnerability.

The reflections of recent events in the last couple weeks were hard to drown out of his mind. Luckily, his Sur's old radio still worked, and he could jam out his favorite music on a classic radio station. Not that his Alpha father appreciated it. Stephen only noticed he was there in the garage with him when he turned it down.

"Ten years didn't repair your hearing, I see," Kane said, resting his body against the work bench. He observed his son on his knees, tightening the bolts on the rear tire.

"There's a lot of things ten years can't repair," Stephen pointed out.

"Don't I know it." Kane studied the work done on his bike so far. "Looks like you're actually making progress."

It took a while for Stephen to process the words, holding several different possible remarks back before he settled on one. "This surprises you?"

"In all honesty, yes."

Stephen curled his lip. "Thanks for the support."

"Listen, you made a lot of progress since you first got home, and that's great. But quit acting like you're the only one who has to adjust to the new you."

The metal wrench dropped from the young Alpha's hand and he stood. After staring into his father's eyes, he smiled gently. "You're right. I can see that." He sighed at Crusher, his old friend, who stared back like a macabre oil painting, running his fingers through his hair.

Kane noticed the sudden drop in pheromones. "What's wrong?"

"This should be a lot farther than it is right now. But having that suspension really screwed up my timeline. Thank Wolf-God we made bank at the event. That's how I got as far as I did but … now I'm going to have to wait another week, if not two. I was hoping to get it going so I could drive it into work today." A look of disappointment washed over him.

"What have you got left to get her up and running?" Kane asked.

"Most of the hard parts I have done. Elbow grease, blood, sweat, and tears took care of most of it. Plugs, connectors, kerosene, oil, and inhibitors did the trick. But I have to get new lights, run a full engine test, and then get the damn thing licensed. So, it's going to be awhile."

Kane twitched his lips in thought and pulled out his wallet. After scanning through several dollar bills, he pulled out a few and held them out. "Here."

Stephen furrowed his brows. "What's this for?"

"The final touches you need to get her up and running. You'll have to put up the rest for the cosmetic stuff I know you're going to want done, but this ought to do it."

The young Alpha took the money in disbelief and counted it. "This is what I paid you for rent."

"Pay it back with your next paycheck, unless you plan on just getting canned." Kane smirked.

Stephen had a hard time keeping a straight face, and he gave his grin back. The gesture and kindness of his Sur had all but been forgotten until now. "Thanks, Dad."

The moment was lost on Kane himself. He wondered what came over him. Whatever it was, he liked it. "What time do you go in today?"

"Not until 5."

Kane checked his watch. "If we get the trailer out now, we might be able to get this done to where you can make your return in style, but we need to be efficient about this. Want to give it a shot?"

A breath of fresh air gave Stephen new life. "More than anything."

"Then, let's go."

***

"He lives!" Bruce shouted as he saw Stephen walk in for the first time in a week.

"You'd know that if you used your phone." The Alpha smiled back and winked. He noticed Bruce take the hint in stride.

James walked over and gave him a welcoming hug. "How ya doin', buddy?"

"Come on, I wanna show you guys something." He beckoned to both Betas who followed him outside and around the corner. There, in decent condition, was Crusher, shining in the afternoon sun like she hadn't in a decade.

"Whoa!" James gasped as he neared the bike, fully inspecting the specs.

"That was *you* in the alley?" Bruce asked in shock. "Thought that was just a passerby trying to cut across."

"Nope. That was me," Stephen said proudly.

"A Gunnolf?!" James remarked. He looked at Stephen with a smirk. "You really *are* a rebel."

"*Was*," the Alpha corrected.

James pushed off his thighs as he stood back up, content with his thorough investigation. "That may be so, but you know the message you send riding around on one of these?"

Stephen shrugged while crossing his arms. "Well aware. People can think what they want. Besides, Crusher's been an important part of my life. No way I was going to get rid of her just because a few small-minded idiots think everyone who owns one of these belong in some sort of biker gang. It's ridiculous."

Both Beta brothers glanced at each other, telepathically agreeing the Alpha had more than just a "few small-minded idiots" to hurdle on the matter. But the burden to convince him otherwise wasn't theirs.

The sound of frantic feet scratching against pavement caught the trio's attention, then the sigh of frustration. Once they were spotted by Alexander, they saw him throw up his arms.

"Does anyone even care a dozen customers are inside with no one manning the bar?!" Alexander was at his wit's end at this point. "I got whistled and snapped at like some sort of callboy while I was in the back dealing with the inventory! And what for? *This*?!" The Omega gestured to the bike, single-handedly reducing it to an insignificant toy. All three men gave their own expression of being shamed in return.

Bruce cleared his throat. "Sorry, Alex. We didn't think we'd been out here that long."

Alexander homed in on Stephen, continuing his attitude. "Can we focus on getting back to work, now? Maybe find some fucking normalcy in this shitty week?" After giving one last death stare to his three hopeless employees, he gave one more look to the motorcycle, then to Stephen. "Nice bike," he complimented while keeping his condescending tone.

Once the Omega was out of sight and back in the bar, the three men exhaled as they attempted to recover from the blow.

"Man," Bruce criticized, "he's been like that all day."

Stephen's pheromone pattern exuded his guilt. "It's all my fault. I'm sure my return today is stressing him out. To be honest, I'm just waiting for the day he decides I'm not worth the hassle." The thought of it hit the pit of his stomach hard.

"No," James interjected, "it's not you at all."

The Alpha's ears perked up with intrigue. "Really?"

"Yeah," Bruce affirmed. "This isn't about you. I'm sure of that."

"What's going on? Something happen?"

"That's just it; we don't know," James confessed helplessly. "Usually, whenever he's in this mood, he makes some sort of comment about what's going on, even if he doesn't give us the exact details. But today," the Beta cocked his head and widened his eyes as he reflected on how both he and Bruce have felt the need to stay out of Alexander's way, "he's just giving off a 'don't fuck with me' vibe. I haven't approached him and I don't think Bruce has either."

"No way," Bruce confirmed. "We're still paying for the city inspection fiasco. So, I'm just glad not to be a target." Then, he corrected, "Until about sixty seconds ago."

"That's gotta be it then," Stephen concluded. "The fact I'm back reminds him of it."

"Nah," James disagreed. "Yesterday, he even made a comment on how he was looking forward to having you back. Said the vibe wasn't the same without you here."

"Hmph." Stephen found the comment ironic. "You wouldn't know that now."

Bruce continued, "That's why we think it's something else."

"Maybe he'll tell you," James hoped. "But Bruce and I are getting the impression we're not invited to try. If anyone's going to get inside that brain of his, it's you."

Stephen furrowed his brows as he thought about the predicament he was getting ready to face. Unfortunately, on the day he was focused solely on reinstating his image, this was an obvious threat to his plan. Hearing the accounts from the brothers as well as their concern for Alexander told him he didn't have a choice.

All three reprimanded employees filed back in the bar with Bruce and James receiving a generous amount of teasing from the patrons who knew they got their asses handed to them. They took it in stride.

Bar talk was nothing more than the practice of growing a thick skin and sharpening a wit which resonated with customers. It was the secret sauce which kept regulars coming in. After all, any bar could recreate a drink which satisfied a thirsty soul. At the end of the day, all patrons wanted a bar to call home with the familiar surroundings and employees who welcome them like they're the golden member of the family. But recreating an alluring atmosphere which provided comfort and entertainment? That was the impossible.

While the Betas tactfully and smoothly reminded the customers of their worth, Stephen bypassed the main room to find Alexander in the back, intentionally avoiding a few turned heads who were surprised to see him again. The customer chatter died in the distance and was replaced with the loud sounds of cardboard boxes being broken down out of frustration. Stephen eyed his boss cautiously as he observed his familiar expression from the alley. "Hey."

Alexander continued his mundane task without looking up. "Hi."

The response didn't give any indication that the Omega's mood had changed any. Stephen started easy. "I'm sorry for causing that. I should have just taken a picture with my phone and brought it in so it didn't leave you high and dry."

"You're fine." The answer was short and anything but sweet.

Not getting any headway, Stephen tried something else. "I know being back here after what happened is challenging enough. Adding that doesn't help me any; I realize that."

The Omega grunted as he struggled to pull two flaps apart on a temperamental box. Finally, the tape gave out with a pop, and he flattened the large container before tossing it into the small pile at his feet. The incessant need for Stephen to put a spotlight on his claim finally forced the Omega to give it the attention it deserved. He relaxed his tone. "Stephen, I mean it: you're not a problem. It's great to have you back. I overreacted out there and I apologize. I'm just..." He hesitated. "I'm just going through something right now."

Stephen scratched his head. "You wanna talk about it?"

Alexander scoffed. "Not really."

The Alpha's face dimmed as he studied the Omega for the first time since arriving. Having been around the Omega enough, he knew Alexander's profile well and being his Fate solidified its recognition. Whatever was going on, it was causing turmoil. A lot of turmoil. Even more than the exasperated expression, Alexander's pheromones were spiking in many different directions, and Stephen could sense it. The biggest concern was the fact the scent was foreign to him. Stephen couldn't narrow down how to interpret it. Anxiety began to creep in as Stephen's instincts and inner wolf wanted to rush in and protect his Fate from whatever harm he was being subjected to or fix whatever problem he was dealing with. Once again, what hurt the most was restraining himself from doing so.

"I'm here if you want me." Stephen deflated. He slowly turned to make his way back out front.

The comment completely took Alexander by surprise. "What?"

Stephen turned back. "To talk. I'm more than willing to listen. Just let me know."

Realizing the context, Alexander felt stupid for thinking it meant anything else. "Oh." An awkward smile ensued from the embarrassment. "Thank you. I'll do that."

The Alpha nodded gently and left with little satisfaction on the matter. Deep inside, he was hoping and praying something would occur to have Alexander let his wall down. Little did he know, the opportunity was going to present itself, and he wasn't going to have to wait very long.

Without being at the bar for the week post the Whitmore's fundraiser, Stephen had no clue the impact it had until now since no one bothered to call or text him about it, or at all. Tonight was his crash course in picking up the routine and then some. By the time nightfall came, the Alpha estimated around thirty customers to be in the joint, and he didn't recognize most of them. Whitmore's influence proved to be everything Alexander and Eric had hoped for. At some point, he exchanged a look with both Bruce and James to indicate the rollercoaster ride was satisfying and the tips were confirming it. Stephen wished Alexander showed the same enthusiasm. Based on the slow increase of his pheromone intensity, the Omega was getting worse. As the night progressed, bar patrons saw less and less of him as it appeared he intentionally was designating himself as the bar back and finding anything to avoid customers.

It was when Stephen caught Alexander pushing the mop bucket toward the bathrooms that he couldn't avoid bringing up the subject again. After finishing a large order for a crowded table, he used the opportunity to slip out and track the Omega down to the bathroom corridor. This time, it was Stephen who carried the attitude.

"What are you doing?" The Alpha crossed his arms and stood over as he watched Alexander set up the caution sign in the open washroom outside the private stalls.

Alexander noticed the tone immediately and shot a look back in confusion. "I'm mopping the floor?"

"At prime time?" Stephen questioned. "Did something happen in there?"

"No... it just needed to get done is all."

Stephen wasn't buying it. "You're going to shut down the bathroom for fifteen minutes when we have a full house here?"

"We have more than one stall, you know." The Omega shook his head in annoyance.

The comment alone was enough for Stephen to break the employer/employee wall and talk candidly like a friend. When he took in the Omega's pungent pheromone again, there was no holding back. With a swift maneuver, the Alpha intercepted the handle of the mop and pulled it from Alexander's hand.

"Give that back!"

"That's my job."

The Omega grimaced. "*Your* job is to provide drinks for that 'full house' we have. Last I checked, I didn't need your permission to do anything here. This is *my* business, and I can do whatever the hell I want!" Equally forceful, Alexander grabbed the mop back and grunted with his first long pass on the tile floor, ignoring the Alpha's presence entirely.

Stephen stared back in disbelief. "What is wrong?" No answer. "Bruce and James are worried about you. *I'm* worried about you. You've been getting worse all night. Your pheromones are completely scrambled, and I can't figure out what you're giving off."

The Omega increased his concentration on his task and avoided Stephen's eye contact. "What business do you have trying to interpret my pheromones?"

"Do you really think I'm the only one who has noticed?"

That caused Alexander to slow his motions to a halt as he thought just how bad his condition must have been. Perhaps in avoiding it himself, he was ignorant of how obvious it really was. He was about to point out no one, not even Bruce nor James spoke up about it, when he realized he didn't do any favors by biting their heads off earlier. No doubt their standoffish approach prevented any customer from making a comment either. Being stubborn again, he went back to the mundane task like the conversation never happened.

"Alex," Stephen began softly. But when the Omega ignored him again, the anger returned to his voice. "Alex!"

"What!" Alexander snapped back. The loud volume rushed throughout the bathroom corridor and trickled back into the bar.

Now at his wit's end, Stephen began a plea. "Why won't you tell me what's wrong?"

The Omega dropped the mop, which smacked the floor with a thud, before turning to finally face Stephen head-on. "Because *I* don't know what's wrong!" he confessed. His lungs heaved hard inside his chest as his eyes began watering. He attempted to make another aimless comment but instead found himself only staring back into Stephen's brown eyes. Instantly, the hurt and confusion dissipated and nothing else mattered. The Omega's heart hitched in his throat as he struggled to figure out what it meant and how to reply.

Stephen instantly noticed the change as well. In the same way, it caught the Alpha off-guard, and he stood there frozen. All he knew was, he didn't want this moment, this connection, and this serenity to end. All the confidence and assurance he came to confront Alexander with melted away in a second. A million different things to say ran through his mind. But, just like Alexander, he found himself lost for words and hoped the Omega could fill in the missing blanks. "What?" he whispered.

"I..."

"Well, well, well!" A shrill of a voice rang through the bar, stopping everyone in their conversations and enjoyment. "First, I hear that South Street came to its senses and got rid of the bastard and now I hear that the famous Omega bar owner lost his mind and rehired the Wolf-Devil himself." Eddie waltzed in like he owned the place, proud with his posse walking in from behind.

"Eddie, you need to bring it down." Bruce's nerves showed his fear of how this was going to end.

"Fuck," Alexander mumbled under his breath. From the opposite end of the building, the Omega hustled up to the front to greet Eddie and his entourage. "We had a deal, Eddie!"

"Nice to see you, Alex. You are looking..." he paused, the sudden intake of the Omega's hormones and visual profile cut off his intended response, "out of sorts." He then eyed Stephen who showed up a moment later. "And there he is!" he marveled condescendingly, studying the Alpha to remind himself what he possessed in stature and strength. "Boy, when you want things to be nothing more than a childish rumor but then they appear right in front of your face." Still entertained by the revelation, he turned to Alexander. "This asshole isn't causing you any trouble, is he?" he growled.

Any other question would have elicited a confident response, but right now, Alexander was on shaky ground. "No... he's not."

Stephen stepped forward. "What trouble do *you* intend to cause?"

From behind Eddie, Craig and his companions gave a light chuckle which pierced the room. "I don't plan on doing nothin'. I had to see for myself whether Alexander was the trailblazing Omega everyone hoped he'd be, or nothing more than the certifiable wreck all the Alphas of the world feared when they caved and allowed

Omegas to sit at the table. Now that you're here, the answer is right in front of me." He took one step toward the Alpha and met him head-on. The intensity sky-rocketed to its limits as it was clear both men were preparing for a brawl. And then, like a light switch, Eddie changed his expression like he was never bothered at all. But the tone left in his voice demonstrated to everyone he knew what he was doing, and he enjoyed every minute of it. "Bartender," he sang, "how about a round of shots for me and my men?" Eddie approached the bar right in front of James, hoping for an instant result.

"I suggest going to the clinic for the shots you need, Eddie," James eloquently protested. Knowing very well the Type 2 Alpha was doing nothing more than banking on bravado and intimidation to get what he wanted, he wasn't in the mood tonight. Even so, the lack of any immediate reaction from Eddie or anyone else in the bar had him secretly wanting to piss himself. After what seemed like an hour, the Alpha finally broke into a guffaw which his friends chimed into shortly after.

"You... you are quite the funny Beta," Eddie squeaked out. "Ah, I miss it here. So, about those drinks..."

"I'm not sure what you're honestly thinking about asking for a drink here. You're banned," Stephen pointed out.

Eddie swiveled his chair. "Banned?" he raspberried. "I'm not banned." Then he whipped back to James. "Come on, Beta. I'm waiting."

"James, forget it," Stephen rushed in.

"James..." Alexander began, "do it."

Stephen turned back, convinced he heard Alexander wrong. "You...you...." The Omega stared at the floor, refusing to say anything in return. "The incident when I first got here... they were banned because of it."

Eddie lifted his finger in protest. "Not even remotely how it happened. Might want to get your head checked." He smirked.

"You want to inform me, then?!" Stephen growled.

Eddie thought for a second. "Sure. Why not? I'm in a good mood." James presented a tray filled with shot glasses as he carried an expression like he wanted to be anywhere but here. Eddie studied the pours, making sure he wasn't short-served. After outlining his mouth with his finger and thumb, he rubbed them together, taking care to decide which one he wanted for himself. He picked one and set it aside. As he gave his explanation, he began to pass the remaining shot glasses out to his friends. "We may have been asked to leave that day, unfairly I'd like to point out, but we were never banned. It got around to us you decided to mess with Alex's mate and that Eric kicked your ass out of here. Everyone deserves a second chance, so we decided to have a chat with Alex in order to come to some sort of understanding. The past week has been an enjoyable reminder of the old days. Boy, having you back changes the atmosphere here. Things were much better without you last week." For good measure, Eddie gestured out his shot glass, offering it to Stephen as he processed the harsh claim. All he received back was a subtle scowl. Eddie hummed to himself and relaxed back in his chair. He raised the shot glass up in a toast and then downed it himself. "Ahhh! That hits the spot."

Once again, Stephen found himself looking at Alexander in disbelief. "You... you want him here?"

"He's a paying customer, Stephen. What don't you get about that? If I banned a customer every single time someone did or said something, I'd have to close this place down in a day. It's business; that's all," Alexander defended.

"You *really* think this is the best move?"

"I don't know what jobs you've had before this where you thought your opinion was law, but this is the second time tonight I've had to remind you about who is in charge here! I don't need your permission to have anyone in my bar, and I don't need to justify any of it to you!" Alexander felt himself reeling from a day he wished he could do over. "This is a nightmare," he mumbled.

"I don't know why you let that jailbird back in here, Alex." Craig added.

"Everyone deserves a second chance." Stephen smarted back, catching Eddie's eye with the timely remark.

Eddie growled. "Sounds to me you have a rodent problem, Omega. I think it's time you let an exterminator take care of it."

Stephen fully knew the comment was for him and shielded Alexander from it. "I'm not going anywhere. Alex wanted me back and now I'm here. If that bothers you so much, I have no problem with you leaving."

Eddie slowly stood at attention. "Hmm. Is that right, Omega? *Do* you want him here?"

The entire tavern was focused on Alexander now. In any predicament, deciding drew a line and sent a message to everyone about how the establishment was run, what was acceptable, and what was not. With the unwanted attention, the Omega froze. "I... I..." All he could see was Stephen getting smaller and smaller. Every fraction of a second made his heart hurt watching it, yet he still couldn't find himself to say anything.

"Alex?" Stephen felt himself on the edge of the cliff getting ready to meet his fate. In all the scenarios of how he imagined being rejected, he didn't see it happening like this. Nowhere close.

"See? What did I say?" Eddie rang out, delighted as he reached into his breast pocket.

With Stephen still locked on him in the devastation, he had no clue what Eddie was preparing to do behind his back. But Alexander did. "STEPHEN!"

Faster than a lightning strike, a bright light bounced off a small blade as it came down hard and fast. Stephen flipped around in a defensive stance but couldn't avoid the sharp metal cutting into his arm. Without any time to register the pain or assess the damage, Stephen's instincts kicked in and his wolf took over. Leaping his entire body forward, his arm grabbed Eddie's wrist, paralyzing it from making another attack. As the arm bent backward, Stephen continued his speed and momentum to completely send Eddie down to the floor on his back, with his body coming down right on top of him.

Instantly, the entire bar erupted. Both Bruce and James pressed their arms down on the bar rail and hoisted themselves over to stop the assault. However, all of Eddie's friends, including Craig, found themselves coming to Eddie's defense which prevented both Betas from intervening. Instead, they found themselves trying to save Stephen from an unfair brutal attack he was sure to lose if he had three additional men jumping him. But securing only two of them allowed the third member to rush over and pull Stephen off Eddie and swipe his fist across his face.

That caused several patrons to come and assist in ending the fray. After all the members of Eddie's group, including Eddie himself were contained, Alexander hurried to Stephen's side to check on him. "Are you okay?"

"I'm fine," Stephen huffed.

Alexander saw a slight red mark on the Alpha's cheek bone. He knew tomorrow that was going to look a lot worse. His gaze then trailed down to see drips of dark red running down his right arm and splashing onto the floor. "Shit!" The Omega grabbed several white towels to help control the bleeding.

"No, really, I'm good," Stephen protested. His words were in vain as he felt the cloth press hard against the long opening in his arm. Now he realized just how much damage was done. "Ah! Easy, easy!"

"Just hold it there!" Alexander commanded.

"This place is nothing but a sorry excuse for a bar that has a fucked-up idea on who to prioritize here. South Street has no business being run by you!" Eddie criticized.

"Bruce... call the police." Alexander then returned to Eddie, studying him and the riffraff who came in with him. "You're right about one thing. I made a mistake in who to let back in here. Eddie, Craig, LeRoy, Todd… you're not to step foot back in here."

"You're a fool, Alex!" Eddie spat back.

"There's more to this place than making sure a few patrons feel as if they have power on who I can hire or let in here. You've wrongfully assumed this is your playground. I was blind to it before, but I'm done with it and I'm done with you." Alexander gave Eddie an apologetic look. "I suggest you tell the police what really happened. With dozens of witnesses here, you're not going to get away with the same shit you've pulled before."

"Plenty of other places around here—a lot better than this." Eddie then addressed the entire bar. "I suggest all of you here find another bar as well!"

A random patron answered, "I won't be going to the one you're at!" A few others vocally joined his opinion.

Eddie and his crew didn't have a response. The low howl of a siren's call in the distance ended his night as he faced the music.

"Get them outside!" Alexander spoke, glad he wasn't going to have to deal with him anymore. Now he was someone else's problem. He once again focused on Stephen, who was trying hard to keep it together. "Are you okay?" Stephen nodded. "You know, it's okay to cry." He smirked. "That's a lot of pain."

"You don't know half of it." The Alpha's body trembled with adrenaline.

"What do you mean?"

"I can't take pain killers!" he confessed. "Right now, I'm still in shock. In an hour, that's when the real pain begins." Alexander's face fell. Based on the response, Stephen knew he realized what he meant. "I'll take the pain of this any day. I have no plans on crying over it. If I was going to cry, it wouldn't be from this."

"What would—" A moment later, the expression on Stephen's face gave him the answer. Unable to look at him, he quietly left the Alpha's side to greet the officers coming in to start their investigation.

"How are you feeling?" Alexander asked as he walked into the ER room.

Stephen sat on the edge of the bed, his arm completely bandaged on a side table. "Do you want the real answer or the one that makes me less of a burden to you?" His pheromone palate displayed the obvious truth.

Alexander sighed. "Of course, I want it to be the truth."

"Twenty-five stitches and a regimen of pills that can barely cure a headache." The frustration of it all caused him to involuntarily flex his arm. Instantly, he regretted it. He winced while cursing himself.

"I see you have some color in your cheek now." The Omega smirked.

"Mhm. I don't think that's what they meant by that expression." He was convinced the shiner on his face did nothing for his looks—not unless Alexander was into brute combat.

Alexander shrugged. "Well, it works." He then contemplated his next words and proceeded carefully. "So, how bad was it to where you can't take the good stuff?"

Stephen chuckled. "Depends who you ask. I have enough people who wouldn't hesitate to say I was some sort of Wolf-Devil looking for a death wish."

"What would the others say?"

The Alpha paused. "I'm not sure if anyone else other than me thought differently. I never did anything to where I was out of control; I know that. But once you get known for doing anything, the assumption is you're doing it all the time and only step away from..." The final word couldn't be said.

"An overdose?" Alexander guessed. Stephen nodded his head. "Is the 'not taking anything' part of some parole thing or rehab?"

"No," Stephen answered. "I have control; I was never an addict. It's not as if testing the theory right now is a smart choice however.

They have the potential to be a gateway for what *will* put me away again, and I have too much to lose."

"You mean your job?" the Omega replied innocently. Stephen gave an expression which read "Really?" Once he realized he couldn't play dumb anymore, he rolled his eyes. "Can we not start this?"

"I'll make a deal with you," the Alpha offered.

Skepticism washed over Alexander, not convinced there was an actual deal but more of a trap being set. Still, the curiosity was too much not to at least hear it. "What deal?" He saw Stephen point to the empty chair next to him. Once again, he was hesitant but chose to oblige the Alpha.

"If you want me to stop pointing out what our destiny is, then I will," the Alpha saw the subtle relief wash over Alexander, but it was short lived, "but on one condition."

Feeling brave after tonight's events, Alexander accepted. "Name it."

"Right before Eddie came into the bar tonight, you and I were having a discussion. It was a heated one, but no less a discussion. And something ... happened." With every slow reveal of where he was going, Stephen studied the Omega, watching every change in his expression and pheromone palate. What was once very prominent before started to come back just a little more with each word. "For a second, your frustration left, and all I could see was you. And I saw you looking back at me; don't lie to me and tell me you saw it any different in that moment."

For the third time tonight, Alexander couldn't believe how transparent he was in revealing his pheromone palate. What made tonight so difficult was the exceptional torment his pheromones were putting him through. Nothing was right ever since the day started. And then, there was the moment Stephen confronted him in the corridor. The Alpha was right; right before Eddie created a nightmare, there was a moment of relief in the way the Omega had never felt before in his life. Yet, he still couldn't explain why his entire mind and body were so offtrack in the first place and why Stephen's momentary domination soothed him. "You did see me, and I did see you." Stephen waited patiently for him to continue. "I was drowning in a cycle I couldn't get myself out of. Hell, I almost decided to bow out before you showed up and go to the doctor myself today."

"Are you okay?" he voiced with concern. "There's a ton of doctors here. Do you want me to call one?" Stephen insisted.

"No, no," Alexander dismissed. "I'm good now. Although I can't explain why."

"You can't?" Stephen pressed.

"Stephen..." The Omega was ready to give the Alpha another condescending explanation of how they were not some destined pair and lay the issue to rest once and for all. But as he stared into Stephen's vulnerable eyes, his breath caught in his throat. He didn't think it was possible, but once again, whatever fleeting moment they shared back in the bar was there once again. The Omega's heart began pumping harder as he felt several parts of his body beginning to vibrate. Specifically, his hand. On and off again. His phone. Breaking his concentration with the Alpha, he looked down to see who the call was from and answered it immediately. "Sean?!" As a stray tear fell down the Omega's face, he stood up and recomposed himself as he realized he had forgotten to call his boyfriend. "No, no, I'm okay!" he insisted, awkwardly laughing the moment off. "You wouldn't believe what I just went through." He slowly took the call in the waiting room, his words fading from the Alpha no longer in front of him.

Stephen sat there in an abrupt silence which hurt more than the noticeable throbbing in his arm. His Omega tore himself away from the connection he was sure they needed in order to finally break down the barrier built by this unknown entity preventing them from being together. Stephen studied his wound covered by the layers of cloth and gauze. With his free hand, he slowly poked and prodded around the area, trying to find where the limitations were. Eventually, he came upon the spot, pain shrieking straight up his arm, down his shoulder, and into his chest. He winced and gritted his teeth. Half of him hated himself for being so careless and foolish in his childish experiment to find the pain. The other half was glad he found something tangible to put his angst and emotions into. Feeling *this* kind of pain was better any day.

It was then Stephen remembered the conversation he had with his Sur and Veo once he revealed to them Alexander was his Fate, and the fate he accepted himself. His shoulders fell in defeat as he realized both his parents were right: Alexander had to make a choice. And right now, Stephen felt he did. The Omega wasn't reciprocating, and he certainly wasn't open to the idea. Sean was the Alpha in his life, and he wasn't going away anytime soon.

Because of that, Stephen was going to have to admit defeat and follow the rules of what it meant to respect an interest who was in a relationship with someone else. That's what was expected of him, and it was absolutely something he knew his parents believed. Heeding his parents' advice, he'd have to be patient and realize the exception to the rule would be if Alexander was in danger. His primal wolf instincts—no, anyone's primal wolf instincts were understood as natural and never expected to be held back from protecting someone he cared about. With Eddie and his pack only going after Stephen, Alexander wasn't in any danger to speak of. If there was opposition to Alexander, an Omega, owning a prolific bar downtown, the resistance was in word only. So far.

Stephen tightened both of his fists to the point to where they both shook. He heard and felt the subtle popping of sutures and medical tape and cared nothing for the damage or pain caused by it. As small pools of blood red flooded the white surface of his bandages, he swore to himself that if he ever saw or even heard of someone causing a fraction of the same pain to his Fated Omega, he was going to unleash the dormant wolf inside who was clawing for the opportunity to show everyone what he was made of. May Wolf-God have pity on the politician, law officer, city official, tavern owner, bar patron, drunk civilian, brute Alpha, confrontational Beta, or even judgmental Omega who messed with Alexander. His Mate. His Omega. His Fate.

*Part II and the conclusion of "Stephen's Second Chance" coming soon! Return to the story to read about Alexander's introduction to the famous Dr. Paul Birowack and the inevitable collision of Stephen's past and present.*

# BOOK CLUB QUESTIONS

1.  What do you think of the established social inequality between Alphas and Omegas Eric and Alexander? (Chapter 1)
2.  Based on Kane and Stephen's interaction, what discussions do you foresee happening between the two in the future? How do you expect each character will react in those scenes? (Chapter 2)
3.  Did Marlon owe it to his son Stephen to reveal what Kane's condition was much earlier or was he justified in keeping it a secret? (Chapter2)
4.  Alexander claims he was venting and criticizes his friend Daniel for claiming a definitive stance on his relationship with Sean. Whose viewpoint do you feel holds more water and why? (Chapter 3)
5.  After Stephen has his confrontation in the bank, what parallels are there between what Alexander experiences as an Omega and an Omega bar owner? Is it justified? Is it fair? (Chapter 4)
6.  Was Stephen's approach to Craig a showmanship in reformation or a calculated manipulation of his former past? (Chapter 5)
7.  What reasons can you surmise of why Alexander continues his relationship with Sean based on what you've read so far? (Chapter 6)

8.  What does the bar confrontation say about Sean's character? How do you think his personality influences his relationship with Alexander? (Chapter 8)
9.  How does Alexander's relationship with his father, Robert, play out in his social/personal life? (Chapter 9)
10. Interpret what it means when Alexander continues to let Stephen work in the bar considering all that has happened thus far. (Chapter 09)
11. Predict how Raymond ("Rat") will affect the story in the future. (Chapter 10)

# AUTHOR BIO:

Lucas LaMont lives near the mountains of Colorado and has been a storyteller since childhood. Throughout the years, he has dabbled in fiction and poetry and in his adult writing, most of his focus has been in gay fiction. Recently, he discovered the Omegaverse genre and is obsessed with it! During the Covid pandemic, he found his favorite series to read: The Adrien English Mysteries by Josh Lanyon (But he is very much a fan of several noteworthy Omegaverse authors). When he's not writing and reading, Lucas loves traveling to fabulous Las Vegas to gamble or staying near the rustic lakes of Minnesota to go fishing. His current focus has been the creation of Boy Love Visual Novels, starting with his first one Fated: Type 6. The goal of his writing has always been to focus on the power of relationships and the journey they take. You can find Lucas Lamont on Facebook, Twitter, Instagram, and Wix.

## Discover more at
## 4HorsemenPublications.com

## 10% off using HORSEMEN10

www.ingramcontent.com/pod-product-compliance
Lightning Source LLC
Chambersburg PA
CBHW061229310726
48971CB00007B/1996